Sharing the Nanny

A Reverse Harem Romance

Krista Wolf

Copyright © 2024 Krista Wolf

All rights reserved. No part of this publication may be reproduced, distributed, or transmitted in any form without prior consent of the author.

Cover photography by Wander Aguiar.

KRISTA'S VIP EMAIL LIST:

Join to get free book offers, and learn release dates for the hottest new titles!

Tap here to sign up: http://eepurl.com/dkWHab

* * *

~ Other Books by Krista Wolf ~

Quadruple Duty
Quadruple Duty II - All or Nothing
Snowed In
Unwrapping Holly
Protecting Dallas
The Arrangement
Three Alpha Romeo
What Happens in Vegas
Sharing Hannah
Unconventional
Saving Savannah
The Christmas Toy
The Wager
The Ex-Boyfriend Agreement
One Lucky Bride
Theirs To Keep
Corrupting Chastity
Stealing Candy
The Boys Who Loved Me
Three Christmas Wishes
Trading with the Boys
Surrogate with Benefits
The Vacation Toy
Nanny for the Army Rangers

Wife to the Marines
The Switching Hour
Secret Wife to the Special Forces
Secret Baby for the Navy SEALs
Given to the Mercenaries
Sharing Second Chances
Baby for the Mercenaries
Best Friends Never Kiss
The Auction
Sharing the Nanny

Chronicles of the Hallowed Order

Book one: Ghosts of Averoigne
Book two: Beyond the Gates of Evermoore
Book three: Claimed by the Pack

~ 1 ~

HARPER

Walking Buffalo's snowplowed sidewalks in January could be fun or miserable, depending upon your outlook. If you weren't bundled to the chin like I was, you could freeze your ass straight off. On the other hand however, the four-foot walls of snow looming on either side of me made it easy to imagine I was walking the trenches of the ice-planet Hoth.

And I *loved* Hoth.

Snap.

Something cracked behind me again. A twig, a stick, maybe a rock. Somebody had stepped on something for sure, though, which brought me to the stark realization that I wasn't imagining things.

I was *definitely* being followed.

Shit.

At this hour and temperature, there were very few people around. Most of the bars were almost closed. The driving ban wouldn't be lifted until tomorrow, but even those who defied it weren't leaving the warmth of their cars to walk sidewalks by any means.

Except for the asshole behind me, closing the distance since the block we crossed.

Silently I wished for my date again, as funny as it seemed. I'd left *that* debacle about six blocks back, when the guy wouldn't take the hint that our evening was over. Then again I should've known better than to swipe right on someone who "taught himself to be a black belt." But I'd been on an epic dry spell, cooped up in my house writing code for months. I was desperate for some fun, some human interaction, and yes, hopefully even some sex.

Instead, my date turned out to be a professional focus group participant and Feng Shui consultant; both of which turned out to be even less interesting than they originally sounded. But right now, with the crunch of footprints against the frozen snow behind me growing ever louder? The karate master part sounded awfully handy.

I picked up the pace, but so did my possible pursuer. Before they got *too* close, I planted one foot and whirled.

"WHY ARE YOU FOLLOWING ME AND WHAT DO YOU WA—"

A nearby streetlight illuminated the man's face. Relief flooded over me in a wave.

"Holy fuck!" I breathed, nearly doubling over. I clutched at my chest. "You scared the hell out of me!"

"Sorry. Didn't mean to."

My ex-date looked nervous and only slightly apologetic. He had his hands up, and they were empty.

"I… I just—"

"Did I forget something back there?" I asked, patting my coat down for my phone and keys.

"No. No, you didn't."

My head tilted curiously. "But our date's over," I said firmly. "So why are you following me?"

Very quickly, I sized him up. He was average height, average build, even average looks. But the man that had seemed so cool and confident in his profile pics now looked lost and conflicted, and downright creepy. Awkwardly, he put his hands down.

"I... just wanted to make sure you got home alright."

My eyes narrowed skeptically. "You sure you weren't just trying to figure out where I live?"

He didn't have an immediate answer. His expression however, told me everything I needed to know.

"Look, Lenny—"

"Lawrence."

"Whatever," I sighed in frustration. "It's late. I need to get home. Let's assume you probably meant well, but as I already told you, I don't need to be walked to my front door."

"Yes, but—"

"So just turn around, head back, and maybe I'll—"

A hand closed over my wrist. It happened fast. Almost with black belt-like reflexes.

"You *really* should see my place," he said, forcing the same smile he'd put on all night. Only that smile was twisted now. And there was something akin to malice behind it. "Like I told you, my roommates are gone. We'd have the whole place to ourselv—"

"Let fucking *go* of me." I seethed.

I pulled abruptly, as hard as I could. Pain flared up my arm. He still had my wrist.

"Are you SERIOUS!?" I shouted as loudly as I could. My frosted breath hung in the air for a moment before dissipating. "ARE YOU REALLY—"

He pulled me in, looking around frantically, and that's when his other hand clamped over my mouth. A second later he was pinning me against his chest. Trying desperately to hold me there as I writhed left and right, working to shake myself loose.

"Harper, PLEASE!" he begged. "Just listen to me for a minute!"

He was losing control fast, I could tell. Everything he'd tried had gone cataclysmically wrong, and now he was merely reacting to a series of miserable failures.

I pulled again, this time even harder, and somehow I broke free. The instant momentum sent me spinning sideways, throwing me completely off balance…

FUCK!

My head hit the lamp post with an explosion of silver stars. I collapsed backward woozily, falling ass-first into the wall of snow. When I looked up again, my attacker was lunging forward. He reached for me with both hands.

"Don't be like this!" he pleaded again. "It's not like I'm trying to—"

The man's sentence ended in a strangled gasp, as he was suddenly and violently flung backwards. Before he could recover, two sets of hands seized hold of him. They shoved him sideways, straight through a narrowly-shoveled area, where he bounced hard off a brick wall.

Thank fucking God.

Absurdly, the worst first date in the universe dropped into some kind of karate fighting stance. His expression was murderous. His eyes were wild, shifting back and forth between my two saviors as they advanced toward him.

Then, wisely, he slipped around the corner and fled down the nearest alleyway.

"I'm on him!"

One of the two men bolted forward in pursuit, quickly disappearing from view. The other turned his attention toward me. Two big hands closed over mine, powerfully yet somehow gently extracting me from the snow bank.

"Hey… are you alright?"

The man pulled off his gloves, and two warm fingers tilted my chin upward so he could get a better look at me. His eyes went immediately wide. His mouth curled instinctively into a half-snarl.

I might've been shocked or offended, if I wasn't already scowling back at him.

"Oh, for fuck's sake!" he growled, as we both took a step back. "YOU?"

~ 2 ~

HARPER

There were small assholes and big assholes, and then there was Jackson Ripley: an asshole of such enormity, he had smaller assholes orbiting around him. He was the king of cockiness. The crown prince of total arrogance, with a head so swollen, no crown would ever fit.

"What the fuck are *you* doing here?" was all I could say.

He was staring down at me like he'd seen a ghost. In a way he had.

"That's how you greet me?" he scoffed. "After I just saved your ass?"

"Saved my ass?" I laughed, pointing. "From *that* loser?"

I was speaking with a lot more confidence than I actually felt, but I couldn't let him know I was grateful. Not Jax. Not ever.

"Well then fuck me for showing up," he grumbled. "Next time I'll just keep walking."

We stared at each other for a moment, probably

because it had been a while. To tell the truth, Jax looked good. Better than good, actually. Even under his jacket I could see he'd put on ten or fifteen pounds of muscle. His arms were thicker, his shoulders broader. But those ice-blue eyes. That smug, condescending smile...

Those things were all the same.

"So, you know who that asshole was?" he asked smartly. "He said your name."

I stared back at him for a moment, then let out a long, resigned sigh.

"He's... my date."

Two dark brows arched upward. "Your date?"

"He was, anyway. Yeah."

Jax laughed, and his laughter was every bit as mocking as I remembered it.

"Well, you sure know how to pick em'!" He scratched at his well-trimmed beard. "Where the hell did you find that guy, anyway?"

I searched for a quick lie, and came up with nothing. His smile widened.

"Ah, Tinder train!"

"Shut up."

"Choo-choo!" he mocked, holding a hand to the side of his mouth. "All aboard!"

"Oh please," I countered. "Like you did any better with what's her name? Melissa?"

He shook his head. "I don't know what you're talking about."

"Yeah," I smiled wryly. "That's it, Melissa! The one who used to wear pajamas when we went out to the movies, and drank from a sippy cup?"

"It *wasn't* a sippy cup."

"And remember that time she put her hair in pigtails?" I forged on. "For no good reason? At twenty-something years old?"

God, I'd forgotten how much I enjoyed watching him squirm. And it was so easy, too. I knew all the right buttons to press.

"Melody, not Melissa," he spat evenly, "is ancient history."

"Oh yeah?" I pressed. "And what'd she do? Did she leave her crayons out all over the table? Color outside the lines? Did she forget to put away her toys, or—"

"She robbed a bank."

He said the words matter-of-factly, I couldn't do anything but chuckle.

"Yeah, right."

"No, seriously," Jax said. "An actual bank. Plastic gun, ski mask. She wrote the teller a note and everything."

I paused, picturing Melissa — no, Melody — in my head again. Then I started laughing, totally uncontrollably. The look of disdain on his face had me laughing even harder.

"So it's not like you're batting a thousand, either," I told him.

"Do you even know what batting a thousand *is?*" he asked glibly.

"No," I admitted. "But I know that you're striking

out."

"Yeah," Jax sniffed, and tilted his head in the direction of the alleyway. "Like you and the karate kid, back there."

The wind picked up, blowing a lock of hair across his square-jawed face. Maybe it was because I hated him so much, but I'd forgotten how good he looked. The last few years appeared to have sharpened his more masculine features.

"You're lucky my roommate and I were out walking tonight," he told me. "I was supposed to be on shift."

"You still swinging that stethoscope, pretending to be a doctor?" I quipped.

"You still playing *Dungeons and Dragons?*" he asked, dragging the last part out snidely.

I shrugged. Shit yeah I was.

"Dick."

"Dork."

"Lame ass, wanna be—"

We both turned, as someone came running back in our direction. My second savior rounded the corner, puffing great white breaths into the icy, almost-midnight air.

"What happened?" Jax demanded.

His friend rested his hands on his knees and shook his head. "He… was just… too fast…"

Jax huffed. He looked at me bitterly.

"Know where that asshat lives?"

"No, not really."

"But you've got his name though, right? I mean, you dated him."

I knew what he was driving at. I didn't like it.

"Look, just let him go," I told him. "It's not even worth it."

Jax shook his full head of thick, dark hair. "Unlike you, I have a hard time letting go. You know that."

I ignored the dig and turned my attention to my other rescuer. The man was shorter than Jax, with dark, curly hair and skin so tan it was almost brown. His face was covered in sexy stubble, and what a handsome face it was, too. Handsome and exotic, but also, somehow familiar…

"This, unfortunately," Jax grumbled, "is Harper Hayes." He jerked an obligatory chin my way.

The other man put out his hand and grinned. "Harper Hayes?" he repeated. "Sounds like a superhero name."

I took his palm. I shook it numbly.

"Super *villains* have names like that too," Jax noted disdainfully.

A scathing retort leapt straight to the tip of my tongue. It died there however, as dim recognition jockeyed valiantly for position at the forefront of my brain.

"Harper, this is Preston."

Preston. Preston…

Oh SHIT!

"Preston!"

I shouted the man's name so abruptly it actually turned Jax's head. In the meantime, Preston's soft brown eyes met mine. They reflected back the same recognition, even if Jax didn't immediately notice it.

"Nice to meet you, Harper Hayes."

The memories came flooding back all at once. A night of speed dating, in a forgotten bar. Nine random men that I had absolutely nothing in common with, followed by one handsome nerd and fellow programmer I connected with on every possible level.

We'd gelled physically, mentally, socially, all the way until the buzzer sounded and our ten minutes were up. After that, we'd ditched the rest of the group and snuck off. The chemistry between us had been instant and electric. We found a dark corner of the bar and made out like teenagers, kissing until our faces hurt, then took off to find the nearest room we could rent by the hour.

Once there, 'Preston' had fucked the absolute daylights out of me, and I him. We screwed ourselves stupid, in total, blissful anonymity. We rode each other wantonly, recklessly, until dawn streamed golden rays of unwanted sunlight through the broken blinds, eroding away the fantasy, and ending our time together.

Afterwards, I intentionally gave him all the wrong contact info. In my defense, I'd only recently gone freelance and my mind was buzzing with all new ideas. I had a ton of work to do. Prototypes to draw up. I just didn't have time for a boyfriend, or a fuck-buddy, or whatever he might turn out to be.

Or at least, that's what I told myself.

As it turned out, I couldn't have changed my mind even if I'd wanted to. I knew very little about him, and the speed dating company wouldn't give out any personal info. All I had was his first name, his likes and dislikes, and the memories of an unforgettable, dripping hot night.

At the moment, Preston's almond-shaped eyes were

staring back at me with the same look of fond recollection, perhaps fucking me all over again in his mind. He kept his expression blank and unreadable, though. It was a discretion I appreciated.

"Anyway…" Jax continued awkwardly, "she dated Adrian for a hot minute."

"Adrian from 3C?" Preston asked.

My gaze snapped back to Jax. "You and Adrian live in the same *building?*"

"Yeah. And by dated, I mean fucked over," Jax went on. "And by fucked over, I mean she rejected him so hard he ended up with someone else entirely. Someone who really, really sucked."

Preston's look went grave. "Do you mean—"

"Yes. The demon queen herself." Jax grimaced. "Before he finally wised up and left her, of course."

Jax's look of smug satisfaction had me shaking my head. "It wasn't like that and you know it."

"Wasn't it?" he shot back.

I tried to think, but my head was still spinning. The history between us seemed ancient now. As Adrian's best friend, the three of us had been around each other so much growing up. Both before and after Adrian told me he loved me.

My thoughts were interrupted by Jax reaching out for me all of a sudden. I pulled back.

"What the hell are you doing?"

"Better let me have a look at your head," he said.

"Why?"

"Because you haven't taken your hand away from it since we got here."

Numbly, I realized he was right. I pulled my palm away, and looked down on it.

"There's no blood," I assured him. "It's fine. But thanks for the assist."

"Assist?" he chortled. "Don't you mean rescue?"

I rolled my eyes dramatically. "If that satisfies your hyper-masculine need for validation, then sure."

Preston chuckled. Jax did too.

"It does, actually."

"Anyway," I continued, "I'd have handled it."

"Maybe," Jax allowed. "Maybe not."

He reached out again, and this time I didn't flinch. Instead I let him fall into EMT mode, assessing me with practiced fingers.

"You've got a nasty bump," he said, scanning me. "Better get some ice on that."

"Fine. I will."

"Come with us then," Preston offered. "We only live two blocks away."

I froze. "With Adrian?"

"Yeah, but don't worry. It's not like he lives in our apartment." Preston winked. "It's a big building."

The wink made my stomach flutter. *Preston*. Here. Now. And somehow, living with Jax!?

Holy fucking shit.

"Ummm... no, but thanks. I've got ice at home."

Preston looked crestfallen. "Are you sure?"

I paused for a moment. Jax grunted.

"Yeah. She's sure."

Our eyes locked one last time, and I saw the judgment and disdain. Those eyes were definitely sneering at me. I returned a similar look, one that was equivalent to being ocularly flipped off.

"See ya, asshole."

Jax nodded, and chuckled gruffly.

"Later, nerd."

~ 3 ~

HARPER

I wasn't just flying, I was soaring. Spinning. Looping through a shining sea of spectacular, glimmering stars. The movements made me giddy, but also dizzy beyond belief. My brain was overloaded with stimulation, and body wasn't accustomed to this much motion. No one's body could be.

Nevertheless, I raised my arms overhead like an Olympic diver to soar even higher, then swept them simultaneously downward, to swoop in low. I swam my way through a vast, multi-colored nebula. Soared past a trio of inky black holes. A large planet approached, red and angry but still breathtakingly beautiful. And that's where I descended downward, straight through the swirl of noxious, sulfurous eddies.

I imagined I could smell those fumes as they burned my nostrils. Feel the sharp sting of them against my eyes. Instead, all I could feel was the intensity of the heat, which by now was making me sweat. It grew stronger and more stifling throughout my descent, until finally, at long last, my feet were touching the ground.

The surface was sharp beneath me, like jagged glass. It

pinched threateningly against my tender soles, but the pain was deadened by the thrilling fact that I could actually, at long last, finally *feel* it.

YES!

I reached down near my feet, and picked up one of the strange, pointed stones. It was warm to the touch, but not hot. I squeezed it in my palm, willing it to get hotter. It did, slowly, and I held it there until I could barely stand the pain.

The clouds above me were rolling in waves now, the skies looking more and more like an alien world. I swung my arm in their direction, and they began spinning even faster. Fascinated, I watched them churning, swirling, changing colors...

BZZZZZZT!

The haptic patches shocked me from every connection, all over my body at once! I flung off my virtual reality headset and pulled out the leads, hurling them away on instinct alone. The wires whipped painfully against my skin before skidding across the room.

"FUCK!"

The curse left my lips a full second and a half after the malfunction, the delay between pain and action a combination of muscle movements reacting to the synapses in my brain.

"Fuck fuck *fuuuuck!*"

My heart was pounding so hard and fast I could barely breathe. As usual, my eyes were darting everywhere. The sudden appearance of the real world made me so dizzy I flopped back to the couch.

What the hell went wrong?

I didn't know, but the whole thing had been finally

working. The haptic patches I'd developed over the past eighteen months were transferring heat and vibration, force and feedback. And they were doing it in all new ways too; ones that were both revolutionary and sophisticated.

Up until a minute ago, anyway.

I waited until the room stopped spinning, and my pupils adjusted to the new levels of light. Then I got up, slid into my computer chair, and punched up the code in question.

It hadn't been easy, working solely for myself. Since quitting two jobs working as a software engineer at two different companies, I'd had to find other ways to make ends meet. There were short-term contracts, debugging gigs, and small, quick projects I could take on through internet sites like Freelancer and Upwork. But that was all just bottom-feeding, really. Making a living from scraps so I could be free to pursue my own projects of my own design.

Either I'd create the greatest VR haptic system ever invented, or I'd fail and go back to writing subroutines and database queries for a placeholder boss at some megacorporation. But if I somehow pulled off the former, and sold that technology to Sony, Meta, and more?

Well, that's when life would get very, *very* uncomplicated.

I put on my headphones, cranked up the music, and started to debug. There were podcasts I loved that I could write code to, and more modern music that went perfectly with system design. But when I was scouring thousands of lines of code for a stubborn, embedded error that was driving me absolutely crazy? Heavy metal was the only way to go.

And in a case like this, the heavier the better.

Ten minutes flew by, then twenty, then more. I looked

up at the time, and realized that more than an hour had passed. Somehow, I hadn't found a single thing out of place. An entire Manowar album later, I was no closer to getting answers.

"I need food."

I pushed back, and realized I hadn't eaten anything since breakfast. Usually my growling stomach gave me a few not-so-subtle reminders. But today, well...

Maybe it did, but you're too distracted.

I folded my arms behind my head and stared at the ceiling. Sometimes the answers were up there. Other times, like right now, they simply weren't. The big empty canvas that was my living room ceiling cleared my head though, at least partially. It gave me time to reflect. Time to realize just why I was so distracted.

And shit, I didn't like the answer one bit.

Jax.

An image of the big asshole barbarian floated to mind. Every encounter with Jax pissed me off, and this time was no exception. But there was something else, though. Something that didn't sit right after our encounter, and it took me a while to figure out what it was:

Adrian was still upset with me.

I stood up and crossed the room, pacing back and forth a few times as the blood returned to my legs. Honestly, I'd thought we'd left on semi-good terms. Adrian and I had been best friends growing up, and then somewhat even more than that. The whole situation had gotten very complicated, very quickly. And then just as suddenly it was over... he was seeing someone else.

For that reason, I figured all was right between us. In

fact, I was happy for him — or at least, I convinced myself that I was. In reality my feelings had gone much deeper. *I felt slighted, much more than he should've.* Which is why, even after all these years, I couldn't believe he was still holding a grudge.

Maybe he's not, though.

I frowned in confusion. Jax wasn't exactly notorious for being right. And as Adrian's other best friend throughout high school, he was implicitly biased. I couldn't count on his opinion of the way things had gone. And if the demon queen was already ancient history…

I slid back into my chair and punched up a browser. Not two minutes later I had Adrian's full information, including the street address of the aforementioned apartment 3C.

Seeing Adrian again after all these years would be wholly cathartic. At the very least, it would clear my head. I'd find out for sure why my old friend was still carrying a grudge, or even if he was.

All that was left to do was grab my coat.

~ 4 ~

HARPER

I'd spent half my life as an introvert, agonizing over the pros and cons of every choice. The other half, I spent taking immediate action. I'm not sure when the switch got flipped, or if there was a specific event that flipped it. All I knew was that my new outlook on life had pretty much stomped out the old one.

And man, did the new philosophy get shit done.

KNOCK KNOCK KNOCK.

The door to 3C opened before I even had time to consider what I'd say. It had been four or five years since I'd last seen Adrian. I didn't even have an icebreaker.

"Oh my God! You've gotta be *kidding* me!"

Luckily, I didn't need one.

"Harper!"

A smile lit up his whole face as Adrian swept me into two very long arms. Those arms were a lot thicker and stronger than I remembered them, but they still folded perfectly around me, just as they'd done a thousand times before.

It was a great hug, a fantastic hug. The most familiar hug in the universe.

"Hi…" I mumbled into his chest. It came out with a muffled chuckle as he squeezed me even tighter.

By the time Adrian pushed me back to get a good look at me, I was already in his apartment. The door had swung shut. I was enveloped in warmth, surrounded by coziness. He took my coat and led me further inside.

"Sorry to just show up like this," I said sheepishly, "but I—"

"Don't even," he interrupted me solemnly. The look in his starfire blue eyes was almost deadly serious. "Time doesn't matter between us. Remember?"

I remembered. It was something we'd said often, growing up. Something we'd sworn to each other while lying on the beach at night, looking up at the stars, wondering where the world might take us. Back then, we'd decided that no matter what paths we'd eventually go down, we would always be in each other's lives.

So much for that plan.

I looked up again and Adrian had slipped into the kitchen, so I snooped nosily around the living room. He had a beautiful place, dimly lit by some overhead lights with a couple of scented candles flickering here and there. There was soft music drifting in. A soothing warmth, emanating from a modern electric fireplace set flush into one of the walls. The place was cozy and awesome and much more conducive to women than his original man-cave apartment, which had been decorated and shared by a few dozen fraternity brothers.

"Harper…" I heard him repeat with a happy sigh. "I can't *believe* you're actually here."

He stood in the doorway to the kitchen, holding a pair of very full wine glasses. I hadn't even heard the popping of a cork.

"Yeah, well, I just… I wanted to…"

Again, I had no words planned out. I was always better just shooting from the hip. Right now though, it was impossible to do anything but stare. And that's because I was finally getting a good overall look at my ex-best friend.

Holy fucking hell.

Adrian was still tall and handsome, but now, years later, it seemed his good looks were on steroids. He had a strong, chiseled jawline. Acres upon acres of luscious, shoulder-length blond hair. His tanned, flawless face broke into a million-dollar smile, behind a pair of plump, beautiful lips I remembered kissing over and over again… but only for one single, fateful night.

My estranged friend was absolutely *gorgeous*, to the point where his looks were distracting. But looking at his body? Shit, that was even worse. Since the last time I'd seen him, Adrian had built his body into something akin to a work of art. His arms, his chest, even his flat, taut stomach — all of it rippled with hard, lean muscle, just beneath the thin fabric of his cotton shorts and T-shirt.

He caught me looking and laughed.

"I guess I look different."

I tried to speak and nearly choked to death.

"Ummm… yeah! You *think?*"

He walked over and handed me my wine. His smile never faded though.

"I got involved in modeling," he shrugged. "Turns out

it pays the bills. I do other stuff too, but before any of that…"

He lifted his glass my way. I toasted him back.

"Here's to old times" he said.

Our glasses clinked.

"And some long-overdue new ones," I added on a whim.

We drank, and I continued drinking him in. I could see him checking me out, as well. We'd been apart for so many years, I guess it couldn't be helped.

Adrian patted a soft leather couch, and together we sat down. It was easy to catch up, but hard not to look at him. I kept getting distracted by how intimidatingly good-looking he'd become, while trying to remind myself this was the same person I'd grown up with. The same friend with whom I'd shared most of my childhood experiences with, up until the moment we drifted apart.

He told me a little about his job, which sounded absolutely magical, and I told him something about mine. We'd taken radically different paths, apparently. Adrian's job had him traveling all over, and to some very exotic places. Mine had me chained to my computer desk like a prisoner, my eyes locked on multiple screens full of letters and numbers instead of staring up at a clear blue sky.

"What made you come?" he finally asked.

"You really wanna know?"

He laughed. "No. Lie to me."

"I ran into Jax."

Adrian's smile turned into a smirk. "Really? Jax?"

"Yeah."

"And he told you to come here?"

"Hell no," I shot back. "But he mentioned you lived in his building, and it felt incredibly wrong not to touch base with you. Especially after what he told me."

He leaned back and set an arm on the back of the couch. "You mean he told you about Erika."

"Yeah. But called her—"

"The queen of demons."

"Well, she is," I said defensively. "It's one of the only things that asshole and I actually agree upon. Queen of demons, demon queen... tomato, tomahto. Whichever way you slice it—"

"You don't have to say anything else," Adrian interjected smoothly. "I'm not denying it. Not now, anyway. Back then of course, when I thought I was in love with her? It was hard to see."

"Hindsight," I agreed with a nod.

"She was awful," Adrian went on. "*Is* awful, actually. But my greatest regret is how especially bad she was to you." His voice went low. "You never deserved that."

"Well, it's not like I didn't give her a chance," I agreed. "Do you remember the last thing she said to me, all those years ago?"

He looked down for a moment. "Yes. Unfortunately."

"I mean, after that how could we still be friends?"

Watching him carefully, I drained the rest of my wine. I wasn't blaming him entirely for what happened, and I never had. But I wanted to know if *he* blamed me for pushing him into Erika's general direction.

"We all make stupid choices," Adrian eventually murmured.

"Yeah," I agreed. "We do."

I looked up at him, and butterflies erupted in my stomach. His eyes told me he knew exactly what I was talking about. We were both thinking exactly the same thing.

"I… I was scared a lot, back then," I added. "I hardly ever pulled the trigger on anything."

"No," he smiled. "You seldom did."

"What we uh, *did* together that night…" I started awkwardly. "I, ummm…"

A hand closed warmly over mine. With his other, he touched my face ever so softly.

"What we did that night was amazing," he said, adding a gentle smile. "Or rather, what we *almost* did."

I let out a nervous chuckle. "We did a *lot*, actually."

"True," he agreed. "But Harper, I think of that night all the time. I think about what you said. About how the friendship was worth more than any short-term pleasure we might get from—"

"I was stupid," I cut in. "And I was wrong. Look what happened. We lost the friendship anyway."

"Only because I foolishly rebounded," he insisted. "And that had nothing to do with you, or me, or—"

"Adrian, you told me you *loved* me," I said.

"I know."

"Right in the middle of… I mean, *almost* in the middle of—"

"I *know,*" he repeated.

"And then I balked," I went on. "I pushed you away. I was scared — no, I was pretty fucking terrified, actually. But not because you came clean about your feelings. Not because I was afraid those words just destroyed our friendship."

He looked confused, now. His eyebrows came together, and even those were magnificent.

"But that's what you told me."

I nodded glumly. "I know that's what I told you… but it's not what I meant. Shit, when do young girls *ever* say what they mean?"

There was an agonizing beat of silence. It went on for too long.

"What was it, then?"

I turned my head to look directly at him. I owed him that much.

"I was scared because I felt those same feelings, too."

For a long moment Adrian did nothing. Centimeter by centimeter however, his mouth dropped open.

"W—Why didn't you *tell* me?"

"Because I was young and dumb and confused," I shrugged. "Back then I lived behind a whole series of walls. It might've well have been a castle!" Guiltily, I shook my head. "I was good at putting them up, too. Great at it, in fact."

I let out an exasperated sigh. This part wasn't going the way I wanted.

"A couple of days went by, and then a week. And you still hadn't called me."

"I was afraid to call you," he admitted. "I wanted to give you space."

"I know. But then it got…"

"Weird."

"Yes."

Adrian leaned back against the couch, stretching his massive body in an unintentionally sexy arch. I saw the delicious ripple of a whole sea of abs, straining beneath his shirt. His biceps and triceps popped out of his too-short sleeves. They looked sculpted and beautiful and hard as rocks.

But he was happy now, even smiling fondly. There was no more confusion in his placid expression. Nothing in the way of ill will.

"We were kids," Adrian shrugged, folding his hands behind his head. "But we were friends, first and foremost. I loved you then, and I love you now. Most of all, I love that you showed up tonight." His grin widened, and I felt myself melt into my side of the couch.

"I'm so glad you're here, Harper."

The warmth of the fireplace, the wine, the music, the candles: it was all so soothing and relaxing. I might've accused him of planning it, if I hadn't shown up so totally out of the blue.

"I'm glad, too." I said. "In fact—"

I whirled, as something moved off to my right. Standing in the hallway, clutching a fuzzy blanket and a red stuffed dragon, was a beautiful, blond-haired little boy.

"Dada?"

Adrian's smile turned fatherly. He stood up, crossed the room, and lifted the toddler into his arms.

A son!

I couldn't believe it.

Adrian has a son.

Oh my God, how could I not have known? I should've internet stalked him better, or Jax should've mentioned it, or any number of other things.

"Hey pal, you're up again?"

His voice was so gentle, so tender, I felt my throat closing up. How could I not have known?

"Brayden, this is my friend, Harper."

The little boy looked my way and smiled, sleepily. When he waved his tiny hand, my heart melted.

"Hi baby!" I called cheerily.

Adrian smiled at me, then smiled back at his son who was fighting to keep awake. The poor little baby was already closing his eyes.

"It's late," Adrian murmured, kissing the boy's smooth, chubby little cheek. "Let's get you back to bed, okay?"

He turned toward the hallway, but not before looking over his shoulder and mouthing three silent words to me:

Be right back.

~ 5 ~

ADRIAN

I couldn't believe she was actually here! Sitting in my living room, waiting for me to return. Her wine glass was almost empty. It was a problem I meant to remedy immediately.

"There you go, buddy. Here's Draco."

I tucked the stuffed dragon between my son's arms, watching as he clutched it to his little chest. My heart swelled. I bent to kiss him for the tenth time.

"Now… go to sleep."

He was already three-quarters there. I covered him from the waist down with his blanket, then ran my hand slowly through the softness of his hair. It was that baby hair you only get once in your life. Once you cut it, it's gone forever.

A minute passed. Two minutes. I kept rubbing his back the whole time, wondering what random stroke of good fortune had brought Harper Hayes to my doorstep. Eventually I decided that I didn't care. I was just glad that it happened.

She looked absolutely incredible of course — even

better than I'd remembered! And truth be told, my memories were fantastic to begin with. I'd thought about her a lot lately, over the long trips and even longer plane rides. Travel tended to do that sometimes. It left you time to dance around in your past. It amplified loneliness.

Once Brayden's breathing became slow and regular, I crept from the room and closed his door halfway. I paused at the end of the hallway though, if for no other reason than to take her in.

Damn.

Harper was standing at my graduated shelving unit, picking up trinkets and putting them down. A cascade of long blonde hair spilled down her slender back, ending just above the curve where her ass met her hips. And those hips were shapely, too. So were her legs. So was everything. I'd seen it all firsthand.

Once.

I watched some more as she shifted her weight from one hip to the other. Her dress went tight on that side, sliding snugly over one rounded cheek of her beautiful ass.

"Got that one in Thailand," I told her, keeping my voice low. "Hand-carved by a hundred-year old man with the warmest eyes I've ever seen."

Very carefully she set down the jade statuette, beside the dozen or so other tchotchkes I'd picked up from around the world. Then she turned to face me. Her empty wine glass still dangled from her delicate fingertips.

"Need another?"

She looked down at it.

"Only if you're having one."

"Oh, I'm having one."

Harper's smile was so hauntingly familiar, it picked me up and hurtled me through time. I was back on Ridley Street with her again, riding bicycles, having adventures. I could smell my mother's cooking. I could feel the warm glow of the streetlamps, kicking on just in time for dinner.

I poured us another as she walked in a slow circle, continuing her inventory of my apartment. If I knew Harper, she was picking up every little detail. She could go home right at this very moment, and a whole month from now, still tell you everything I owned.

"You never told me you had a son," she said, reaching out to accept the glass I offered.

"You weren't around," I shrugged. "We lost touch."

"Still. We were friends."

"We *are* friends," I corrected her.

Harper made her way back to the couch and sighed softly. "Didn't seem like it for a while."

"No," I agreed somberly. "I guess it didn't."

I watched her go through the motions of sitting down. Even that seemed so wonderfully nostalgic.

"Erika takes the blame for that, I suppose."

"No," I jumped in. "That's *my* fault, and mine alone. *I* was the one who cut out my previous life in order to make her happy." I sighed into my glass. "Only she was never happy. There was no satisfying that woman, ever, no matter what I gave up for her. No matter how many sacrifices I made."

"Did you ever end up marrying her?" Harper asked.

"No. Gave her a ring, but we never set a date."

"How come?"

"Well, you know how couples get closer the longer they're together? How their lives sort of become one?"

She let out a little laugh. "In theory, sure."

"Erika and I were the opposite," I said. "The more time we spent together, the further we drifted apart. We had different goals, different hobbies, different lifestyles. At one point, I was about to break up with her. And then…"

I stopped. Harper nodded. "She got pregnant."

"Yes."

"And you tried to make it work."

"I know it sounds cliché, but I thought it was the right thing to do," I told her. "I figured this would be common ground for us, that boy or girl, we could build a whole new life around our child. And then Brayden was born, and things only got worse." I hesitated, before looking down. "*Way* worse."

Harper waited until I looked back at her again. When I did, her return gaze was deep with understanding.

"What exactly happened?"

"Honestly?" I asked. "I'm not even sure. I thought having a baby would bring out some maternal instincts, but she became like a whole different person. Erika went from mad to worse, blaming me for anything and everything that ever went wrong, no matter how big or small. It was like she hated me for putting the baby inside her."

"So… demon queen mode," she smiled.

"Yes." I couldn't help but laugh. "Turns out Jax was right all along."

"We were *all* right," she pointed out. "Not trying to

rub your nose in it, but…"

"I know, I know," I conceded. "And trust me, you were. Even so, I tried to make the best of it. I turned my focus on our son for a while, thinking this pure new love could fill the hole in my heart. But then Erika did something I couldn't abide by. Something I couldn't possibly ignore."

Harper stiffened, waiting for the other shoe to drop.

"She cheated."

My best friend growing up frowned, then bit her lip. "Bitch," she swore.

"Yeah."

"Demon bitch."

"Something like that." I let up a shrug. "At that point it was a relief, really. A blessing in disguise. While Erika was busy falling for her next potential victim, I took everything and moved right the fuck out. With the help of a mediator we worked out shared parental custody of Brayden."

"And what's that like?"

"Not terrible," I conceded. "Erika's been unreasonably flexible with my schedule, I have to admit. Probably because any time her new boyfriend takes her away she's eager to pawn him off on me." I smiled in the direction of the hallway. "Of course, I'm always thrilled for any extra time I get with him."

"Yeah, well he's absolutely adorable," Harper grinned. "Soo…"

She took a slow, deep sip of her wine. I had to wonder if she caught me staring as it slid down her pretty throat.

"Jax makes an amazing uncle, by the way," I added

slyly, just to gauge her reaction. "Not to mention, he's also a pretty great da—"

Three sharp raps turned us both in the direction of the door. Harper looked at me curiously.

"You expecting another long lost friend tonight?"

"Not that I know of, no."

I stood up halfway to get the door, but I didn't need to. It opened all on its own, and my friend barged in wearing his EMT uniform.

"Hey man, listen," said Jax. As usual he was halfway into the living room, while already mid-sentence. "I almost forget to tell you, I ran into—"

Upon seeing Harper he stopped dead in his tracks. Staring down at the couch, he looked like he'd seen a ghost.

"You're kidding, right!?" he demanded of the both of us. "Tell me you're kidding? Tell me I'm dreaming!"

"Not kidding," I chuckled. "Not dreaming."

Both hands went to his head, which he was already shaking back and forth. His expression was abject misery.

"Awww, *fuck*."

~ 6 ~

HARPER

"You?" I asked again, incredulously. "*You're* a dad?"

The news was punch-you-in-the-face, no fucking way, totally unbelievable. At least to me.

"Umm-hmm."

"You…" I repeated again, looking at Jax.

"Yes, me," Jax replied sharply. For a second, he actually appeared wounded. "Why? Don't you think I could —"

"Oh, it's not that you couldn't," I interjected quickly. "I'm quite sure that you *could*. Physically, anyway. I just, well… I guess I just don't see you in that role."

He'd been here for twenty whole minutes that felt like an hour. In that time I'd learned a lot of things about both of them, and them about me. We'd filled in some gaps, caught up on some missing time. With a bit of prompting on Adrian's part, I'd even told them a little something about my project. The one I'd left two perfectly good jobs to work on.

"So what poor woman carried *your* child?" I asked, still

not totally believing him. "And do I know her? I'd like to send her some flowers, or my condolences, or…"

My sentence died a slow death as I saw their faces. Adrian and Jax were staring at each other, with two of the most somber expressions I'd ever seen.

"What?"

None of them spoke, further deepening the mystery. My eyebrows damn near knitted themselves right off.

"C'mon, you're putting me on, right?"

Another few seconds passed. I was starting to get worried.

"Well, I'd love to stay for more of this rampant nerd-fest, but I've gotta run," Jax said abruptly. He bounced up from the chair he was sitting in, and headed for the door. "Call me if she drowns you in boredom," he told Adrian.

"You look good leaving," I shot back. "Great, in fact."

"And you look very pretty," Jax smirked. "Not at all gross, tonight. At all."

The door closed, and silence descended over the cozy apartment. I turned toward Adrian.

"What the hell was *that* all about?"

He stared at the door for a moment, perhaps waiting to make sure his friend was gone. Eventually he turned to look back at me.

"Jax's daughter's name is Emma," he said, in a low and even tone. "He has her three nights a week, and every other weekend."

"Wow, I'm shocked," I admitted. "But I still don't—"

"She's both his daughter… *and* his niece."

The statement didn't register immediately. I had to process it more than once.

When I did, my heart leapt into my throat.

"You mean…"

"Jax lost his brother Jason, recently," said Adrian. "Car accident. Totally fucking brutal. Had to be a year ago, now."

A wave of nausea swept over me. "Oh my God. That's awful."

"It is, but it gets worse," Adrian sighed. "His sister-in-law died in the crash, too. Emma wasn't in the car, thank God. But the accident left her parentless."

I felt like total and complete shit now. All I could do was look at the door.

"Jax was able to co-adopt his niece, along with his sister-in-law's sister, Jennifer. She's got primary custody of Emma, actually. But since she's a trauma nurse, and almost always on call, they split the time according to their busy schedules."

My mouth was suddenly so dry I could barely speak. "How old is she?"

"She's two. Just a couple months older than Brayden." Adrian smiled. "She's so beautiful, too, Harper. You should see her. She's the sweetest, most wide-eyed little girl you'd ever want to meet."

I shook my head, wondering how life could be so unnecessarily cruel at such a young age. All those people who went around saying 'everything happens for a reason' never seemed to have a reason for things like this.

"How does he do it?" she asked.

"One day at a time," Adrian shrugged. "Same as I do it. For me, traveling is the toughest. We were sharing childcare for a while, but our nanny quit when he moved back to Florida. He was a good guy, too. Funny and sweet. The kids really loved him."

Adrian *and* Jax: both of them, fathers. It still hadn't fully hit me.

"You need to find someone who can be flexible to your crazy schedules," I said. "That's a tough one. But with so many people working from home these days, maybe you could find… I don't know, a responsible college student? Someone trustworthy, looking to make some extra cash, but who also…"

Adrian was staring at me, smiling strangely. I tilted my head.

"What? Wait… no."

"No, what?"

"*Me?*"

"Sure, why not you?" he said, leaning forward excitedly. "You were the one who just put the idea in my head!"

"No I didn't."

"Sure you did," he continued to smile. "You said it yourself earlier; you're having trouble making ends meet. You're trying to develop this new technology, but until you do, you're swimming in bills."

"I know," I conceded. "But—"

"Those were your exact words: swimming in bills. You said you're taking all these odd jobs, and they pay virtually nothing. You have to stack them all up, just to scrape some cash together. It's not sustainable. You're losing time, keeping track of them all."

I'd said these things, sure, but I hadn't expected him to throw them back at me. But is that really what he was doing? And after all, wasn't he right?

"Do you have any idea what we paid our old nanny to watch our kids?" he asked.

"None."

He told me. My eyes went wide.

"Holy shit. Seriously?"

"Yeah seriously," Adrian smiled. "And with that kind of money, you wouldn't need to do all the Upwork gigs you told me about, right? You could stop chasing all that nonsense?"

"In a heartbeat," I conceded.

"So then what's the problem?" he asked. "I'd much rather leave Brayden with someone I love and trust, instead of a stranger. And if the money's helping *you* out, wouldn't that be a win-win?"

"But… but I don't know anything about taking care of kids."

"No one ever does," Adrian shrugged. "Until you have one, that is. And then you learn hands-on. Like every other parent in the world." He glanced back in the direction little Brayden had come earlier. "We were about to hire someone from a service, Jax and I."

"Jax doesn't want anything to do with me," I smirked, "much less trust me with his kid."

"Bah. That's an act."

"Is it? Besides, I don't want anything to do with him, either."

Adrian rolled his eyes dismissively. "You wouldn't be dealing with him at all, really. Besides, Emma's only here about half the time."

I fingered the stem of my wine glass, rolling it between my fingers. How many gigs was I working on at once right now? Twelve? Fifteen?

"I— I can't," I protested. "I'm sorry, it's just that I've got so much work of my own to do."

"Do you own a laptop?"

I laughed. "I have *five* of them."

"Awesome," smiled Adrian. "Do some of your work here, between naps and feeding and stuff. You'd be making money while you make money. I could clear out a nice workspace for you, and set up a desk."

I stopped talking and started glancing around. I was still looking for reasons to say no, but I was rapidly running out of them.

"Look, no pressure," Adrian said apologetically. "If kids aren't your thing…"

"No," I stopped him. "No, it's not that."

"Then sleep on it," he shrugged. "You could always try it out, give it a shot. And if it turns out it isn't for you, no hard feelings."

His ensuing smile stopped me dead in my tracks, obliterating all current avenues of protest. Had Adrian turned on the charm just now? Or had he been charming the whole time?

I couldn't tell, to be honest. I was too busy picturing myself crushed up against his chest, or imagining myself being held in those granite-like arms. Maybe I couldn't think straight because I was still conjuring up the fading memories of actually kissing him. And of him kissing me… in hot, secret places that made me instantly wet.

"But if it *is* for you," he smiled hopefully, "well, you'd be helping us out big time. And maybe helping yourself out in the process."

Helping myself out, I thought silently, looking his gorgeous male body up and down.

Yeah, maybe that part could be fun.

~ 7 ~

HARPER

Three days: that's how long it took me to catch up on my work. And by work I meant *paying* work, because anything I did involving my haptic research wasn't work at all. Designing and building the new system was thrilling. It was rewarding. It was…

Expensive?

Yeah, it was definitely that, too. I had all sorts of electronic components already lying around; transistors and resistors and tiny circuit boards, most of which I'd managed to salvage from old projects or 'liberate' from previous job sites. But now, this far into my research, I needed new stuff too. You couldn't build a cutting-edge prototype from yesterday's tech. And no matter how fast or streamlined my code was, the system could only move at the highest speed the equipment would physically let it.

It had been three snowy days since I'd taken an Uber home from Adrian's apartment, across the Cazenovia Creek to my little Cape Cod on Portland Street. I'd spent those days sulking, then doing the math, then sulking some more. I abstained from wine — a financial decision more than a moral one. I ate leftovers, and kept the lights and heat turned low to avoid a huge electric bill.

Eventually though, I came to a grim, bitter realization. If I wanted to keep this modest house I'd bought a few years back, to celebrate my most recent promotion for a job I no longer had, I'd have to start earning a full salary again. Which meant, of course, that I'd need to go back to work.

Bullshit.

My phone buzzed; as a text message came through. Immediately I thought of Adrian. I hadn't been able to get him out of my head, really. Not that I'd tried too hard to begin with. He'd already sent two messages over the past couple of days, and just seeing his name in my phone had made me excited. In one, he told me how great it was to catch up with me again. In the other, he'd sent a pic of his son. Brayden was eating — no, smearing — some kind of rust-colored baby food all over his hands and face in the photo. His onesie, pure white and practically unblemished, was lettered with the words:

FEELING CUTE, MIGHT SHIT MYSELF LATER.

I'd laughed my ass off at that one, and the laughter felt unreasonably good. Adrian himself was stuck in my mind. He looked so incredible now; a lot like the old Adrian, but radically different, too. I marveled at his body. I could still smell the scent of him, sitting so close to me on that leather couch…

The phone buzzed again, and I woke from my daydream. The message wasn't from Adrian at all. It was from one of my mentors and closest contacts — but also someone I'd ironically never met. A fellow programmer and developer I'd run into on one of the deeper forums, in the nerdiest corner of the internet.

***

> Hey! Still looking for those micro pneumatic adapters?

I was shocked. The post I'd put up a few weeks back was long-buried by now, and after a complete lack of response I didn't think anyone had even noticed it.

> Hey you! I sure as hell am.
> But I'll probably have to put them off for a while.

The person I knew only as Telengard had exchanged phone numbers with me a while back, when I'd helped them debug a bunch of interface code for some music software. We shared a love for virtual reality, C++, and vintage Star Wars Lego sets.

> Why put them off when I already have them?

My mouth dropped open. The blanket cinched up around my shoulders to keep me warm fell to the floor.

> Shoot me your address. I'll get them out.

As thrilled as I initially was, I had to temper my rising excitement with reality.

***

> I, umm… I'm kinda short on cash at the moment.

The ellipses started blinking immediately as Telengard began typing back. Outside, just beyond my window, new snow was falling. It was beautiful, even if I knew it meant more shoveling.

> No cash necessary. Let's say I was able to trade for these.
> Besides, I still owe you one. Remember?

My breath caught in my throat. Free stuff was always good, but these components were particularly hard to find. Ordering them could take months, even if I had the money. And now they'd just fallen into my lap.

> I don't know what to say!
> Other than thank you, thank you, THANK YOU!

I sent over my address, my fingers moving so quickly I screwed it up two or three times. Eventually I got it right.

> Welcome! Lego-maniacs always look out for each other.

Telengard ended the conversation with a smiley-faced wink emoji, and I pushed back in my chair. With the adapters taken care of, I could move forward into the next phase of testing. My kinesthetic perception software was on point, and the tactile feedback loops I'd agonized so much over had finally been perfected. I was getting closer, week by week. Everything was coming together.

A shiver swept over me, as I glanced up at the thermostat. It was sixty-four degrees. I had the thermostat set to sixty-six, which could only mean one thing: I'd run out of oil. Again.

Well, almost everything.

The phone was still in my hand. I punched up my conversation with Adrian, and scrolled to the photo of Brayden, sitting there in his high chair. He looked beyond cute. Totally adorable! Just like his father…

My finger hovered over the contact button, but only for a second or two.

Then I pushed it.

~ 8 ~

HARPER

I'd been a waitress, a dishwasher, an apprentice baker for a mom-and-pop bakery. I'd worked as a lifeguard during my teenage years, and served as the night clerk at a bed-and-breakfast.

But I'd never, not even once, imagined myself as a nanny.

None of those things mattered much now, but I'd figured them out as I went. With a little luck, I expected the same kind of learning curve here. If I was going to be a nanny, I'd be the most kickass nanny this side of Niagara Falls. Maybe even in the whole universe.

Easy, killer.

Not only that, but I was also putting my best foot forward, so to speak. I wore a low-cut but comfortable blouse, with trendy pre-torn jeans that hugged my hips and accentuated my ass. I looked good, and I smelled even better. Most of all, I intended upon impressing the hell out of Adrian. I wanted to semi-seduce him; make him as physically crazy for me as I was for him. Some of it was to make up the time we missed out on. A sort of apology for what happened when we were younger, and more naive, and not always able to make good decisions.

And if my sexy ex-best friend happened to be up for a second-chance rendezvous as much as I was? Well, then he'd get to nail the nanny. To the nearest wall, if that were an option. But, more preferably, in his nice, soft bed.

In short, I wanted to make up for lost time. I wanted to finish what the two of us had started, all those years ago.

An entire catalog of those memories were still swirling through my mind as Adrian answered the door. He looked absolutely incredible, dressed in a button-down shirt and sports jacket. Cool casual. Perfect for whatever business he happened to be taking care of on a snowy weekday evening.

As it turns out, I wasn't the only one checking somebody out. Adrian's eyes lingered on me in all sorts of strategic places, both before and after he took my coat.

"Where's the little one?" I asked.

"He's in the kitchen, strapped into his high chair."

"Should I feed him?"

Adrian smirked. "Well… he's learning how to feed himself. And he's fiercely determined, so you'll need to clean him up afterward for sure."

I chuckled and made my way to the kitchen. The mess, by then, was damn near apocalyptic.

"Sorry," Adrian apologized. He ran for the sink. "Let me—"

"No, no," I told him. "I've got it. You finish getting ready."

I could tell he was in the process of getting dressed because he was still barefoot, and holding a pair of socks. He thanked me and disappeared into the hallway, leaving me with the cutest little baby I'd seen in forever.

"You *can* get some in your mouth, you know."

Little Brayden looked up at me curiously, all wide-eyed and covered in goop. His little face broke into a smile, and my heart nearly exploded.

Five minutes and half a roll of paper towels later, I had everything cleaned up. He'd need a bath to get the puree out of his hair before it hardened, but he was otherwise no worse for wear.

"You and I are gonna be good pals, kid."

Brayden clapped his hands. I clapped mine back.

"Now get over here…"

I lifted him into my arms, marveling at how small and light he was. Beneath the scent of liquefied carrots, he smelled like baby. It was the kind of thing you couldn't really describe unless you'd smelled it yourself.

"You guys make it through?"

A deep, masculine laugh came from the doorway. Adrian was twisting away at a pair of silver cufflinks. He was having trouble with them, though.

"Here, hold this monster."

I handed his son over, then went to work. There was something inherently sexy about doing a man's cufflinks. Kinda like wearing his shirt… with nothing underneath it.

Adrian watched as I finished up, then shook his sleeves straight. His face broke into a panty-melting smile.

"Follow me. I'll show you where you can set up."

I shadowed him down the hall, and into the first room on the left. It was decorated like an office. A large desk against the window had been totally cleared, and a large surge-protector plugged in to offer me ten or twelve outlets.

"What do you think I'm running here? A Bitcoin mining operation?"

"Hmmm?"

I laughed. "Never mind. This is actually perfect. Thank you."

"I figured it's quiet, it's open, and it's across from Brayden's bedroom so you'll be able to hear him when you need to," said Adrian. "There's a small baby monitor in the nursery, too. It's portable, so you can just take it with you after putting him down."

He then started telling me about his internet connection, but the truth was I'd already checked it out myself. The bandwidth was good, and the bps speeds were suitable for my needs. I'd mostly be debugging here, anyway.

"Any questions?"

He was bouncing Brayden off his hip with practiced ease, and his son was laughing harder with every bounce.

"Yeah," I smiled. "Let's talk baby stuff."

We went over food, snacks, baths, bedtime, and changes of clothing. We also discussed the overall schedule, which might change at a moment's notice depending upon when and where he was needed. There could be overnights too, but only if Erika couldn't take the baby that particular night. That possibility had driven away other potential nannies, but I told him I was perfectly okay with it.

"I can't tell you how much this means to me," he said finally. "I mean, it's one thing getting someone to watch your kid. But when it's someone you love, someone you trust…"

"Save it," I smiled, pointing at the door. "Go on, I've got this. Do your thing. You've probably got—"

Almost on cue, there was a low rap at the door. Adrian smiled, handed Brayden back to me, and made his way over. He opened the door, and embraced the tiny brunette who ushered herself inside.

"Hi!" she waved at me merrily, over his shoulder.

"Ummm… hi?"

The woman had short-cropped hair, and big round eyes that seemed too big for her slender face. Still, I couldn't deny that face was pretty. Her smile was perfectly straight and ridiculously white, framed by symmetrical lips that were plump and full.

"I'm Amy," she said enthusiastically. "You're Heather, right? The babysitter?"

"The *Nanny,*" I shot back. "And I'm not—"

"Amy," Adrian jumped in quickly, "this is *Harper*. She's a good friend of mine, who's going to be watching Brayden for me."

Amy, still smiling and chewing gum, reached out to shake my hand. It was the last fucking thing in the world I wanted to do.

I took it and shook it anyway.

"Pleased to meet you, Amy."

Amy was wearing a green dress, matching shoes, and enough rings, bracelets, and earrings to open a small jewelry store. She shuffled two steps closer to Adrian in a series of jingles and jangles.

"You ready?"

It was all coming together now; Adrian, all dressed up. Going out on a weeknight, cufflinks and all.

And of course me, standing here, holding his son. My hands still smelling like peas and carrots.

"I'm ready," Adrian said.

He leaned in close, like was going to kiss me goodbye. For an awkward moment I froze there… then realized he was only kissing his son on the cheek.

My God, I felt so stupid.

"Have a great night," Adrian said to me. He added a wink. "I'll call in a bit, to make sure the two of you are getting along."

"Yeah," I smirked. "And I'll do the same."

Amy blew a perfect bubble, then popped it with her tongue. She waved to me as they walked out the door, her bracelets sounding like sleighbells as they rang about her wrists.

Then the door closed, leaving me standing there all alone. Holding the baby in silence.

That is, until Brayden giggled and spit up on my shoulder.

~ 9 ~

HARPER

The door opened on the second knock. Which I was grateful for, because there wasn't going to be a third.

"Oh… hey." Jax stood there in his EMT uniform, looking wholly confused. "Did Comic Con let out early, or—"

"Where do you keep your wine?"

I swept past him and into his apartment, without being invited. The unit was a mirror of Adrian's, only more cluttered and with mismatched furniture. The kitchen was dark, but backlit by under-the-counter lighting. I found a bottle of red and slid it from a rack on the wall.

"Corkscrew?"

Jax's eyes narrowed. "Third drawer down."

"Thanks."

Neither of us said anything as I trimmed off the seal and pulled out the cork. Jax provided two glasses. He set them down before me, and I poured an aggressive amount into each.

"You're not fucking around, are you?"

"Nope."

"Mind telling me what happ—"

"I just got done watching Brayden upstairs," I said, grabbing my glass. "I thought Adrian needed a nanny."

"He *does* need a nanny," said Jax. "So do—"

"He doesn't need a nanny, he needs a babysitter," I shot back. "So he can go out with Jingle Jangles."

Recognition suddenly dawned on Jax's face. His lips curled into a smile.

"Ahhh, I get it."

I hated that fucking smile.

"You thought—"

"Who the fuck wears eighty-six bracelets and necklaces?" I demanded. "She looks absolutely ridiculous! Jingling and jangling all over the place, with every fucking step…"

I brought the glass to my lips and gulped down the merlot, or cabernet, or whatever the fuck it was. I hadn't even checked the bottle. It didn't matter.

"And all that *gum*," I said, curling my lip. "What was that, Bubblicious?"

"I think it's Bubble Yum," Jax answered. "Grape."

"Grape. Yeah."

"I see you've met Amy."

I shook my head and walked around him, making my way to the couch. On the way, I almost tripped over a brightly-colored Playskool Bounce and Ride.

"Do you have Emma tonight?" I asked, looking around.

Jax took a slow pull of his wine. "Nah. Not my night."

I scanned the apartment and found the hallway, a mirror image of the one upstairs.

"Preston's already sleeping?"

Jax snickered. "Well it *is* midnight."

"Yeah," I conceded. "Guess so."

"But no, Preston's not here," Jax went on. "He and his friends usually play cards tonight. *Magic* cards."

He said the second part with such disdain, the word might've well have tasted like earwax.

"So let me get this straight," he said, joining me on the couch. "You came here thinking you and Adrian would somehow pick up where you left off." He chuckled gruffly. "After all these years."

I shot him an intense look of total hatred. He responded with a dismissive sigh.

"For such a nerd, you're not very smart."

God, I wanted to kick him! More than that, I wanted to kick myself.

But fuck. He was right.

Five hours. That's how long Adrian had been gone. He'd returned to his apartment alone, thankfully, and even offered me a drink before I left. I'd told him I was tired and got out of there as fast as humanly possible.

Stopping down here on the way out, though…

It was already starting to look like a bad decision.

"You look like shit," Jax told me.

"And you smell like hot dog water," I sneered back.

He laughed. "Yeah, well I should. I've been on shift almost fifteen hours." He pointed somewhere near my neck. "But I wasn't talking about you, I was referring to your shirt."

I looked down. The mixture of baby food and toddler vomit was still a chalky outline on my shoulder, despite my best attempts to clean it up.

"This *was* a nice shirt," I lamented.

"You shouldn't wear nice shirts around toddlers," Jax admonished. "A good nanny knows that." He smiled wryly. "But we both know you didn't wear that blouse for Brayden, now don't we?"

I opened my mouth to speak, but he'd already stood up. Jax reached down with one big hand.

"Give it here."

"What?"

"Your shirt. I'll wash it."

I laughed and shook my head. "Yeah, no. I'm good, thanks."

Undaunted, Jax set his wine glass down on the coffee table and began unbuttoning his own shirt. He got down around his navel when I balked.

"What the hell are you doing?"

"Laundry," he answered.

"But—"

"Look, I'm washing my uniform anyway. I could

throw your shirt in too, if you weren't such a prude."

I frowned, but didn't look away as he peeled off his button-down shirt and undershirt. His slacks came next. He pulled a black leather belt through the loops and dropped them easily, revealing a pair of legs that were surprisingly toned and muscular.

He caught me staring at him, head to toe. I quickly put the glass to my face and took another long drink.

"See anything you like?"

"Only a pair of legs so pale they'd make a vampire look tan."

My comments were merely a thin veil beneath which I stole a few quick glances at his physique. I'd definitely been right about the muscle. Like Adrian, Jax had put on a lot of a it, and in all the right places. His broad shoulders flared out to two very big, annoyingly toned arms. I started to low-key hate myself for even looking.

My host snickered and dipped down the hallway for a moment. He came back still wearing nothing except boxer briefs, but now carrying a small stack of clothing. Extending one arm, he dangled a clean T-shirt my way.

"Last chance."

I paused for a moment, reading the judgment in his eyes. Then, defiantly, I began wriggling my way out of my shirt.

"Don't look, perv," I instructed him.

He turned his head away in an expression of mock disgust. "Don't worry."

I watched him through the corner of one eye. Did he sneak a peek? Should it even matter? I still had a bra on.

Despite his opinion, I was the furthest thing from prudish.

A few seconds later I was wearing the T-shirt he'd provided, which was black and red and printed with the words 'Bronx Zoo'. It was tremendous on me, of course, and came down to my knees. But at least it was clean.

"You could say thanks, asshole," he chastised me.

"Thanks, asshole."

"You're very welcome."

The washer and dryer were stacked on top of each other, just inside the hallway. Jax loaded the machine, as I tried to keep my eyes from his troublesomely tight ass. It was a battle I was unfortunately losing.

He started the cycle, and our clothes began dancing away.

"You gonna put something on?" I scoffed.

"Sure. After I shower."

I laughed bitterly and stood up. "Yeah, well I'm not sitting around while—"

"Yes you are."

The sudden command in his voice caught my attention. But when I looked into those ice-blue eyes, I could swear I saw them soften.

"I'm covered in six different bodily fluids right now, including the miracle of childbirth," he said wearily. "Relax and drink the rest of your wine. Then drink *my* glass of wine, and pour me a whiskey from up there."

He pointed to a pile of bottles at the end of the counter that doubled as a makeshift bar.

"But for fuck's sake, let me shower."

~ 10 ~

HARPER

I'm not really sure why I stayed. It certainly wasn't because the conversation was good, and the wine was even worse. It was late, I was tired, and I wasn't even wearing my own clothes.

I think I just needed the company. Even if that company happened to be Jackson Ripley.

He left the door open of course, like a dog marking its territory. Steam from the shower rolled into the hallway, billowing outward in clouds of warm moisture. I'd tried sneaking a peek for the pure fuck of it, or maybe even to get him back for looking when I had my shirt off. But there was too much steam. The shower was just too hot.

Instead I occupied myself with touring the apartment, much as I'd done at Adrian's. I could tell right away which parts of the decor belonged to Jax, and which had been brought in by Preston. Their clash of styles blended the place into a geek-chic bachelor pad that, oddly enough, was sorta right up my alley.

Dutifully I drank my wine, and poured the rest of Jax's

glass into my own as instructed. Then, begrudgingly, I found the glassware and even fixed him a whiskey.

By the time I returned to the living room, the shower was off and the steam was gone. Moving silently, I edged closer to the bathroom doorway. I heard nothing, but sensed movement.

Maybe you should just—

I risked a split-second glance, and in that glance I saw it all. Jax's wide, naked back was thankfully turned to me, giving me full view of the two tight globes that made up his very nice, well-rounded ass. And I got a glimpse of something else as he was toweling off, too. Something that swung heavily against his inner thigh as he turned sideways, perhaps sensing my own presence...

In a flash of movement I was back on the couch again, my heart racing a mile a minute. I set down his whiskey in the spot where his wine had been, and pulled out my phone so I could pretend to be on it.

He returned to the room still warm and flush from the shower. Only now he was wearing a T-shirt, and a pair of loose-fitting sweat-shorts.

"All better?" I smirked, without looking up.

"Much."

I watched as he sank tiredly back to the couch, the cushions spitting out air beneath the weight of his bulk. Eventually he reached for his whiskey.

"What are you doing here, Harper?"

It was a good question. I wasn't so sure myself.

"What do you mean?"

"I mean you show up here at midnight, after getting rejected upstairs—"

"I did *not* get rejected upstairs."

He made another smug face. I shot him an even scarier-than-before glance.

"Whatever."

There was truth in what he said, of course. I *had* shown up to Adrian's apartment tonight looking for something more than a nanny gig. We both knew that. Just as we both knew I'd been surprised and angered by Amy's presence.

Still, I had no right to be. Up until last week, I hadn't spoken to either of these men in years. Adrian owed me absolutely nothing. I hadn't asked him about his personal life, so he'd never really lied. I'd just assumed that since he was separated from the mother of his child, he was single.

That didn't make the whole thing any less bitter for me, though. Sitting in his empty apartment, taking care of his son while he was out with someone else? It was a tough pill to swallow. The only consolation, really, had been Brayden himself. The little boy was smart, sweet, and heartbreakingly adorable. We'd bonded instantly he and I, laughing and playing together until, finally exhausted, he'd fallen asleep in my arms.

"I don't know what the fuck I'm doing here," I finally admitted. "But now that I am here, I *did* want to tell you something."

"Your Star Wars socks finally came in the mail?" he quipped.

I shook my head slowly. "I wanted to say I'm sorry about your brother."

Jax paused for a long moment, but his expression

didn't change. Eventually he tilted his glass back and drank all his whiskey at once.

"You didn't put ice in this," he said, matter-of-factly.

"You didn't ask for ice."

"Ice in whiskey is implied, unless specifically—"

"God, why are you such an asshole?"

He sat there doing nothing. Just staring back at me.

"I'm serious!" I shouted, practically into his face. "Every time we've ever talked, it's all sarcasm and insults and quips and—"

"You ever think maybe I just don't like you?"

I glared back at him scathingly. "Ever think maybe you're just a belligerent dick?"

"Nah."

I could feel my temperature rising with each passing second. He was so infuriating!

"Asshole."

"Skank."

"Fuckface!"

"Dorky, cosplaying wanna-be —"

"I fucked your roommate."

The words spilled scathingly from my lips: a confession, meant to be an insult. Meant to shock him, or hurt him, or somehow—"

"*Preston?*" he asked incredulously.

I nodded silently, gauging his reaction.

"You fucked Preston?"

"And he fucked me, yes."

Jax laughed. "And you did this to get *back* at me?"

Wait. What? He wasn't getting this at all!

"No."

"You did it to make me jealous, then?"

"Hell no!" I cried. "Think I give a shit what you think?"

"Well, if you're going out of your way to fuck my roommate—"

"It happened more than a year ago!" I shouted. "We met at a bar, at this… this stupid hookup thing."

Jax just sat there, shaking his head and smirking. "Sounds romantic."

"It was a one-shot deal. We never saw each other again."

"Shit, now it sounds even *more* romantic."

He leaned back casually, spreading his arms over the back of the couch. He looked pleased with himself. I was ready to kill him.

"Did you hear *anything* I just said!?" I demanded, leaning in. "Are you really so thickheaded you're gonna pretend—"

"About what!?" he screamed, leaning forward to meet me. "That I care? That I give even the tiniest shit *what* you do?"

We were suddenly nose to nose, face to face, his ice-blue eyes locked tightly on my own. I could feel the raw intensity of his presence. Smell the rich, toffee-like scent of the whiskey on his hot breath.

"You're right about one thing!" I growled, half getting up. "Why the hell am I even here? Why would I think for a single second that—"

Jax's lips crashed into mine, kissing me violently, destroying all else. There was no shock. No recoil. No second thoughts.

Because instantaneously, I was kissing him *back*.

Our tongues began some fiery duel, our mouths devouring each other hungrily, angrily, as our hands rushed forward to complete our embrace. Jax's palms went to the sides of my cheeks. My fingers slipped through the thick forest of his dark hair, all the way to the back of his head, pulling him in. Keeping him locked so tightly against me, he couldn't possibly retreat until I'd drank my fill.

Fuck…

This was a necessary evil, I knew. A more primal outlet for our rage, our hatred, our general disdain for each other. Jax wasn't just kissing me, he was conquering me… and I, him. I knew it by the way I half-climbed, was half-pulled on top of him, until I was straddling him on the couch.

I just hadn't expected to enjoy it *this* fucking much.

Our hands and mouths grew even more frantic as they started to roam. I pulled his tongue deep into my eager mouth, trapping it there mercilessly, sucking on it until he let out a deep, sexy grunt. In the meantime, his hands were everywhere at once. They were on the small of my back, the curve of my ass. They slid over my hips and then downward, to the sensitive spot in the soft flesh of my lower abdomen. Right where my cute satin thong rode up to meet my waist.

I jumped when he plucked it like a guitar string.

Jax was kissing me like the toy he'd always wanted — the one he'd waited so very long for, and might not ever be willing to give up. That part frightened me, but in a thrilling way. It only served to make me hotter, as his calloused fingers slid up the sides of my neck to roughly and definitively possess my face.

"You're such an asshole," I murmured into his mouth.

"And you're such a bitch."

A searing heat flowed through me, compelling me to kiss him even harder. I wasn't just straddling him now, I was grinding into him. Pressing my chest tightly against his hard, shower-fresh body, as I grabbed his hands and pinned them to either side of the back of the couch.

What are you doing here, Harper?

His words echoed loudly in my horny little mind. Was it really disdain I'd heard in his voice? Had he really been angry I showed up?

No, seriously. What the fuck are you doing?

I realized too late the voice I heard was my own. Because by then I was lifted into the air, and pinned to a giant shoulder by one iron-like arm. I was being carried down the hallway and into the shadows, before being dumped unceremoniously — and gratefully — onto a soft, warm bed.

~ 11 ~

JAX

Kissing her on the couch was one thing. Spreading her out in the bedroom was quite another. And yet here I was, kneeling over her lithe, supine body. My fingers undid the button of her jeans, then battled the zipper. I tugged once, and nothing.

I tugged a second time… and she lifted her hips.

Holy FUCK.

I hated her. I despised her. I couldn't wait to be rid of her!

Maybe that's why kissing her had been the hottest thing in the world.

I peeled the denim from the smoothness of her toned legs, and was back to those lips in seconds, before she could change her mind. Before I could change *my* mind.

What the hell are you thinking?

There was no time to think. No room for rationalization or consequences. There was only the softness of her lips. The movements of her warm, feminine body, writhing beneath me. There was only the roll of her hips, the heat of her thighs…

I sat up again and peeled my shirt off, and everything else just followed. I watched as Harper observed my every move, her eyes now crawling over my body. They lingered on every new inch of exposed skin. They widened ever-so-slightly, as the rock-hardness of my swollen manhood swung free from my boxers.

Then those blue eyes locked on mine, and I saw the fire behind them. I could still sense her general hatred for me. The conflict of what we were about to do, battling the long history of derision and disdain between us.

But there was something else now, too. Something deeper, buried just beneath that facade of utter contempt…

Her eyes were a lot like mine, I realized. The color. The ferocity. The starfire flecks of darker blue, radiating outward against a shimmering, azure sea.

That fire flickered as I rolled her panties down, so tiny they were barely panties at all. I hefted them in the palm of my hand, feeling their dampness, gauging her arousal.

She didn't even flinch as I tossed them over my shoulder. Never breaking eye contact, I shifted my body weight forward and nudged her thighs apart.

"If you don't say something," I warned her ominously. "We're gonna fuck."

God, I was *throbbing* with the need to be inside her! So hard it actually fucking hurt. Nestled snugly between us, my erection jumped and leapt with every heartbeat. And those beats were getting faster and closer together with each passing second.

But she wasn't looking at my manhood, as impressive

as it was. Her gaze was still locked tightly on mine. She still hadn't said anything.

"I'm serious, Harper."

The look in those smoldering blue eyes was fearsome and defiant. But there was also challenge in them, as her upper lip curled back in an almost-sneer.

"Last chance…"

Inching myself forward, I encountered something warm and wet and wonderful. My hand trembled as I reached down and gripped my thickness by the base. Ever so slowly, I began dragging just the tip through her slick, molten folds.

Good, sweet fuck.

Harper's hungry eyes were still searching mine. They burned even brighter, even bluer.

And then all at once her body relaxed, sinking further into the bed. Those thighs parted wide, opening herself for me…

My sigh turned into a cry of rapture as I plunged into her.

~ 12 ~

HARPER

My heart was racing, pounding, pumping me full of blood and adrenaline as Jax climbed between my legs. There should've been a hundred reasons why we should stop this. I had a thousand angry voices screaming in my head, brutally chastising me. They were calling me a hypocrite, a lunatic, a horny asshole...

But every last one of them gasped as he shoved himself home.

Yesssssss...

My eyes rolled back, and I knew instantly I'd made the right decision. I knew it in the way my thighs automatically parted, in the satisfying way my hips cracked. I knew it in the way my legs took on a mind of their own; wrapping themselves around his tightly-shredded flanks. My heels locked and began pulling him in. Driving him deeper and more fully inside me, with every successive stroke.

Mother of God, YES.

My whole body didn't just tingle, it vibrated. My muscles were surging, twisting, pumping. My skin was on fire.

And through it all, we never broke eye contact.

Fuuuuck.

I hated that it was happening, but I hated it even more that I was so fucking grateful for it. I needed this. I needed *him*. The sad truth was, I hadn't been laid in forever. And I hadn't been properly laid since... well, since...

Since Preston.

I shoved all other thoughts aside as Jax increased his speed and angle, pile-driving me deep into the bed. Forehead to forehead, eye to eye, I fucked him back. No words were said. An entire ocean of understanding passed silently between us, without a single word being uttered.

It was as if our bodies had finally taken things over, and they were doing all the talking now.

Slowly I relinquished personal control, letting go of the last of my resolve. Fine, we were fucking. So what? It didn't mean jack shit in the grand scheme of things. In fact, it would be stupid of us *not* to fuck, especially tonight, especially now. At this point in the relationship, or friendship, or whatever the fuck it was, we had two choices, really: blow off some steam, or totally blow the fuck up.

Right now, with Jax and I pounding away at each other, it felt like both.

His hands were on either side of my face, supporting his bulk, giving him leverage. That left my own hands to roam his shoulders, his arms, his upper body. I raked my nails down the sides of his tremendous biceps and triceps, wondering if I'd leave marks, smirking at him the whole time. Happily knowing, in my heart of hearts, that he was powerless to stop a single thing.

The headboard cracked hard against the wall. The

breath was driven from my lungs. Jax was hate-fucking me now, eliciting gasps and whimpers I could no longer hold back. In sweet retribution I squeezed his arms even tighter, driving my nails in. Not even caring what he did to me, or what even came next.

I... I'm gonna..

My orgasm ripped through me like a bomb, rolling up so quickly and unexpectedly I didn't even have time to react. There was no holding back. No denying the pleasure he was giving me as, for the first time since we'd started, I was forced to look away.

Shit...

My mouth opened in a silent 'O' as I screwed my eyes shut and climaxed all over Jax Ripley's thick, unmercifully thrusting shaft. I couldn't hide it, or keep anything that powerful to myself. I could only grip him tightly, and grind harder against him. I dug my heels into his flanks like that of a horse, surging happily through my climax, riding the guilty waves of pleasure he delivered with such expertly-tailored thrusts.

I came to groggily, my body still rocking forward and back as Jax continued digging me out. If he was hate-fucking me, it was certainly working. I hated that I came first. I almost hated that I came at all. I hated that I even cared what he thought of this whole sordid event, or how he might use this night to lord power over me in the future. We were lovers now, and we couldn't go back. For the rest of our lives, whenever we looked into each other's eyes? We'd always remember... we totally, totally *fucked*.

Good.

I blinked a few times, struggling to catch my breath. *Good?*

I turned my head to find my body on its side, completely stretched out, my legs scissored apart. Jax was hovering over me, fucking me sideways, supporting his entire body weight on his two big, extended arms. If I craned my neck I could even watch, and the watching part was *hot*. His shaft glistened with wetness as he glided in and out of me, disappearing again and again into the valley formed by the two plump globes of my ass.

Okay, maybe it is good.

The new position put our faces together, enabling us to kiss just as deeply as before. That happened immediately, magnetically, our lips crashing together like we couldn't wait to start up again. And weirdly enough, it might've been the most wonderful part of all.

For one, kissing Jax required both of us to keep our mouths shut, so to speak. We couldn't talk, so we couldn't trade insults. Instead, we fought with our lips; kissing, nibbling, even biting at times. His hot tongue slid through every corner of my eager, breathless mouth, and the very moment it finished, my own tongue was exploring his.

Kissing him at all should've been taboo, really. It seemed something reserved for two people forging a more intimate, loving connection. We could've been content to hate-fuck the shit out of each other, without ever making eye contact. Without even touching our lips together, too.

Instead, we seemed to revel in both.

A hand closed over my wrist, twisting my arm forward, pressing my palm against something hard and smooth. When I looked up, I knew what he wanted me to do. I grabbed the headboard with both hands, arched my back, and shoved my ass back in his direction. With my hair spilling down my back, it must've looked obscenely hot.

"Finish already."

I growled the words as a challenge, and Jax took that challenge immediately. He impaled me from behind, wrapping one hand so deep in my hair my mind began spinning with the possibilities.

Then he began fucking me even harder than before...

... and pulled.

FUCK!

I wanted to hate it, but I simply couldn't. The exquisite stretching, the borderline pain. The breathless pace of the intense, furious pounding he was giving me — I loved it all way more than I expected to. My God, I'd so fucking wanted this! And I didn't just want it, I'd *needed* it, too.

Paint chips flew as the headboard banged violently into the wall, causing me to shove myself backward against his ferocious thrusts. Jax had stamina. He had control. He had technique too, whether I begrudgingly wanted to admit it or not. But the main reason he was drilling me so hard, and fucking me so well, was perhaps because after all these years of going off on me verbally, it was finally his chance to go off on me physically, as well.

I looked back at him over my shoulder, and once again our eyes locked. Silently, wordlessly, I *ordered* him to come. I expected him to defy me, or maybe even go harder. To my surprise however, he actually nodded.

OhmyGod...

With one final grunt he pulled out and came all over me, showering my ass and back with his warm, sticky heat. It was incredible, watching him come. Jax became lost in the moment, his face twisted in ecstasy. I felt oddly powerful, in the face of his vulnerability.

We collapsed to the bed side by side, our bodies touching, the both of us heaving from the exertion of our release. For long minutes, neither one of us said a thing. In the warmth and the stillness, there was nothing to be said, really.

Then my eyelids grew heavier, the bed grew softer, and the shadows closed in from all sides.

~ 13 ~

HARPER

I woke up alone, naked and sticky in the empty bed, straddling a whole mess of blankets. Last night had been frenzied. Crazy. Totally reckless.

But also, insanely amazing.

"Hey, Harper."

The voice that came from the doorway sounded different today. Maybe that's because everything *was* different, whether I liked it or not.

"Is there any particular reason you're naked in my bed?"

I whirled in a panic, flipping the blankets off entirely by accident as I turned to face the foreign voice. When I saw who it was, I grabbed for the blankets again, to cover up.

"Holy SHIT!"

Preston stood in the doorway, casually chowing down on a bowl of very granola-looking cereal. He pointed his spoon at me.

"I mean, if this is a sexy surprise thing, I'm totally into it," he said. "Let me shower first, though. I've been out all night—"

"*YOUR* bed?" I cried.

"Yup."

I bolted upright, noticing now that the walls glowed dimly with the yellow light of dawn. Preston stared down at the mess and shook his head.

"Jax took you in here, didn't he?" He let out a sigh. "That fucker."

"W—What time is it?"

"A little after five."

He walked over, and I clutched the sheets even tighter against me. But Preston wasn't interested in me. He was reaching out to inspect the damage his headboard had done to the wall.

"Oh man," he groaned, thumbing the badly-dented sheetrock. More chips of paint flaked away. "There goes the security deposit."

I scanned the room for my clothes. They were scattered in a circle around the bed, exactly where Jax had taken them off. When I looked up again, Preston was noticing the same thing.

"Look, I ummm…. I'm really sorry," I said awkwardly. "I had no idea this was your bedroom."

Preston laughed, and for some reason his laughter made everything better. He took another scoop of cereal.

"I came here last night, we had a few drinks…"

"Yeah, yeah. I get it."

In the almost-daylight I could see it all now; the pristine toys, the graded comics. The posters framed neatly on the walls, of obscure sci-fi movies that only someone like me would've seen. There was a stack of worn Dungeons & Dragons books piled on the corner of a nearby dresser. The ones you'd need to not only play a campaign, but actually run one.

"Fourth edition?" I noted.

Preston nodded, looking impressed. "My friends and I have been rolling the dice for a long time. We like to keep it oldschool."

"Oldschool would be second edition, at the very least."

"True, but then you're missing out on a lot of new classes, races and spells."

I smiled at him. "Three or four Comic-Cons ago I cosplayed as an elven war-mage. Took second place in my category."

He eyed me over with an appreciative wink. "I would've liked to have seen that."

All of a sudden I remembered I was naked. Beneath the blankets, anyway.

"You've seen enough," I admonished him. "Hand me my clothes?"

"Yes, milady."

He gathered my things, panties and all, then chivalrously turned around so I could get dressed. I suppose I should've been embarrassed, especially when he handed me my thong. But none of it was anything he hadn't seen before.

"You sure you didn't come here last night looking for me?" Preston asked.

"Why?"

"Because I can't imagine you came looking for Jax."

I slid to the edge of the bed and slipped on my underwear. I felt a little better, but not much.

"I was in a weird mood last night," I admitted. "If you were the one who had been here, instead of him? I'd probably have ended up in this bed anyway."

"Unlucky me," Preston chuckled.

"Uh huh. I hope a night of Magic the Gathering was worth it." While he was still turned around, I kissed him on the cheek. "Now be a doll and check the dryer? I should have a shirt in there."

It took a minute, but Preston eventually returned with my blouse. He began breaking down the bed. Gathering the sheets, the blankets, the pillowcases.

I felt so guilty, I actually started helping him.

"Again, I'm sorry," I apologized. "After being out all night I'm sure you're exhausted. The last thing you want to do right now is strip your bed and do laundry."

"Pretty much," he smirked. "But screw it, another couple of hours won't kill me. I've got code to write anyway."

"Don't we all," I agreed.

The parts of my body that remembered his touch began sizing him up all over again. I'd nearly forgotten how sexy he was, with that flawless mocha skin and thick, dark hair. I'd spent hours running my fingers through that hair on the night we hooked up. He'd looked so beautiful and exotic, compared to the rest of the speed dating pool. Actually, with his five-in-the-morning stubble, he looked pretty fucking fantastic right now.

"So what happened?" he asked abruptly.

"Last night? I told you—"

"No," said Preston. "With us."

It was the question I'd been dreading. But of course I owed him an answer.

"I know I blew you off with all the wrong contact info," I admitted. "But believe me, it wasn't because I didn't want to see you again. It was because I *did* want to see you, actually. I wanted to see you too much."

He stopped in the middle of taking his pillowcase off. "Too much?"

"Yes."

"That's a new one. You're going to have to enlighten me, here."

I bit my lip. "It's just that I was busy," I explained. "Overwhelmed. I convinced myself I didn't have time for a boyfriend, and so..."

"You ditched."

"Yeah."

He paused, shrugged, and went back to gathering up the dirty sheets.

"Look, it totally wasn't you. I just wasn't looking for anything serious at the time." I dropped the sheets to the bed and sighed. "See, I'm working on this thing—"

"Your haptic software," he jumped in.

"And hardware," I added mechanically. I looked up at him, suddenly wide-eyed. "Wow, you remember?"

"Of course I remember! You had some great fucking

ideas."

Preston's chocolate brown eyes met mine, and I fought back a swell of pride. Why the hell did I not call this guy, again?

"So did you ever get it going?" he asked.

"Yes! I'm in the thick of it, actually."

"Prototype?"

I nodded eagerly. "Two."

"Well shit, Harper. You need to *show* me."

"I... Okay. I will."

My answer came entirely without thinking. Pitfalls? Consequences? Why worry about those insignificant little annoyances, when I could just say whatever the hell I wanted?

"There's a diner up the block," said Preston. "It generally sucks, but how bad could they fuck up some eggs?"

"Are you asking me to breakfast?"

He laughed. "What do you think?"

Breakfast. With Preston.

My stomach rumbled noisily.

"I think I'm one hot shower and about forty-five minutes of coding behind on my day already," I told him gently. "But... raincheck?"

Grinning smugly, he unlocked his phone and handed it over to me. This time I put in my proper info.

"I really *do* want to show you my work, by the way," I told him.

Together we stepped from his bedroom. Preston

began stuffing the washing machine, while I stared at a door at the end of the hall.

"Is that…"

"Jax?" Preston nodded. "Yeah, he's gonna sleep until three in the afternoon."

Maybe even later, I thought naughtily.

"I really should kick his door in and dump him out of bed," said Preston.

"You should," I agreed wholeheartedly. "The asshole deserves it."

Preston added soap, turned the dial, and the wash cycle kicked in. As the machine began rolling noisily, he looked at me and grinned.

"Don't worry too much about it," he said with a wink. "We'll get him back."

~ 14 ~

HARPER

There wasn't a hot enough shower in the world to wash away the fact I'd slept with Jackson Ripley, so I didn't even try. I needed a DeLorean, or a time machine, or that flashy pen thing they used to memory-wipe people in *Men in Black*. But since I had access to none of those things — at least not at this point in my life — all I could do was promise myself to never, ever think about it again.

But first, I thought about it. A lot.

Fuck.

I'd obviously gone down to that apartment because I felt slighted by Adrian, but there was more to it than that. For one, I was lonely as I'd ever been. Turns out sealing yourself in your house and shunning the rest of society to write code tended to put a huge dent in your social life.

But there were other reasons I stopped downstairs too, and some were deeper and darker than I liked to admit. There was a good chance I'd kissed Jax just to make Adrian jealous. That was bad enough, but there was also a chance I'd kissed him because I *wanted* to. Maybe I hadn't intended upon ending the night on my hands and knees, getting my hair pulled back as I left scratch marks on poor Preston's headboard. But I hadn't exactly stopped that situation from happening, either.

And then of course, there was Preston. I hadn't yet processed how I felt about him being cycled back into my life, but those warm brown eyes and that authentic smile had me questioning my previous decision to cut him out. Besides, it seemed like he could really help me. And didn't I just agree to have breakfast with him?

All these things tumbled randomly through my mind, throughout the day, as I went back to work debugging the feedback subroutine that had so rudely shocked me. I gained a little ground, and tweaked a few function calls. Some time after lunch I dropped into my couch for an episode of *Columbo*, but after an unanticipated cat nap I realized I'd have to watch the whole episode over again.

Finally, sometime after five, I headed over to Adrian's place. He had some kind of work meeting lined up for tonight, and wouldn't need me *that* long, so I didn't even bring my laptop. Already I was looking forward to seeing Brayden's smiling face again. Adrian, too, I begrudgingly admitted.

The walk to the car was bone-chillingly cold. I spent five miserable minutes shivering in the front seat, waiting for the defrost to kick in. Each winter I kept reminding myself to invest in an automatic starter. My bank account kept reminding me to fuck off.

A few minutes later I was raising my knuckles to Adrian's door, but it opened before I could even knock. He ushered me in with a smile, took my coat, and kissed me on the cheek. The whole thing happened in one smooth motion.

"Where's the baby?" I asked, looking around eagerly.

"Sleeping already. You hungry?"

I tried masking my disappointment. The apartment was every bit as cozy as it always was, except now it was filled with the smell of something utterly delicious. Two place settings rested opposite each other at the kitchen table. Before I could even answer, Adrian began piling thick strands of fettuccine on both plates.

"You made dinner?" I asked, incredulously.

"I did."

"Why?"

He chuckled as he set down the bowl of white pasta. "I know it's been a while, but you still eat dinner, don't you?"

"Yes. Yes, I do."

"Good. Could you grab us the garlic bread over there?"

Steam was still rising from the warm loaf of buttery, garlicky bread on the nearby butcher's block. I brought it strategically past my nostrils before setting it on the table. My stomach practically ate itself.

"You didn't have to do this, you know," I told him. "You've gotta leave here in what... five minutes?"

He poured us each a glass of water and a glass of wine. "More like five minutes *ago*, but yeah."

I'd gotten the call from Adrian not long ago. His meeting tonight was impromptu and late because there was a big storm sweeping in, and they wanted to beat it. Now it looked like he might be even later.

"Adrian—"

"Look, I figured it was the least I could do, after... you know. Last night."

I didn't know what to say, so I didn't say anything. I picked up my fork and began twirling.

"By the way, here. Take this."

He slid something across the table. I didn't see what it was until he took his hand away.

"What's this?"

"The key to my place," he shrugged. "If you're here watching my son, you should certainly have one."

"Oh. Okay."

I took the key and bit into the fettuccine, which was covered in a delicious cream sauce and tasted very familiar. It was also cooked perfectly al dente. Exactly like—

"Is this from a foil *pouch?*" I laughed. "The ones your mother made us as kids?"

"Knorr," he smiled. "Sure is."

The taste was unmistakable now, just as the memories that came with it. My father left when I was only ten, and my mother mentally checked out immediately afterward. Dinner at home, the few times my brother and I actually got it, was always a shitshow. It's probably why I was at Adrian's house so often.

"Screw it," I swore digging back in. "If it ain't broke…"

For the next few minutes we ate like we used to, scarfing down cheap food while laughing and talking about old times. Adrian's parents didn't have much, but they'd always been good to me. Their house had always felt like a second home.

"Look, I felt terrible after you left last night," said

Adrian. "I felt like you went home angry."

I kept my eyes on my plate, wondering what he'd say if he knew the truth. That I hadn't gone home at all.

"I should've been more forthcoming about Amy," he went on. "I mean, it's not like we're *dating* dating. We're just sort of, I don't know, figuring things out."

"Yeah, sure. With your genitals," I joked, slurping some fettuccine.

He frowned wryly. "It's not like that."

"No?"

"Not yet, no."

I blinked in surprise. It wasn't like him. Or was it? Shit, I didn't even know anymore. So much time had passed between us. We had history, but it was old history. Of his new life, I knew practically nothing.

Adrian dabbed his cloth napkin at one corner of his pretty mouth. He looked like a connoisseur at some Michelin Star restaurant, rather than a guy eating instant noodles covered in powdered cheese.

The image was too much for me. I broke out laughing.

"What?"

"Nothing."

He shook his head at me and grinned. "No, seriously, Harper. Give it up."

"I was just thinking about that one time you came to *my* house for dinner. And my mom made a 'meatloaf' by unwrapping a package of chop meat, slapping it onto a pan, and baking it for two hours."

Adrian's grin stretched from ear to ear. "It caught on fire if I remember, didn't it?"

"No, but it smoldered like hell. Eventually it set off the smoke alarms, and we ended up in the back yard."

"I remember," he chuckled. "You grabbed Max, and I grabbed the dog. She came out through a big swirl of smoke, holding a blackened pan."

"With a burnt hockey puck-looking thing in the center, yes."

Holy shit, the visuals. The memories! Adrian's laughter brought me even further back, to all the incredible times we'd spent together. On the couch in his basement, watching movies. Spending our summers at the town pool. He'd come to all my soccer games, back when my mom was still driving me to them. And I'd watched just about every one of his lacrosse matches, even after Jax made it nearly unbearable by joining the team.

We'd become so close over the years, even when new friends and different interests led us in opposite directions. Not long after graduating, it made me sad to think at how quickly and easily we lost track.

The nostalgia faded as an alarm chimed on his phone. I checked the time on mine.

"You know you *really* should go."

Adrian was still staring at me, lost perhaps in the same places I was. He was dressed for business today; all clean cut and freshly-shaved. He smelled and looked absolutely delicious. I wanted a bite.

"You sure you're okay?"

I threw my hand dismissively. "Are you serious? Of

course I am. Come on, you never owed me an explanation to begin with."

"Yes I did," he said firmly. "I owe you a hell of a lot, Harper. More than you realize. And if for any reason this thing isn't working for you," he pointed around, "just say the word. I'd totally understand."

"You would, huh?"

He nodded slowly. "I can't have you mad at me. I've missed you way too much."

Butterflies took flight in my stomach. Guilty ones.

"I've... missed you too," I admitted.

He stood up and embraced me, and the hug felt better than ten-thousand apologies. Not that I wanted an apology at all. I just wanted... well...

Him?

"I'll be back before midnight," he promised. "Try and get some work done."

I frowned at the lack of my laptop. And at the lack of something else.

"You wanna know the one thing I actually *am* angry about?" I asked him.

He froze halfway through the process of putting his coat on. "Of course."

"I'm mad you put that baby down before I got here. I was gonna snuggle the hell out of him."

The fatherly smile on Adrian's face melted me all over again.

"That baby was so tired he put *himself* down," he

chuckled. "But if he happens to wake up? Feel free to snuggle away."

Pulling the rest of his coat on, he opened the door and looked back.

"I wouldn't mind if you saved one for me, too," he said with a wink.

~ 15 ~

HARPER

Snow.

For most people, it was a huge inconvenience. It meant shoveling, scraping, plowing yourself out. Putting on layer after layer to keep warm as you battled the elements, then peeling off those wet clothes as you stood, shivering, trying to get warm again.

Snow triggered claustrophobia in those who rarely felt it, for the simple reason that the right storm or blizzard could trap you in your house. With someone like me, however? I *counted* on those blizzards. They were the perfect excuse to start a fire, get cozy, and write code until my fingers were ready to fall off. I could drink guilt-free hot chocolate. Read an entire book, or start a movie marathon. Winter storms let me put off anything and everything that normally took me away from my work, or distracted me from my computer screens.

And especially; up here in a place like Buffalo? They were a free, multi-day pass to be totally anti-social.

The snowstorm raging over the past two days had swallowed up my driveway, nearly covered my windows, and blissfully ended any reasons for me leaving the house. I had the little wood stove between my kitchen and living room glowing white-hot, burning with such heat and ferocity that, at one point, I actually started sweating.

As it turned out, that was not only fine, it was actually ideal. The haptics I was currently testing required patches fixed directly to the skin. I could simulate an entire haptic suit by connecting leads to the pads fixed on my arms, legs, thighs, and stomach. I had pads affixed up and down my ribcage. Pads from my shoulders down to the tops of my breasts, just above the nipple, where current iterations of Virtual Reality software wouldn't dare to send signals.

But not *my* software.

Inevitably, as VR continued its evolution, people meeting virtually instead of in-person would feel the basic human need to *touch*. It wasn't enough to just see each other anymore, or feel the pressure on your fingertips as someone on the other side of the world reached for your hand. No, you needed to feel the tingle as they slid their palm into yours. The butterflies that came with lying atop each other, chest to chest, stomach to stomach, even pelvis to pelvis.

I'd written *kissing* software; one with extremely intricate and delicate receptors that interfaced with the eleven different muscles of your upper and lower lip. I hadn't tested out both sides of that one yet, but I was more than ready to. I just wasn't willing to part with my prototypes. At least not until I had the next generational version built.

And so there I was, standing in my underwear, a few dozen wires dangling from all different parts of my exposed skin. I was running low on firewood, and frozen pizzas, and bottled water. Testing my most recent bug, I was running even lower on patience, when suddenly:

Knock KNOCK.

On any other day the raps at my front door would be unmistakable. But they had to be mistaken, because—

"C'mon, egghead. Open up!"

I pulled out the leads as quickly as possible, which even then took practically forever, then ran to get dressed. I recognized the voice immediately, of course. And I knew ignoring that voice wouldn't make it go away.

KNOCK KNOCK KNOCK!

"Alright, already!" I called back.

Is he serious?

I was both annoyed and excited as I threw open the door. I hated being interrupted while I was making progress. At the same time, I hadn't seen another human in days.

"How the hell did you—"

Framed by the still-falling snow, I was shocked to find Preston standing in my doorway. He was covered head to toe in big, thick snowflakes, and wearing gloves that were caked with little balls of ice. Right behind him, holding a pair of snow shovels, was Jax.

"C'mon, it's freezing out here!"

The icy wind practically blew them inside. I had to shoulder the door closed.

"Holy shit," I shivered.

They began stripping down, and shaking themselves off. Both men were soaking wet. I knew immediately it wasn't only from the storm.

"Did you just shovel me *out?*" I asked incredulously.

"Your car, your walkway, your driveway," Preston smiled.

"And you're welcome," spat Jax.

"How the hell did you even *get* here?" I marveled.

Jax jerked a thumb his roommate's way. "He's got these obnoxiously oversized tires on his Bronco. I think he might be trying to compensate for something."

I shot Preston a surreptitious wink and grinned. "Trust me, he's not."

Jax's expression went temporarily sour. He made a 'walked right into that one' face and rolled his eyes. "Oh yeah. Right."

"Look, let's not pretend I don't know what the two of *you* did the other night, either," Preston replied dryly. "And on my *bed,* no less."

"On your bed, *in* your bed..." Jax smirked. "Up against your bed—"

"Territorial pissings," I sighed and shook my head.

Jax squinted curiously. "You mean the Nirvana song?"

"No, I mean enough with the two of you, lifting your legs like dogs to mark out your territory." I folded my arms. "There *is* no territory. Got it?"

They looked at me together now, two ex-lovers sizing me up in much the same way. I had to admit, there was a small part of me that actually liked it. I'd never been in a situation like this before.

"Can we talk about these hooker boots then?" Jax asked, as he pulled his own off.

He was holding up my highest leather boots, picked

from a pile of footwear in the corner. To be honest, they were pretty fucking fantastic.

"They're *not* hooker boots," I somewhat lied.

"Do they come up past your knees?"

I hesitated a little too long. "Well, yes. But—"

"Then they're hooker boots," Jax smiled victoriously. "End of story."

God, he could be such an asshole! Sometimes. Sort of.

"Let's get back to how the two of you arrived at my doorstep in the middle of this crazy blizzard."

It seemed unbelievable that they'd be out driving in this, much less come all the way here. They'd risked getting stuck in some very terrible conditions. Hell, they'd even shoveled me out.

"We already told you," Jax started up again. "He's got—"

"I know, but *why?*" I finally asked.

Jax was busy pulling his wet socks off, one by one. Preston just smiled and pointed.

"I wanted to see *that.*"

I turned, and found myself staring at my prototype. Already Preston was making his way toward it.

"It's—it's not nearly ready, yet," I stammered. "The input code is wonky as hell. Even when the tactile connectors *are* firing in sequence, there's still a ton of delay issues."

"Can I try it?"

Preston's eyes weren't just wide, they were eager and

full of excitement. They scanned left and right over my workbench area, stopping in all the same places my own eyes would stop, if I were in his shoes. He looked like a kid on Christmas.

"Well..."

Jax, on the other hand, had produced an eighteen-pack of beer. It was soggy from apparently sitting in the snow for the past half hour or more, but also, ice-cold.

"This was all his idea," he said, nodding toward Preston. "He told me you guys were gonna do nerd stuff all night. I told him I'd tag along, but there was no way I was going to face this geekfest sober."

He cracked a beer, then held it out to me. "Here dork."

To my surprise, I found myself taking it. "Thanks, dick."

I tilted it back, and the liquid was so cold it slid right down my throat. I finished half the can before coming up for air, that's how thirsty I was.

When I looked back at them, glassy eyed, they were staring at me. Preston's look was especially pleading.

"Ummm... okay," I shrugged. "Sure, why not? Let's get you hooked up."

~ 16 ~

HARPER

"Oh my God…"

"DUCK!"

Preston ducked, twisting left and out of the way. The dragon's fire just barely missed him. On the monitor, we could see his avatar was actually singed, as the winged beast climbed back into the smoke-swirled sky.

"I felt the *heat!*" Preston cried, whirling around. His arms were held outward, gripping an imaginary sword and shield. Haptic leads sprang from his body in every direction. The VR headset was secured tightly to his face.

"On the right side of my body, I could actually feel the —"

His sentence ended abruptly as he dropped to his knees, jolted there by an earthquake that only he could feel. The dragon's tail had slammed the cobblestone courtyard of the ancient castle, sending bricks and mortar flying everywhere.

"My legs… you *shocked* them!"

"No!" I said loudly, so he could hear me through the

headset. Then, with a renewed sense of pride: "It only feels that way."

Preston had been hooked up to the game for nearly an hour now; a custom-modded version that I'd created myself. He'd made his way through a medieval town, and completed the dungeon crawl. He'd climbed the hill, and found the castle.

The dragon was bearing down on him again. The flapping of its wings took up the entire screen.

"What do I do? What do I DO!?"

"Kick it in the balls!" Jax cried from the couch. By now, he'd put away a significant number of beers. His eyes were half-lidded as they watched the monitor.

"It does have balls, doesn't it?" Jax asked me confidentially.

I didn't answer. I was too busy watching Preston's reaction as the dragon soared over him. The haptic patches on his shoulders and upper arms would be giving him tingles now, just enough to simulate a wind.

"Holy shit, Harper…" he swore, turning another one-eighty. "This is *incredible!*"

My pride swelled even more, but I couldn't focus on enjoying it. And that's because I was too fixated on Preston's mostly-naked body.

Damn…

I'd gotten a little excited, watching him strip down to his boxers so I could put the leads on him. I'd gotten even hotter applying the temporary patches to his bare stretches of beautifully-striated muscle. His mocha skin was smooth and blemishless. His six-pack abdominals weren't just well-defined, they were hard, sculpted works of individual art.

He might've noticed how badly my fingers trembled, affixing the patches there. Because he'd covered my wrist with his, flashed those bright white teeth, and gently dragged my hand downward... over the lower part of his belly.

Then he winked at me, and I actually *felt* myself get wet.

I'd put patches on his broad chest, the wings of his rib cage, and the sides of his warm, beautiful neck. Flashbacks came; moving images of our night together. All the kissing there, on his neck and mine. All the goosebumps that erupted across our bodies, right before we came together, stripped down, and fucked each other's brains out.

I hadn't gotten to *really* see his body in action. Not twisting and jumping and swinging a sword, like he was right now. For the first few minutes I nervously watched the leads, keeping an eye on a separate monitor to see how the reactional data was being fed back real-time. But very soon I became mesmerized, just watching the movements of his body.

If Jax noticed, it was hard to tell. He was his usual dickish self, throwing back beers and dropping crude comments as I applied the leads to Preston's inner and outer thighs. Eventually these leads would be fed into a full-body suit, and that suit would become the last generation prototype. Jax, of course, couldn't see the light at the end of that tunnel. And so he made even more comments about Preston looking like a naked porcupine.

The screen changed again, and a yellow light filled the living room. The dragon breathed. Preston cried out. The flames turned to smoke, and the smoke formed the words GAME OVER.

"You're barbecue!" Jax laughed.

Preston's shoulders were slumped in defeat as he

removed the headset. I took it from him, and began disconnecting the leads.

"Don't feel bad," I told him. "No one beats the dragon on the first try."

"Nobody, huh?" he smirked. "Did you beat him?"

"Well yeah," I chuckled. "But I wrote the code for most of his behavioral patterns, so…"

A few minutes later the last of the haptic patches had been removed, and the lead wires had all been hung in their proper places on the master board. Preston searched his body for any I might've missed before pulling on his shirt. When he stepped into his jeans again, I actually mourned the moment.

"That was *really* something spectacular," Preston swore. "And trust me, I've played on a *lot* of VR systems. Oculus. Valve. Sony. Meta…"

"Well that's the plan," I admitted. "Once I get the tech right, I can pitch it to the bigger companies. The hope is, at least one of them should bite."

He shook his head in slow admiration. Face to face, I could see my pride reflected back in his smooth brown eyes.

"Bite?" he murmured. "Harper, they're going to be fighting over you."

I shrugged. "Maybe."

"You're going to be *rich*."

I swallowed dryly. "Well, it's not like—"

A loud noise turned us both in the direction of the couch. Jax was face down, passed out, and snoring loudly.

"Wow," I said. "That's incredible."

"What is?"

"I don't think I've ever seen him with his mouth shut."

Preston laughed. "In his defense, he's not even that drunk. He worked two doubles in the past three days, and we came straight here from his last shift."

"I see. Does he always sound like a chainsaw when he sleeps?"

"Not always," Preston smirked. "Sometimes he sounds more like a broken lawnmower."

I wrinkled my nose at a particularly loud exhale. "How do you *live* with this?"

Preston tapped his ears. "Noise-canceling headset."

We were standing on the other side of the living room now, nearest the glowing wood stove. Jax had been feeding it firewood for the past hour. It was still cherry red. The warmth was soothing.

"I guess you're staying here tonight," I said, in the form of a non-question.

Preston glanced at the snow-caked window, then back at Jax.

"Sure looks that way, yeah."

There was a pregnant pause as we stared at each other for a long, silent moment. The fire crackled. Jax snorted.

"Do you have a spare air-mattress or—"

"Hey, you wanna see something weird?"

I asked the question at almost the same time he spoke. Preston tilted his head curiously.

"Really?"

"Yeah, really."

He shrugged and grinned. "Is there a guy on Earth who would say no to something like that?"

~ 17 ~

PRESTON

It wasn't a room, it was an outright museum. And not just any museum either, but one lovingly dedicated to every single one of my deepest, darkest, vices.

Or fantasies, depending upon how you looked at it.

"Harper!" I swore.

The room was light and dark, good and evil, Jedi and Sith. The shelves and built-ins were stocked with everything Star Wars. There were figures, vehicles, models and lightsabers. Movie posters lined every square inch of the walls, wherever they weren't covered with in-the-box, 1977, Kenner original toys.

Some of the posters were even signed by the cast.

"HARPER!"

The room was backlit in blue and red, by well-hidden LED lighting strips. A full-sized set of stormtrooper armor stood menacingly in one corner, blaster drawn. On the other side, a life-sized model of Luke Skywalker opposed it, all shrouded in Jedi robes and sporting a black-gloved hand.

There were Star Wars Lego kits everywhere. Old ones. Discontinued ones. Ones that I never even *knew* of. She had the AT-AT Walker, the Falcon, the Imperial Star Destroyer from the Ultimate Collector Series. Rare mini-figures from over a decade ago worth hundreds of dollars each, displayed in clear Lucite cases, their weapons held high.

"I know, I know," she finally sighed. "It's a disease."

If it was a disease, I certainly had it too. Her case might just be terminal, though.

"Is... Is that—"

I pointed to a frame within a frame. A tiny piece of plastic, enshrouded within a shadowbox.

"That's not... that can't be—"

"Yes," she said, her voice filled with pride. "It is."

The certificate of authenticity told me what I already knew. Standing before me, at eye-level, was a tiny piece of gray foam carved meticulously by hand. An original, screen-used section of the Death Star's surface.

"I... I..."

"You need to hold it, don't you?"

I whirled on her. Standing in the doorway, arms held overhead, she looked strikingly beautiful. Like the goddess of geeks.

"If you're teasing me..."

"Go ahead," she chuckled. "Open it."

I moved slowly, removing the artifact with the care of a surgeon. I held it in my palm. My whole body shivered.

"This... this is a piece of history."

"Sure is."

I treated the moment as the religious experience it actually was. Then, reverently, I returned the piece to its protective case. Staring at it was like staring back through time.

"I knew you were a fan," I swore. "But I had no idea you were *this* far into it."

Harper crossed her arms and grinned. "Just wait 'till you see the Lord of the Rings room."

My jaw scraped the floor. *"You have a Lord of the RINGS room?!"*

"No," she laughed evilly. "But wouldn't it be awesome if I did?"

I spent the next twenty or so minutes touring her collection, with Harper pointing out any of the little details I might've missed. She was a woman after my own heart. Someone dedicated to all the same things I was, with brains and beauty to spare.

Beyond it all, there was an inherent sexiness about her that made my blood boil. It was the way she walked, the way she talked, the way she laughed her cute little laugh. I saw it in her eyes, whenever she'd look at me. I felt it in her touch earlier on, when her fingers lingered all over my body while hooking me up to the fruits of her labor.

One night. That's all I'd had with her. One incredible, beautiful night…

And then she was gone.

"This *would've* been the guest room," she said apologetically. "But obviously I got rid of the bed."

"That's okay."

"Follow me to my room though," she continued. "I should have all kinds of extra blankets and pillows somewhere in the closet."

This certainly wasn't a request she had to make twice. Harper led me into a small, cozy bedroom, decorated in neutral but warm tones. There were a few more dorky collectibles in here, as well. I recognized every piece.

"Nice Doomhammer," I grinned, pointing. "World of Warcraft. Epic weapon replica."

Harper returned a similar grin, obviously impressed. "I actually won that thing. It's heavy as hell."

She lifted it from its mount, and swung the big war hammer over her shoulder. By the way her body tilted, I could tell it was *heavy*.

"You wanna see my Doomhammer?" Harper teased. She was obviously enjoying herself.

"Well, you've already seen mine, so…"

"Here then."

She swung it down, intending to give it to me handle-first, but it was just *too* heavy. Instead she pitched forward, crying out as the hammer slipped from her hands and thudded heavily to the floor. She would've been on the floor too, but I reacted too quickly and she ended up in my arms.

I wasted absolutely no time in kissing her.

Fuck…

She smelled like vanilla and sugar and all things delicious, as her hot mouth churned against mine. Harper was kissing me back so greedily, so furiously, I had to question whether she'd fallen in the first place, or simply flung herself willfully into my arms.

Either way, the two of us were all in.

I worked her body with my hands, the tips of my fingers remembering her every delicate curve and crevasse. Harper gasped as I slipped my fingers down her back and beyond her waistband. The warmth of her thong-covered ass felt incredible against my palms and I squeezed possessively, devouring the resulting moans and whimpers as I remembered *other* places that were even warmer.

We tripped our way to the bed then fell shamelessly into it, the last of our inhibitions gone. Our bodies began grinding obscenely. Our mouths moved over places we both knew well, as I began peeling my clothes off for the second time tonight.

But what about—

What, Jax? I shoved the intrusive thought from my head. Jax had certainly taken her, but this wasn't Jax's girl. If anything I had first dibs, having planted my flag long before him.

Besides, Jax and Harper totally fucking hated each other. On separate occasions, they'd *both* told me so. Yeah, okay, they'd had sex. But so what? The way Jax described it, I saw it as a heat of the moment thing. A necessary letting off of steam, after more than a decade of swapping insults and hard infighting.

Ultimately, it was Jax's friend Adrian that had created this powder keg in the first place. She'd grown up with him, she knew him well. If anything she was *his* girl, and not ours. Or maybe, just like she said, Harper was no one's girl at all. No marking of territory needed.

But fuck… I wasn't leaving here without marking *something*.

A delicate hand slipped through the leg of my boxer briefs. Eager fingers wrapped around my thickening shaft before extracting me, slapping my manhood heavily down the side of one leg.

Harper stared at her handiwork, lips slightly parted, her sapphire eyes fixed on my erection like she'd seen an old friend. A second later she was kissing me even more deeply, swirling her smooth pink tongue through my mouth as she spread her legs wide for me. I buried my face between those incredible thighs, then inhaled her through the thin fabric of her tiny thong.

Fuck yes.

Her scent was husky, sweet, ambrosial — exactly as I remembered it. Her panties were totally adorable. I couldn't wait to destroy them.

I looked down into those beautiful, lust-filled eyes. Harper bit her lip and smiled. She gave me the nod…

THUMP!

We jumped off the bed so fast the springs squeaked! The noise had been loud and unmistakable. With a protective arm out, I kept her behind me as we crept in the direction of the doorway. We peered down the hall, into the living room…

Jax was flopping around and groaning, spread eagle across the floor.

He'd rolled off the couch.

"He's up?" Harper whispered.

Her near-naked body was pressed into me from behind, awakening my every last animalistic instinct. It was almost impossible to suppress them.

"Nah," I assured her. "The four horsemen of the

apocalypse could ride through your living room right now, and he'd still be asleep."

This happened often I knew, especially after he'd worked so many hours in a row. Jax's body desperately needed rest, but his mind was still racing, still awake. And sometimes, still hungry too. This combination had caused all kinds of midnight chaos back at our place, usually in the kitchen.

Jax groaned again, then flopped over. He tried to get up, but apparently his legs said no.

"Does he sleepwalk?" Harper asked.

"Sometimes," I admitted. "Usually when he's exhausted like this. I've found him in all different rooms, doing all different things. Once he was sitting in the corner, trying to play cards with himself."

On cue, Jax mumbled something loudly. It was a half-sentence of gibberish, followed by an all-new round of snoring.

I turned to face Harper. She stood there in her underwear, all soft and vulnerable, staring back at me. Her expression was unsure.

"Maybe... Maybe we shouldn't do this," she murmured. "Right now, I mean."

Her blue eyes were soft and apologetic as she took my hand.

"If he wakes up, it just wouldn't be—"

"I know."

I squeezed her hands in mine, then kissed her softly. I wanted her to be comfortable. I wanted her to feel safe. I wanted to ravage the everliving fuck out of her hot little body, but if it were anything like the last time, neither one of us could possibly keep quiet.

We got dressed slowly and reluctantly, but we still got dressed. Harper eventually ducked into her closet and came out with pillows and blankets. On the way back into the living room, she dropped them abruptly and slid her body against mine.

"Hey…" she whispered, nuzzling into my chest. "Preston, I'm sorry. I really am."

I hugged her as tightly as I dared, then tilted her chin upward with the gentle guide of my fingers.

"Harper Hayes," I sighed softly, "you might just be the most perfect girl I've ever met."

Her skin flushed a slightly darker shade of pink. Staring into her eyes, my face broke into a smile.

"But I'm sort of getting used to the idea that I can't have you."

~ 18 ~

HARPER

"No!" I cried. "No no no no nooooo!"

The resulting chuckle was gleeful, almost even triumphant. But I was too far away. It was too late for me to do anything, but watch the horror unfold.

Looking me dead in the eye, Emma added a sinister smile as she dumped her Cheerios right over Brayden's freshly-washed head. The milk slid down his shoulders, soaking his onesie front and back. For a moment, the little boy's eyes went wide with shock. Then, joining his partner in crime, he began giggling right alongside Emma.

Damn.

I considered chastising the toddler, but I couldn't bring myself to do it. For one, Jax's adopted daughter was just too damn cute. But more important that that, *I* was the idiot who gave her a full bowl of milk to begin with.

"Lesson learned," I sighed.

I grabbed a fresh roll of paper towels and cleaned Brayden up first, then I got down on my hands and knees.

Pulling out long sections of Brawny and ripping them off seemed to amuse them. Emma began clapping her hands, and the two babies began laughing even harder.

"You like that, huh?"

They squealed and clapped some more, so I made funny faces and exaggerated motions from the floor. Eventually I had the mess cleaned up. My knees popped loudly as I got up, and they began mimicking my resulting grunt.

"Oh yeah?" I taunted. "Well one day your little knees are gonna pop too."

It had been a long night. I figured watching two children wouldn't be that much more difficult than watching one. Instead, it was more than twice as hard. The little ones had obviously been around each other a lot. They worked together like partners in crime, taking off in opposite directions whenever I turned my head. They laughed like crazy as I chased them down on their shaky little legs, while moving from one mess to another.

We tried playing games, but they were interested for no more than ten seconds at a clip. I tried reading to them, but they only had so much interest. On Adrian's suggestion, I cordoned off the little play mat area he'd set up using the interlocking baby gates he stored in the coat closet. But five minutes after I put them in there to play, Emma had scratched Brayden's face.

It wasn't intentional, but her sharp little baby nails left a tiny red line across the boy's cheek. He cried for a few minutes, then snuggled me adorably for a few more. I couldn't enjoy the moment though, because Emma hung off my leg, demanding the same kind of attention.

Washing my hands, I turned back to the two clapping babies in the high chair. Brayden was still soaked, his hair all matted with milk. Which really sucked, because I'd *just* bathed him.

"Lesson two," I chided myself. "Bathe the kid *after* you give him a bath."

He reached for me as I began unclipping his high chair, so Emma began reaching too. She was no longer laughing. In wriggling and struggling to free herself, her expression was one of growing panic and frustration.

In that moment, I caught a strange, familiar glimpse…

My God… she looks just like Jax!

She really did! Or at least, she looked like her biological father. Jax's brother had been a few years older than us, so I hadn't been around him much. Jason had been a three-letter athlete, and almost always at some kind of practice. He'd run in different circles, growing up.

KNOCK KNOCK.

I whirled in the direction of the front door, halfway through picking up the baby. Emma was still holding her little arms out, her tiny hands opening and closing.

"Ummm…"

KNOCK KNOCK KNOCK!

The knocking grew louder and much more insistent. Leaving Emma strapped securely in her high chair, I carried Brayden with me to the front door and peered through the peephole.

A woman stood on the other side.

She was small, and so bundled in jackets and scarves I could barely make her out. She was alone in the hall, though, so I cracked the door.

"Can I help yo—"

I never got to finish. Without a single word she shoved her way inside, with a strength and speed that surprised me. To my horror, she reached for Brayden and slid her hands beneath his arms.

"EXCUSE ME!" I shouted, twisting away. But the baby was reaching for her. And as the scarf fell away I saw her face, and slowly, vaguely remembered...

The demon queen.

"Erika?"

She was a little older, a little thinner, and a lot more angry looking than I remembered.

"Of course, Erika!" she shot back. "Who else would I be? Now give me my son!"

Reluctantly, I handed him over. Brayden went willingly enough, but once in her arms, he began reaching back for me again.

"So who the hell are *you?*" Erika demanded. "And where's Adrian?"

"He's out. At work."

"Work!?" she scoffed. Just then, a baby began screaming loudly. Her cries carried in from the kitchen.

Emma!

"Whose baby is *that?*" Erika roared. Her mean eyes narrowed. "Are you running some kind of a daycare here, or —"

"One second!"

I ran back, scooped Emma from the high chair, and

dried the tears on her little cheeks. She clutched me tenderly, her tiny fingers clenching and unclenching on my shirt. My heart felt like it would literally melt.

"Is this *milk?*"

Adrian's ex-fiancée stood in the doorway to the kitchen now, her lip curled back in disgust. She was holding her son with one hand, and sifting his matted hair with the other.

"Yes, actually."

"How did—"

"Look, it just happened. I'm going to bathe him. In fact, I was just about to—"

"Oh you're not doing anything of the sort," Erika laughed bitterly. "I'm taking my son home. It's obvious he's not getting proper care here, and he was supposed to be visiting his *father* anyway."

She scanned around, sniffing the place like she'd never been this far inside. As far as I knew, maybe she hadn't.

"You don't recognize me, do you?" I asked her.

Her gaze finished its circuit of the kitchen and fixed tiredly back on mine.

"No. Should I?"

"C'mon Erika," I sighed. "It's me. Harper."

She shook her head, looking bored.

"Harper *Hayes.*"

If I hadn't been looking I would've missed the quick flash of recognition in her eyes. It happened lightning fast, but disappeared just as quickly as she suppressed it immediately.

"Look, it's been years," I told her. "If I'm going to be

watching Brayden from time to time, we should probably learn to—"

"Is this is SCRATCH?" Erika shouted suddenly. "On his *FACE?*"

Taking a finger, she tried rubbing the red line off her son's tiny cheek. It only served to upset him. Little Brayden swatted her away repeatedly. His eyes teared up and he began crying.

"About that—"

"You're forbidden from watching him!" Erika shouted. "Do you hear me? Never again!"

Her face was contorted in anger, but I sensed it was mostly a mock outrage. She'd obviously been caught off guard. She hadn't expected to find me here, and my presence enraged her. And now her finger was in my face.

For Brayden's sake, I resisted the urge to grab it.

"Look, Adrian said you'd be away for a few days," I said evenly. "He told me he had the baby until—"

"Well, I came back early," Erika snapped.

"And that's fine," I said placatingly. "But you can't just show up and *take* him."

Her eyes went so wide they looked like something straight from a horror movie. It actually frightened me.

"I mean you *can*, of course," I amended quickly. "But at least let me call Adrian, so you can tell him you're—"

"SHUT UP!"

Her frantic screams were affecting both children, of course. Brayden's tears flowed freely now, and Emma was crying openly again. I'd gotten her to stop by bouncing her off my hip, but now she was cowering against me, looking fearfully back at Erika.

I didn't try stop her as she stormed off. All I could do was watch Brayden stare back at me over her shoulder, wondering why our fun little playdate was so suddenly and violently over. He sniffed miserably, his eyes welling with tears as he reached back for us both.

The last thing I saw was his expression of pure misery as his mother slammed the door behind her. I turned to Emma for comfort, her tiny lip quivering wildly.

We were both in tears as I reached for my phone.

~ 19 ~

HARPER

Once the tears started flowing, I couldn't stop them. I had to though, for the sake of Emma.

Her precious little eyes watched my every move, willing me to smile, to somehow feel better, to comfort her in all the same ways she was comforting me. After making the phone call I took her back into the kitchen, and finished feeding her. Emma ate very little. She kept pointing to the empty high chair, beside her.

"Bray?"

"Yes, honey," I'd assured her with a smile. "Brayden's fine. He went to see his mommy."

My words calmed her, and eventually I was able to clean her up and get her into her sleep sack. Jax's daughter was loving, trusting, and incredibly sweet. This was only my second time watching her, and yet the two of us had connected on a deep, special level that seemed to supersede everything else. Somehow, I could sense that I filled a void for her. It was in the way she clutched me, the way she looked at me. The way she'd held so tightly onto me, as Adrian's bitch of an ex-fiancée ranted like a lunatic in front of two little kids.

And I had to admit, the tiny toddler did the same for me. There was a hole in my heart I never even knew existed; and that void was suddenly filled to overflowing by the love of this incredible little girl. I must've kissed her a hundred times as we sat there on the couch, calming each other down. When she fell asleep against my chest, I kept her there for a long while, just watching the slow rise and fall of her tiny body in rhythm with her breathing.

Adrian flew through the door about an hour after I called him. Which was remarkable, considering he was nearly an hour and a half away.

"Harper, I'm sooo sorry!"

I shushed him with a finger against my lips. He saw Emma and began tiptoeing immediately.

"I— I had no idea Erika was—"

"It's okay," I whispered. "Here. Help me get up."

He extended an arm, and pulled me easily to my feet without disturbing the sleeping baby. Together we stared at her for a few quiet moments.

"She's a trooper," I murmured.

"She is."

"Let me get her to bed."

Moving slowly I carried her down the hall and into the nursery; where Adrian and Jax had set up a second crib. Emma was big for her age. Soon she'd be reaching up with her tiny arms and climbing out, and then they'd have to get her a little bed with rails. I remembered my brother Max doing exactly that. Of course, as a big sister, I often saw it as my duty to help him escape…

Max.

My heart hurt a little, just thinking about my brother. I remember the day he'd turned nineteen and moved to Oahu, determined to learn how to surf. He'd come back several weeks later, only to tell my mother and I that he'd be moving there indefinitely. Hawaii was like that, he told us. It sucked you in. Kept you from wanting to be *anywhere* else.

I couldn't count the number of times I'd wanted to drop everything and join him.

Reaching down, I painstakingly managed to transfer Emma to the crib without waking her up. She twisted around a little, though. I pulled her little blanket up over her legs, and spent the next several minutes gently rubbing her back. Eventually she stopped moving and lay still, sleeping peacefully as I crept from the room.

I reentered the living room to find the lights dimmed, and candles lit. Adrian had already eradicated the mess in the kitchen I'd intended to tackle. He'd cleaned up, taken out the garbage, and done the dishes. He'd also changed from the button-down shirt and slacks to a pair of mesh basketball shorts and the softest-looking T-shirt in the universe.

"You tired?" he asked.

"Not even a little bit."

"Good, me neither. Sit down and relax. I'll be right back."

I sank into the couch, just as he returned with a bag of microwave popcorn. The blue lettering on the side read 'extra butter.' Just like old times.

"Pick a movie," he told me, dropping the remote in my lap.

I scooted over as he sat down beside me. Two empty glasses rested on the coffee table before us. And between them…

"You brought the bottle," I smiled wearily, nodding toward an uncorked merlot.

"Sure did."

"Good move."

"The *only* move," Adrian grinned, "on a night like this."

He poured, we clinked glasses, and we proceeded to stretch out. I surfed briefly with the remote, then stopped on the first comedy I saw, which happened to be *Stepbrothers*.

Anything to make me laugh, I figured.

"Listen, Harper…"

"You're going to tell me you're sorry about your ex showing up here," I headed him off. "That you didn't know she was even in town, much less coming to get Brayden."

"Well, yes."

"It's fine," I told him. "I'll admit, I was a little rattled when she ripped the baby out of here like she was carrying the nuclear football. And even I was shocked at the all-new levels of bitchdom she's obtained. But then again, Erika was always a bitch, Adrian. I still don't know what you saw in her."

Purely out of reflex, I went to extend my legs over his, like we'd done hundreds of times before. But that was so many years ago. I stopped myself halfway.

"Here."

He reached out and took my legs, putting them exactly where they always went. As I settled back into the arm of the couch, his hand began kneading my foot.

"I'll just say this," Adrian began absently. "It won't ever happen again. She took the baby during *my* visitation, and I've already documented it with the police and my lawyer."

My eyebrow arched. "The police?"

"Nothing big," Adrian said dismissively. "But when she breaks custody rules, it's always good to get a report. With enough reports, the judge can change things. Maybe get her to stop the ridiculous behavior."

He wasn't just kneading now, he was full-blown rubbing my foot, rolling the ball of his thumb into the hollow just above my heel. I'd forgotten how good he was at it, too. As the tension left, and pleasure flooded in to take its place, my eyes half-closed in pure ecstasy.

"The funny part is, I would've given her the baby if she'd only just called me," he said. "I've never kept Brayden from his mother, ever. And I never will."

"You…" I sighed. "You're very…"

God, I was in absolute *heaven* now. Drifting through clouds of pure—

"How was it tonight, watching the both of them?" he asked.

I took a sip of my wine and sighed into the glass. "Fun, actually," I smiled. "They're great kids, and they adore each other. They feed off each other, too."

Adrian's handsome face broke into a fatherly smile that was overtly sexy, even if he didn't know it. "Yeah, well thanks for taking them on such short notice. Especially with Jax getting called in for someone else's shift."

He'd set his wine glass down, now. Hopefully so he could work my foot with two hands.

"How was work for you?" I somehow managed to ask.

He shrugged his massive shoulders. "Work was good. I'm still getting into the client side of things, which is all about meeting people and making contacts. It requires a lot of face time, though. A lot of late dinners, and getting drinks afterward…"

"Sounds a lot more glamorous than what I'm doing."

"To an extent," Adrian agreed. "It takes me away from here in the evenings, though. I love that I get to spend time with Brayden during the day, but I miss putting him down at night. He's always cutest right before he falls asleep."

Adrian lifted his glass again and took a long, deep pull. When he returned it to the coffee table, he began rubbing my foot with both hands.

"Amy is history, by the way," he said, casually.

His words didn't register immediately. When they did, they tore me rudely from my rapturous haze.

"Wait, *what?*"

"We only had a few dates, and the dates we had pretty much sucked," he chuckled. "We have almost nothing in common. Not like you and me."

His eyes found mine as he realized what he'd just said. I watched his skin go flush.

"Besides, she never stopped chewing that fucking gum."

I blinked a few times, then broke out laughing, almost snorting my wine. "What was *up* with that gum!?"

He shook his head and laughed along with me. "I

wish I knew. It wasn't just the gum, though. It was all those —"

"Bracelets? Necklaces?"

He chuckled and shook his head. "Too many, huh?"

"Are you kidding? Jax and I refer to her as Jingle Jangles." At that bit of information, I could tell he looked almost embarrassed. "Why did you even date her in the first place?"

Adrian paused, while switching from one foot to the other. The second his warm hands closed over my toes, I let out an unmistakably sexual moan.

"I dunno," he said eventually. "I guess I was lonely."

"You," I smirked, looking him over. "Lonely."

"Yes."

"Adrian, have you looked in the mirror lately?" I demanded. "You could get any girl you want. Any time you want."

"Maybe," he agreed. "But a bunch of empty sex wouldn't make me any less lonely."

"I'd take empty sex right now any day of the week," I replied, without thinking.

The hands rubbing my feet squeezed tight for a moment and then stopped. "You would, huh?"

"Over my current sex life?" I mused, doing my damnedest to mentally omit my tryst with Jax. "Yes."

Adrian's eyes were on my body, now. They crawled downward, over my legs, just as his hands moved from my foot to my calf muscle.

"What about meaningful sex?" he asked plainly.

"Meaningful?"

"Yes," he reiterated. "As in sex with someone you love and care about. Sex with someone you actually connect with."

The room was suddenly very warm. The candles, the wine, the strong hands kneading my tired muscles — it was all starting to stack up. His fingers weren't just feeling good anymore, they were feeling electric.

"You're talking about when we almost hooked up," I murmured softly.

Adrian shrugged. "Could be."

~ 20 ~

HARPER

My mind wandered back to *the* night. It was a night I'd thought about so many, many times. A night I wished I could somehow have back, to do it all over again.

To do it right.

"We *should've* hooked up," I eventually admitted.

"We sorta did hook up," he smiled.

Slowly I drained my glass, thinking back to the night of the most severe thunderstorm of our young lives. We'd been caught outside, a few blocks from home. We'd run through sheets of rain, buckets even, until we arrived back at Adrian's house, breathless and soaked.

But he'd forgotten his key. His parents weren't home. Grabbing my hand, Adrian had led me through his backyard and into the pool house, where we quickly shed our clothes and tossed them straight in the dryer.

I remember the flash of lightning that illuminated our near-naked, shivering bodies. We stood there with our chests heaving, our eyes devouring each other with full permission, the walls and inhibitions of our platonic friendship temporarily stripped away. We came together with the very next thunderclap, kissing and writhing. Touching and feeling and exploring all the hot, secret places that had been so forbidden during our countless hangouts, our movie nights, our times together.

I remember falling onto the little pool house couch, as Adrian's mouth slid methodically down my neck. He kissed my shoulders, my breasts, my flat, quivering stomach. He'd kissed me until the cold of the rain was gone, and only the heat of our twisting, grinding bodies remained.

I remember trembling as he took my thighs in his hands. He spread my legs. Pulled my panties to the side…

And then he went down on me, burying his hot tongue so achingly deep inside me I could only grab his head and scream.

I remember seeing stars. I saw planets and universes and entire fucking galaxies as Adrian devoured me, so very hotly, from his knees. The pleasure washing over my brain was all-consuming, almost terrifying in its totality. My fingers went from sifting his hair, to scratching his back, to clutching the pillows beneath me so hard my nails were piercing the fabric.

Up until then, no one had ever done this to me. Even now, no one has ever done it *nearly* so well. I screamed like a banshee as I came, convulsing wildly, clutching Adrian's hungry mouth against my surging, throbbing womanhood until I flooded him with my warmth and wetness. I bucked and screamed as lightning split the sky, but Adrian wrapped his arms around my thighs and hung on for dear life.

When it was finally over I looked into his eyes, thoroughly spent. Adrian knelt over me, gloriously naked. He was hard as a railroad spike and twice as thick. In that moment, I was totally *his*. I would've done anything in the world he wanted. Anything at all.

And then he told me he loved me…

And my young heart leapt into my throat.

"My God, I was *this* close to having you," Adrian murmured, his voice snapping me back to reality. He held up his thumb and forefinger, barely touching.

"You were even closer than that," I chuckled. "Way closer than you think."

His hands returned to massaging and kneading me. They were higher than ever now. Past my knee.

"If only I hadn't said what I said," he smirked, shaking his head. "Such awful timing. So, so stupid."

"It wasn't stupid, it was actually kind of adorable," I corrected him. "But you're right. If only you'd kept your mouth shut, you would've gotten seriously laid."

His hands were on my thigh now. Kneading. Rubbing. Touching places they hadn't touched since that night at the pool house.

"We were young," he said wistfully. "We were around each other so much, but still afraid to ask for what we wanted."

I could see the arousal in his eyes now, just as I'd seen it all those years before. Only this time it was backed by model good looks, roguish charm, and an unfailing confidence. And this time, it was backed by action.

Butterflies exploded deep in my belly as Adrian's fingers crept even higher, moving closer to his ultimate goal. I wasn't about to stop him. Not again. Not ever.

"And… what is it that you wanted?" I finally dared to ask.

Adrian leaned in, his hand sliding boldly inside the leg of my cozy sweatpants. His mouth closed over mine, taking my breath away with the first of a hundred searing hot kisses.

"*This…*" he murmured, his fingers brushing my mound.

~ 21 ~

ADRIAN

I kissed her for as long as I dared, and I dared for a long time. Inhaling her scent, feeling her beneath me, my heart raced with excitement. My whole body vibrated with the anticipation of having her, of being *inside* her, of finally, after all these years, making her mine.

As far as I was concerned, Harper had been mine for as long I could remember. I'd shared more with her than with any other woman, even the ones I'd dated, even the nut-job I almost married.

Bullet dodged.

But no, my beautiful friend and neighbor had always been the one who got away. I'd had merely a taste of her; a tantalizing glimpse into what might've been. Harper and I had shared secrets together. We'd shared hopes and fears and far-flung future plans, all while maintaining the veil of platonic closeness. Back then I saw our restraint as a strength. An impenetrable barrier by which we'd keep our friendship forever safe, only it hadn't been safe, it had been torn straight to pieces by the very situation we'd tried so hard to avoid.

But now...

Now it seems I'd been given a rare second chance to do things the right way.

I continued kissing her deeply, our tongues swirling, sifting her hair with one hand and rubbing her through her thong until she was so wet her panties were soaked through. I wanted so much to inhale her again. To bury my face between those supple thighs and gorge myself on the sweetest-tasting honey I'd ever had the pleasure of plunging my tongue through.

But I'd done all that already. And this time, I had far more extensive plans.

Picking her up, I carried Harper to my room and threw her onto the bed. I wasted no time in stripping her naked. I wasted even less time in peeling my own clothes off.

One by one, our garments hit the floor. Yet between the two of us, not a single word was said.

I can't believe this...

Harper was stretched out on her back, thighs parted, looking up at me from my soft down comforter. She had one hand draped across her ample chest. With the other, she dipped a hand teasingly down her belly.

God, she's beautiful.

Not just beautiful, but absolutely gorgeous. Her skin was flush, her lips plump from being so thoroughly kissed. Her hair fanned out beneath her, across my pillow, the very pillow of my very bed.

I still can't believe—

She crooked a finger, and I climbed between her legs. There would be nothing stopping us this time. Nothing between my thick, raging hard-on and the beautiful, lightly golden 'V' that formed at the junction of those long, beautiful legs.

I pushed forward, parting her slightly, stopping against her wetness. My eyes scanned every beautiful, majestic detail of the scene before me. I wanted to sear it into my brain, so I could remember it forever.

"I still love you, you know," I smiled down at her.

Harper laughed. "You're such an asshole."

"And your point?"

She sighed softly, squirming into the comforter, spreading her legs even wider. Then she reached down, wrapped one hand around me, and guided me home.

"I love you too," she whispered, her eyes locked on mine.

"Now *fuck* me."

Finally, I leapt.

Harper groaned as I plunged into her, driving the air from her lungs as I bottomed out in the hottest, most molten place in the universe. It was every bit as good as I imagined. Worth every last moment I'd spent dreaming about what could've been, what should've been, and what now, at long last, finally *was*.

Our bodies connected perfectly as I surged into her again and again, grinding myself deeper inside her at the end of every thrust. I was up on my arms, looking down into that beautiful face. Down below, Harper had her hands clamped on my ass. The stab of her fingernails felt surprisingly good as she squeezed me tightly, perhaps making sure I wasn't going anywhere, anytime soon.

Our eyes met again, but there were no words to mark this monumental event. There was only the rhythm of our bodies, the heat of her core. The gentle forward and back shift as we slowly, methodically fucked, enjoying the moment, rolling comfortably against one another as the magnitude of what we were doing gradually sank in.

This is perfect, I thought to myself. *This is—*

My reflections were interrupted by the greatest kiss of all time. Harper's lips surged softly against mine, her tongue piercing my teeth, rolling its way lovingly through my open mouth as I kissed her back. It meant so much that we were still so intimately connected, still fucking each other. I rocked her soft, feminine body beneath mine, crushing her against me, as she whimpered and cooed and inhaled my every breath into her wet, waiting mouth.

Eventually she took what she wanted, rolling me onto my back. Harper mounted me with a wicked gleam in her eye. Her lips were wet and pursed with pleasure as she sank down on me, impaling herself to the hilt. From there she rode me slowly, deeply, opening and closing her eyes. I guided her hands to my hard stomach, listening to the gasp of air as she inhaled, fingers splayed. She cried out as I bucked upward, piercing her to the core, then bore down on me with her hips, swallowing me wholly and completely inside her. Eventually she looked at me, and smiled.

"What are you thinking about?" she whispered.

I pulled her face to mine and kissed her some more, still thrusting slowly in and out of her.

"I'm thinking I've imagined this so many times," I murmured against her lips. "That I'm finally realizing the dream of being inside you."

Her expression was adoration, endearment, even love.

Harper moved her hands to my face and kissed me some more. Our eyes were locked, our souls connected. Our smiles grew wide with the pure thrill of sharing each other on such deep, fathomless levels, until our faces contorted in our eventual, mutual climax.

  I erupted inside Harper at the exact moment she contracted around me, moaning, groaning, clawing my chest as I filled her from beneath. She kissed me even more fiercely, throughout our orgasm, until expressions of joy were plastered across both of our faces.

  And my universe was finally right again.

~ 22 ~

HARPER

It was the first semi-warm day in a long time, and I meant to seize it. The sun was out, and shining brilliantly. The contact warmth it provided was enough to bundle the kids up tight, shuffle them downstairs, and walk them across the street to the nearby park.

"And you spent the whole night with him?"

At the moment I was sitting on a bench in the toddler's play area, watching Brayden and Emma worm their way through a series of yellow plastic tubes. The static electricity was making their hair stand up adorably. I'd already taken a thousand pictures.

"I didn't plan to," I admitted. "But yes. I slept until the sun came up, and crept out of there before Jax came to get Emma."

Sophia wrinkled her nose. "Jax..." she repeated. "That's the one who hates you, right?"

"Something like that."

My friend sipped her latte and shook her head. "I

can't imagine anyone who wouldn't like you."

I laughed. "I know, right?"

"Except for Matt. And Jacob. And that guy from sys-admin, who you locked out of your computer while he was actively telnetting into your personal drive."

"Yeah, well he was a dick, so—"

"And Marjorie, of course. Man oh man, she *despised* you. In fact she still talks about you sometimes. And when she does, she makes this face like—"

"Alright, already," I cut her off with a chuckle. "I get it."

Sophia was cool and loyal to a fault, but she also liked to tease. It was one of the more unique things about her.

"So they're friends, then?" she asked. "Jax and Adrian?"

"We're all friends," I explained. "Well, sort of. We grew up together, or in Jax's case, at least around each other. But it's been a long time since I've seen either of them."

Sophia leaned back into the hard metal bench, letting the sun kiss her face. Her sunglasses were comically big. So much so, they made her seem like a bug.

"So, do you like him?"

"Who, Adrian?" I shrugged. "Actually I love him."

This seemed to get her attention. She leaned forward and gripped her coffee with both mittens.

"You *love* him?" she swore. "Really?"

"I've always loved him," I told her. "There was a time in our lives when we hung out every day. We were best friends."

"Hung out or hung *out?*"

"The first one," I answered. "Sort of. Except for this one time." I sighed and bit my lip. "It's… complicated."

My friend chuckled conspiratorially. "It always is."

It was a hard thing, explaining your life to someone relatively new to it. Sophia and I had met at work, not even two years ago. We quickly bonded over being female in a male-dominated industry, but we also shared many of the same likes, dislikes and personality traits.

And just like me, Sophia had a very complicated history with men.

"So what are you going to do?" she asked.

I sighed wearily. It was a great fucking question.

"For now I don't plan on doing anything," I declared. "I'm nannying for both of these men, and it's a really good gig. Plus, Adrian and I just got back in touch. There's no way I want to lose that."

My gaze still hadn't left the playground, all throughout our conversation. Emma was running in circles around Brayden, who was trying desperately to catch her. Their little rubber play area was limited, though. The snow had been shoveled back only thirty feet in all directions.

"And what do you think *he* wants?"

Honestly, I didn't know. Outside of wanting to finish what we'd started in his family's pool house so many years ago, I didn't know what Adrian expected out of this whole thing. And maybe it wasn't a thing it all. Maybe it was a very long, very beautiful, one-shot deal. Unfinished business, finally taken care of.

"Can I see him at least?" asked Sophia. "If I'm giving advice on this guy, I'm gonna need a visual."

I pulled out my phone. Though I didn't have any photos of Adrian, I knew one of the photography websites he'd done some modeling for. I pulled it up, clicked his portfolio, and handed it over.

Sophia's mouth opened so wide she could've swallowed a truck.

"*Him?*"

I nodded, turning two shades redder in the process. I had to admit, I'd perved over the same photos myself.

"You're watching *his* baby?" She scrolled back and forth through the photos in abject shock. "If I were you, I'd be *carrying* his baby!" Sophia swore. "I'd let him put as many of his babies inside me as he wanted!"

She handed my phone back, albeit reluctantly, then shook her head again.

"Holy fuck, Harper," she swore. "You didn't tell me he looked like *that*."

"Why?" I challenged. "Does it change things?"

Sophia huffed. "Nice guy, great job, beautiful son..." she nodded toward the playground. "Plus the two of you are already friends. You have history together. And what did you tell me earlier? You came so hard you woke up in a different time zone?"

I smiled, thinking back to our night together. I'd been so hot, so wet, so incredibly fucking horny for him. Adrian and I hadn't just fucked, we'd made love. We hadn't just gotten our rocks off, we'd taken things slow; savoring the heat, relishing in the warmth and feel of our naked bodies finally, at long last, crushed tightly against one other.

I'd been worried it might be weird, the two of us being so platonic, for so long. But the second he entered me, I knew it was going to be beyond belief. We kissed like long-lost lovers, rather than friends. All the waiting, all the anticipation — these things had created unimaginable levels of raw physical attraction, to go along with the mental and emotional bonds that were already so strong.

And it wasn't *just* making love. We'd done that for sure, finishing gloriously together in a way that connected us on newly-discovered levels I hadn't even anticipated. We'd fucked slowly, kissed softly, ultimately curling our bodies against one another as I'd fallen asleep, safe and secure, in my best friend's strong, beautiful arms.

But then I'd stirred, sometime in the wee hours of the morning… and I had another agenda entirely.

I woke Adrian with my mouth, sucking and stroking him hard, tasting the musky aftermath of our lovemaking on his thick, sleep-warm shaft. It turned me on even more, knowing what we'd done. But I wanted something else, too. Something beyond the amazingly slow, sensuous lovemaking we'd experienced an hour or two earlier.

I really wanted to get *fucked* fucked.

My intentions were made clear as he woke, sleepily, sifting his fingers through my sex-tousled hair. I turned around, shoving myself face-first into his bed. I was face-down, ass-up, ready for business. I waved my naked rump back and forth at him provocatively, until he seized my hips and drove himself into me from behind.

FUCK.

I absolutely *loved* that he'd loved me, adored me, and

that he'd taken things slow. But now... now I needed to get the demons out. I'd twisted my body to intentionally grip the headboard, just as I'd done with Jax, and Adrian took the hint. Soon I was screwing myself backwards and into him, bucking wildly, urging him to pound me with every last ounce of strength and energy, the way his friend had done. It was almost like a kind of twisted penance, for me. Like I could somehow erase the memory of what happened with his best friend, by screwing him even harder and better than I'd done with Jax.

For the next fifteen or so minutes we went totally nuts on each other, rutting and fucking like animals. For every slow, loving stroke he'd driven inside me during our earlier lovemaking, I took three or four of his fast, frenzied thrusts. Adrian grabbed my hips and dug in so hard his fingers curled painfully into my flesh. There would be bruises there the next day; nine of them actually. I counted and treasured each one, wearing them as a badge of a honor, a rite of passage. Proof that we could not only connect in such a slow, loving way, but that we could, when required, fuck each other absolutely, positively senseless.

I'd woken again a short time later, after the two of us had collapsed into a come-soaked heap. Extracting myself without waking him had been tricky. Even trickier though, was processing my feelings. The conflicted thoughts I seemed to be having... and perhaps, not only for Adrian.

Yes, I'd gotten exactly what I wanted. And yes, I'd screwed the memory of Jax into far-flung oblivion.

But had I *really?*

"Look," said Sophia, breaking me of my daydream. "If I were you, I'd try to enjoy this. Don't push it. Don't rush it. Don't expect anything."

My friend flipped her long, curly dark hair over the

opposite shoulder and pointed her coffee at me.

"If this man has true feelings for you, he won't be able to fight them. So let him come around. Let him be the one who approaches you, and don't make any sudden moves."

I pictured a hungry wolf approaching an outstretched hand, but warily. It made sense.

"And if he doesn't come around?" I asked. "If he was carrying the torch all these years, *just* to hook up with me?"

"Then have as much fun as you want with *this*," Sophia grinned, tapping my phone, "for as long as you can."

~ 23 ~

HARPER

I spent two days working, day and night. Forty-eight straight hours of splicing, soldering, and working with wires so small, so delicate, my eyes actually hurt.

Of course, I worked on the coding part of things too, intermittently. Over the years I'd learned that taking short breaks and then switching things up was the key to productivity, especially if you wanted to keep your mind sharp and your problem-solving skills honed like a samurai's blade.

Eventually though, as always, I just had to get out of the house. I'd caught up on everything I wanted to see on Netflix, Amazon, Apple, and all the other channels I was currently addicted to. Right now, I just needed to escape. I needed some fresh air to clear my head.

I debated grabbing some fast food, but ended up driving by all my favorites without ordering anything. Pulling into these places was a bad habit, and I was intent upon breaking it. Instead, I drove aimlessly through town for a while, just checking things out. My mind finally drifted away from work, but my thoughts kept returning intrusively back to Adrian, and Jax, and even Preston.

There were so many feelings to unpack, I didn't know where to begin.

Adrian and I had exchanged texts and even spoken a few times since we'd hooked up, but we hadn't *really* talked about anything. The conversations had been fun and flirty, and somewhat productive. The only problem was, he'd been called out of town for the next week or more. Something about a last-minute shoot in Australia.

I was half-jealous he was going someplace so warm and exotic, and totally broken-hearted that I wouldn't be seeing Brayden. The little guy was staying with his mother, and I knew I'd miss him terribly. His father too, but for much different reasons.

That left me on Emma duty, in Jax's apartment. Depending upon his ever-changing schedule, of course.

Jax…

It was almost easy to forget Jax, because his work schedule was so wonky. There was a time he was slated to go to medical school, but then his father got into a bad way. Things went from awful to even worse when the old man sold practically everything their family owned to support a terrible drug habit, including any money set aside for Jax's schooling. Without a cosigner, loans fell through. Jax became an EMT — and ultimately even a paramedic — hoping the hands-on experience would one day help him. But in the end, like so many other dreams in the face of adulthood, his were pushed to the side.

And then there was Preston, who was stuck like a thorn in the forefront my mind. I'd come so achingly close to being with him again, and I was shocked by how much I'd actually wanted it to happen. Preston *got* me. Of all the people in my life right now, he might just be the most relatable. After exchanging numbers — real numbers, this time — we'd text messaged dozens of times, and actually bounced a few things off of each other. In a perfect world, the two of us would be hanging out. We could be doing real things. Fun things. Things like cosplay and Comic-Con and catching the Hylian Loach while playing Legend of Zelda, the Ocarina of Time.

And, admittedly, there were *other* things I wanted to do with him, too.

Preston had found four different coding errors for me so far, and had even re-written one of my most frequently-used function calls. His code was sharp and concise enough to shave a few milliseconds off the reaction return time for most of my data. And as everyone in our circles already knew, those milliseconds added up.

At the moment, I didn't need work. I didn't need men. I needed a drink, and a stiff one, too.

And that's how I ended up at the Ragged Monkey.

The place sat at the end of town, tucked out of the way between one of the commercial districts and the river. I took a stool, ordered a beer, and drank it slowly, all while observing the handful of somber patrons throwing down alcohol alongside me. And most of them looked, well… ragged.

In here, it was easy to battle the urge to think about everything else. I'd been born inherently nosy, and had a knack for silently butting into people's business and overhearing everyone else's conversations. There was a truck driver chatting up a local waitress. Three friends stood in the corner, playing darts, discussing their upcoming trip to Toronto. Over the low din of the NHL game on the TV behind the bar, I could barely make out the words of a young couple in the middle of a bad fight. She was looking to break up with him. He was making his sales pitch to keep her around. Eventually she stood up, ready to leave, and I turned left so my eyes could follow her out the door...

"Well, well," said a familiar voice. "Look what the cat dragged in."

I was totally dumbfounded to find Jax sitting right next to me. He was still in his work uniform, his dark hair tousled, his normally-trimmed goatee exploding into a full-blown five-o'clock shadow. The pint of beer he had clutched in his hand was already three-quarters empty.

"I had no idea this place was turning into a nerd bar," he spat, disappointedly. "There goes the neighborhood."

"What the fuck?" I swore. "How the hell did you—"

"Been here five full minutes," he headed me off, with an annoying chuckle. "Seems like you noticed everyone in the bar but me."

I wrinkled my nose in disgust. "Have you considered maybe you're not worth noticing?"

"Yeah," he replied, draining his beer. "Once or twice."

He called the bartender by name and ordered two more pints, which irritated me even further. The last thing I wanted was him buying me drinks.

"So did you stalk me all the way here?" I asked politely. "Or did you just *happen* to see my car in the parking lot, and decide to—"

"Don't flatter yourself," Jax sneered. "I'm here two or three times a week."

He shifted some more, and that's when I noticed his face. Jax had fresh bruising under one eye, and a minor cut above his eyebrow. There were scratches over the whole left side of his cheek, too.

"Finally someone punched you in the face, huh?" I quipped.

He received his beer, slid the other one my way, and slowly nodded. "A woman."

I laughed. "Really? I'm jealous."

"You are?"

"Yeah. I'm jealous she got to do it and I didn't."

Jax drank as I gave him a secret once-over. He looked tired, sore, beat up. However long his shift had been, it hadn't been kind to him. At the moment, he looked even more ragged than the rest of the patrons here.

Still…

There was something intrinsically sexy about this man sitting here at the bar, a cold beer in his hand at the end of a long, shitty day. Setting my hate for him aside for the moment, Jax was admittedly edgy. Refreshingly raw. He wasn't trying to be something or someone he wasn't, and made no apologies for the person he was. Ever.

We drank in silence for a while, as I tried not to remember our night together. I couldn't help it, though. The coppery scent of him, the heat of his presence on the barstool beside me… these things just wouldn't let me forget.

"So, what did you do to her?" I finally asked.

"Who?"

"The woman who rearranged your face."

Jax slid a hand through his hopelessly tangled mop of hair before returning it to the side of his pint glass. Sighing wearily, he stared down into his beer.

"Yeah, well she was on PCP, and her boyfriend was ODing on God knows what," he began slowly. "Then she started beating on me as I was trying to resuscitate him, and that's when he threw up in my mouth."

Every inch of my exposed skin broke out in goosebumps. I sat there in stunned silence.

"Jesus."

"Yeah, he was there too," Jax said wearily. "I know this, because the guy took every drug on the fucking planet and somehow he lived."

I tried picturing the scene in my mind's eye, but just couldn't. Jax had been riding in ambulances for a long time. I hadn't thought much about it before, but it occurred to me now that he'd seen some serious shit.

"Sounds like the guy lived because you saved him," was all I could say.

"Yeah, whatever."

"And he... he threw up in your *mouth?*"

"Sure did," he somehow managed to smirk. "On the inhale, too. Worst care scenario."

"My God..."

"Which reminds me, I'm gonna need at least one more beer to forget the taste."

Jax drained his glass, ordered another, then slid from his stool. I sat transfixed as he crossed the bar and entered the men's room. The door swung shut behind him.

Five seconds passed. Ten. Fifteen.

The decision to hop and follow him wasn't a conscious decision at all.

~ 24 ~

HARPER

I knew where my legs were taking me, I just didn't know why. Something told me it didn't matter. This was something that just had to be done.

CLICK.

Jax looked up as I engaged the bathroom's deadbolt, locking the door behind us. He was standing with his hands on the sink, staring directly into the mirror. His whole face was wet. His stubbled chin still dripped with water.

"Jax…"

His gaze shifted to mine, still within the confines of the mirror. But he hadn't moved. I could see the stress coiled in his arms, his shoulders, even his face. I could see the battlescars on his cheek, and around his eye.

He'd saved a life. Dozens, most likely.

He'd unselfishly taken on the role of father.

What in the world was I—

"Jax, I—"

He whirled on me and we crashed together, kissing like crazy, our hands fumbling with each other's clothing almost immediately. Nothing else existed. There was only the heat, the attraction, the mutually-assured destruction we'd silently decided upon. We were both here for a singular reason: to take what we wanted. To use each other in ways that satisfied our most basic and primal of all needs, and nothing more.

My panties were already soaked as he yanked them down, along with my jeans, rolling the whole bunched up mess all the way to my ankles. I yelped as he lifted me up, spun me around, and bent me over the sink.

There was the jangle of a belt buckle. The hurried rush of a zipper…

He sank into me almost immediately.

Fuuuuuck!

Jax set a forceful hand on my back, shoving me forward, bending me so far over I could only grip the sink. Then he began pounding away. The whole sordid act was hot, dirty, totally raw. His hands slid to my hips so he could exert more control, and all I could do was clench my teeth, close my eyes, and enjoy the feeling of being absolutely *plundered*.

It was a little frightening, how easily we fell into such a hot, filthy rhythm. It was even more unbelievable that I was here in the men's room of this shitty little bar, staring into the mirror, watching myself get so thoroughly and ferociously fucked. Our bodies picked up speed, until something began to rattle. My fingers clutched the porcelain, as I practically tore the sink from the wall.

I hated that I was enjoying the view, as Jackson Ripley drilled me from behind. It bothered me that it all felt so fucking good, I had to bite my lip to keep from screaming. We made eye contact once, somewhere in the thick of it all, and the fierce animosity between us only made the whole thing that much hotter for me. I hated that part, too, come to think of it.

But at the same time, I totally fucking *loved* it.

This wasn't a long affair. It wouldn't go on for minutes. Eventually I stopped fighting my orgasm and just let go, surging around him, milking him to a completion that was only a few seconds behind. Jax finished inside me, his thick shaft pulsing violently. The fingers digging into my hips twisted into the same spots left by Adrian, and the ensuing pain only made me feel dirtier, filthier, and somehow, even more amazing.

We stood there in the moments after, the both of us heaving and out of breath. That's when I noticed the sink had been rattled loose, and was hanging an inch or two lower than before. Jax leaned over my back, still buried deep inside me. Staring into the mirror together, we glared at each other, ferociously.

"God, I hate you," he breathed into my ear. "You know that?"

I swallowed hard, then reached down to roll my panties and jeans back up. Everything was a hot fucking mess.

"Ditto," I whispered back at him, curling my lip.

Down between my legs, everything was throbbing. Jax was running down my thighs. My heart was pounding so hard I could feel it beating in my ears.

All of a sudden I felt his hot lips on my neck. Jax kissed me there; somewhat forcefully, but also with a lingering slowness and sweetness I didn't expect. Then he zipped up, buckled his belt, and unlocked the door.

A full minute after he left I was still gripping the sink, staring into the mirror, wondering what the fuck was wrong with me.

~ 25 ~

HARPER

The YouTube video played itself out on my big screen, cast to my television the instant I'd gotten the notification that it had dropped. I was three minutes in. There were nine minutes left.

Already, I felt sick to my stomach.

The demonstration was mostly on-screen footage of the VR end product, interlaced with some close-ups of the connectivity and narrated throughout. It wasn't so much the haptic features that got me, it was the fluidity of the entire system. Everything moved so *fast*, with such a near-instant response time, I didn't know whether to be angry or jealous or both.

Worst of all, the creator was a kid, much younger than myself. He hadn't developed his own hardware, he'd modded an existing rig and was using it to demonstrate features I'd spent months working on in secret. And yet somehow, he had many of the same ideas I did.

My first thoughts were that he'd somehow stolen my ideas. I quickly dismissed this, because my development computer was eternally air-gapped. There was no way of accessing any of my files, because that particular machine had no IP address, no internet connection, and no outside access to the hard-drive.

I watched the video twice, then watched the three others I'd seen earlier on the same channel. Almost everything sent up red flags. The kid's techniques were radically different, just like mine. They weren't exactly the same, though. There were subtle differences in the way he was sending and receiving data that seemed totally fucking genius or outright impossible.

I couldn't tell which though, without seeing the code.

"He could be a genius, or he could be a hack," Telengard had written to me, in an email this morning. He'd been the one who'd originally alerted me to the channel. He promised to look deeper into the creator and keep me updated on what he found, but I didn't expect much. Other than the demonstrations seen within the videos, there was very little outside information

For the next half-hour I paced back and forth in my living room, trying every trick I knew to calm myself down. Maybe my ideas weren't as new and cutting-edge as I thought. Could that be? Had I missed my window of opportunity, in taking too long to deliver a finished product?

Fuck!

I hurried to my development computer and looked over my entire project, top to bottom. It *seemed* like theft, but it could also be sheer coincidence. I wasn't the only person working to improve the fledgling VR genre. Entire teams of programmers were working in all different directions to create new graphics, new experiences, and all new visual, physiological, and tactile sensations.

But shit, mine was the fucking best.

Up until now…

Shaking my head, I shoved the doubts away and made a cup of tea to quell the sick feeling in my stomach. Fuck it, I was still cutting edge. My system *worked*, and the haptics were so sharp, so incredible, they'd blow away whatever I was seeing on this random kid's YouTube channel. Besides, how did I know his system even operated at all? Because it *looked* like it did? Was I supposed to trust his narration, his data, the return speeds he was reporting verbally, rather than showing on screen?

Rather than let it get me down, I used the video as a motivational tool. For the next several hours I channeled my energy, pounding out new code and sifting through errors until I'd rooted out some of the more long-standing problems that I'd been dreading having to fix. When my ass got tired I jumped on the treadmill and walked a fifteen-percent incline until my mind was clear again and my thighs were burning. Then I ate a little something, brewed some more tea, and pulled up enough code on three different computer screens to make Cypher from the *Matrix* look like a rank fucking amateur.

It was past midnight by the time I finally stopped. I was drained. Fried. Exhausted mentally, but physically hopped up on caffeine and still totally exhilarated. I felt like I could conquer the world. Right now though, with sleep an impossibility for a few more hours at the very least, I'd settle for watching a movie.

And that's when my phone went off.

It hadn't buzzed all night, which was fine by me. I picked it up curiously, wondering who was sending me a text message at this time of night. My heart picked up speed almost immediately as I saw Jax's name:

* * *

> Put on your hooker boots and meet me at the motel.

An electric shiver rocketed its way through my body, starting at the base of my neck. It shot down my arms, my legs, then bounced back up to gather in my lower belly, just below my navel. The warm, secret place where everything seemed to collide at once.

I glanced over to my boots, still sitting in the corner. All of a sudden I was very warm.

> Which one?

I sent words without even thinking. It was almost like someone else typed them entirely.

> You know which one.

I did, actually. Growing up together, we all knew the place well. And we all ended up there, at one time or another.

> Leave now.
> I'll send you the room number before you get here.

My heart was a jackhammer, pounding against the walls of my chest. My mind screamed at me to stop. To put an end to this bullshit; to not even consider what I knew in my heart I was about to do.

But my body just felt so fucking *alive*.

Okay.

It was just one word. A single, solitary word that decided the difference between winding down with a movie on the couch, or winding up in a dirty, filthy, sordid place that rented exultation by the hour.

My eyes flitted from the couch, to the boots, and to the couch again. I could still say no. I could reply that I was simply too tired, or too drunk, or just plain not interested…

But fuck it, I'd seen just about every movie anyway.

~ 26 ~

HARPER

It wasn't easy driving in thigh-high boots with three-inch heels on. But at this hour the roads were clearer than my conscience, and my conscience was pretty damn clear. There was no conflict this time, because I knew exactly what I was doing. I was driving to the cheapest motel in town, in the dead of night, for the oldest reason in the world.

Not a soul was around as I pulled in and rolled silently through the snow-shrouded parking lot. I pulled up beside Jax's truck in front of room 121, killed the engine, and stepped out and into the biting cold. My breath left trails of white vapor in the frozen, midnight air.

You're an asshole, Harper.

Yeah. I definitely was.

But I was an asshole who was about to get spectacularly laid.

It was only a few steps to the room's metal door, which was good because I could barely walk in my tight leather mini-skirt. I looked like a hooker. I *felt* like a hooker. Instead of it bothering me, it actually turned me on. It made me seriously hot to think I'd been ordered to this place like a pizza, by some hungry patron. With a little luck, I was about to be devoured like one.

I took a deep breath, letting the crisp air bite sharply at my lungs as I reached out and knocked. The door opened almost immediately. Jax paused in the doorway to look me over, his eyes obviously happy with what he saw.

"You wanna do this out here, or…"

He laughed gruffly before stepping aside. "Get that ass in here."

I strutted in. He'd sprung for the bigger of the shitty motel rooms, but it was the same as any other room in the place. Faux wood-paneled walls. Worn-out commercial carpet. Popcorn ceilings, an uncomfortable-looking chair, and, of course, a bed built purely for fucking.

I dropped my coat, revealing the rest of my outfit which consisted of my tightest black shirt stretched over my sluttiest bra. Jax had loose-fitting shorts and a T-shirt on. He also wore the strangest grin.

I noticed a significant bulge already forming in those shorts. I reached for him… but he deftly stepped aside.

"Are we here to play games," I sighed in frustration, "Or—"

My breath caught in my throat. My heart skipped a beat.

Standing just behind Jax, also in a T-shirt and shorts, stood Preston. For a long moment, I was totally speechless.

"No," I finally squeaked.

Both men had their hands on their hips. Each wore shit-eating grins. They were eying me hungrily, like a favorite piece of candy.

"Oh, no," I murmured, shaking my head. "No, no, no. Not a chance. No fucking way—"

"And why not?" Jax challenged, crossing his arms.

I didn't have an immediate answer. I looked to Preston for help, but he was still devouring me, rather unapologetically, with his eyes.

"Look, you're here," said Jax. "You're horny. You're dressed for sex."

"Are you kidding?!" I gasped. "I—"

"You've already fucked us both," he pointed out, bluntly. "The damage is done, right? So what's the harm?"

Before I could utter another word, he began peeling his shirt off. In solidarity, Preston did the same. I don't know if they worked out together before they showed up, or what, but their muscles were totally *pumped*. I could only watch in awe as a forest of big arms, a mountain of broad shoulders, and a pair of deliciously bare chests slid into view.

"I know what you *almost* did with Preston the other night," Jax went on. "And he knows what we've been doing, too. We're not just roommates, Harper. We're friends. We share practically everything…"

He stepped forward and into me, his body now dangerously close to mine. Somehow, I didn't move a muscle. My heart was beating so fast I was scared it might actually explode.

"But…"

Preston moved next, sliding past his friend. He set his hand on my hip, just above my skirt, and stepped around me in a heady whoosh of musk and cologne. His touch was absolute

Sharing the Nanny

fire. It added to the growing heat in my loins.

"I—I *can't,*" I managed to say, somewhat pleadingly. "This isn't…"

My sentence trailed off totally unfinished, distracted by the sight of the two of them. I wasn't even sure what I was about to say.

"This isn't what?" Jax teased, softly. "This isn't what you *want?*"

I was shivering. Shuddering. Trembling. But with excitement, not cold.

"I… I just can't," I finally finished.

Jax paused, looked back at me, and eventually shrugged. "Alright, then. Fine. Go."

He stepped aside. So did Preston. Together, they gave me a clear path to the door.

But I didn't move.

My jacket was right there, draped over the chair. All I needed to do was grab it. Again I tried to speak, but my words failed me. So did my legs.

Jax chuckled wickedly.

"We notice you haven't left yet."

They stepped in again, and this time I didn't utter a word of protest. Jax leaned in, his face hovering near mine. At the same time, Preston pressed against me from behind. His body was miraculously warm. His exposed flesh, as smooth and beautiful as I remembered.

Holy FUCK, Harper.

A wall dropped; a whole curtain of inhibitions just

dissolving away. It was in that moment I realized I *wanted* them. I wanted the both of them… more than anything I'd ever wanted before.

"Spin around for us," said Jax. "Let's see what's beneath that skirt."

I hesitated, but only for a moment. Then I turned, bit my lip, and spun in a complete circle.

The skirt was tight, and it hugged the tops of my thighs. It didn't flare out a single inch.

"Hmmm."

Two pairs of hands were on my hips now, and I felt Preston's fingers dip below the hem. They lifted the leather up and over my asscheeks, exposing me completely from behind.

"Bro," he said, speaking for the first time since I'd arrived. "You need to see this."

His hands took my hips and physically seized me. I shuddered with the realization he was spinning me around, so Jax could see.

"I thought as much," Jax growled, his voice starting to show his growing arousal. "These don't look like the panties of a girl who *can't*."

He was referring to my almost non-existent G-string, which of course matched my bra. My ass was completely naked, totally on display. Hands began roaming it, softly at first. Then, more aggressively, as I was groped and grabbed.

I inhaled sharply, and then Jax was kissing me hotly, in full view of his friend. I could sense Preston watching, his hands slowly roaming up and down my body. They stopped beneath my breasts, cupping them, feeling them, pulling my shirt upward and off.

Oh my GOD…

And then I felt his mouth too, as it closed over my bare shoulder. It was warm. Wet. Wonderful.

I was being kissed by two men at once… on my neck, my shoulder, my mouth. It was everything I could've ever imagined it would be. And then some.

This is nuts!

I moaned into Jax's mouth, just as a set of fingers grazed high along the inside of my thigh. I didn't know whose fingers they were. The not knowing part made everything *that* much hotter.

"Get this off," I heard someone grumble. "This too."

My skirt dropped. My bra was pulled away. I'd been undressed eagerly by men before, but apparently everything tended to happen a lot faster when getting me naked was a team effort.

None of it mattered, though. I was all in.

A second or two later I was lifted into the air and tossed onto the bed, face down. Someone pulled my G-string all the way back and let go, snapping it against my ass.

"This thing is coming off, one way or the other," I heard Jax snarl.

The whole room tilted as the boys dropped heavily to the bed, one on either side of me. Their hands and mouths were everywhere at once.

"The hooker boots stay on, though."

~ 27 ~

HARPER

I should've been scared, to be honest. It should've been intimidating, being ravaged by two horny lovers who'd already had the pleasure of being inside me. It wasn't though. Not even in the slightest.

And that's because once I'd accepted what was about to happen, I realized I wanted it sooo much fucking more than they did.

Staring up at the motel room's popcorn ceiling, I went with the flow. I ran my eager fingers through two heads of dark, luscious hair, while enjoying the hands and mouths and everything else that slid tantalizingly over every inch of my exposed skin. The boys sandwiched me from either side, pressing their firm bodies against mine. I felt their manhoods uncoil like snakes against the exposed skin of my hips and thighs, as they grew harder and more excited.

And it all felt so oddly fucking powerful.

I made out with them for a long, long time, lolling my head back and forth, enjoying the rising heat of our twisting bodies. Eventually they kissed their way down my chest, their movements so synchronized it was as if they were performing a routine. I had Jax on the left, Preston on the right. As my two pert nipples disappeared into two hot mouths, I bucked my hips into the pair of strong, eager hands competing between my legs.

Fuck yes.

My eyes crossed, and the popcorn ceiling spun away. It left me wondering just how many other girls had experienced something like this, right here, maybe on this very bed, staring up at the same shitty ceiling. How many different women had done something *this* dirty, this filthy, this perverted. This amazingly, wholly liberating, and totally fucking awesome.

Those thoughts faded just as quickly, as a pair of long fingers slipped inside me. They curled mischievously upward, into that thrilling, wonderful place that sent shockwaves of pleasure rippling through my body. I writhed so hard that my ass left the bed. A hand closed over my lower abdomen, seizing control, pushing me down again.

Holy fuck...

The boys were still feeding on my breasts as those fingers began plunging in and out of me. A second hand, independent of the first, began thumbing my swollen clit. It felt so good I could scream. And then I *did* scream, and a hand clapped itself authoritatively over my mouth.

I surrendered, rolling my fingers into their hair, squeezing their heads against my chest. There was nothing else I could do. Nowhere to go but to escape deep into my mind, where everything was so carnal, so sensuous, the excitement was building to off-the-chart levels that had my whole body trembling.

I was already close to climaxing when they flipped me over. Two powerful hands grabbed my hips, and another pair sifted through my hair. I was on my hands and knees as one of the boys fed himself to me, pushing straight past my lips and deep into the back of my throat. I sucked him eagerly, rolling my tongue beneath his hard shaft. Moaning and whimpering around his sizable thickness, as my second lover buried himself all the way inside me in a single, rapturous thrust.

My body was pinned between them, still wearing my hooker boots, stuffed happily from either side. It was a holy shit moment for everyone. I could tell, because none of us moved for a good three or four seconds of pure silence.

Then, slowly, they began pumping in and out of me.

Ohhhhhhhhhhh...

It was even hotter than I'd ever imagined. Better than any one of my raunchiest, most secret fantasies. The feel of their bodies, the excitement of their thrusts — it was almost too much to take in all at once. I marveled at the sheer impact of what I was doing, and how unspeakably good it felt... as two of the hottest guys I knew continued spitroasting me from both ends.

It was crazy. Stupid. Amazing — all at the same time. Yet deep within the sex-soaked confusion that had become the whirlwind of my mind, there was only one thing I was absolutely sure of:

There was nothing on planet earth better than this.

~ 28 ~

JAX

It was insane really, how much she truly loved it. But had I expected any different? Had I really thought Harper would balk at the idea of sleeping with the two of us at once, especially when I was springing it on her like some dirty, midnight trick?

No, actually I hadn't.

And that's because somehow, in some way, I *knew* she'd be down for it.

Right now she wasn't just going along with it, she was moaning and groaning and totally fucking absorbed. I gripped her hips with the same level of ferocity she was bucking back into me. I had only to glance down, to see myself disappearing inside her again and again…

But shit, half the time, I couldn't help but watch her blowing Preston.

It turned me on like crazy, watching her with someone else. But the unexpected jealousy also felt like a hot knife, twisting away in my gut. It was strange, how my feelings for Harper were changing so rapidly. It was in the way she looked, the way she talked. The weird way she kissed me after following me into the bathroom back at the bar, with feeling and passion and actual emotion rather than just kissing me all angry and horny, eager to get her rocks off.

And yeah, she'd gotten her rocks off for sure. So had I. But something had happened in that bathroom that changed the way I looked at and felt about her. Something between us... I dunno. Something just *clicked*.

I'd been thinking about her a lot, but then again, so had Preston. Earlier in the night, over a couple of beers, I'd managed to get their story out of him. I'd been both envious and strangely turned on as he'd told me all about their speed dating tryst. And when I'd reciprocated, telling him how she followed me into the bathroom and nearly fucked the soul out of me? I saw the same jealous look in his eyes.

I knew Preston had been dying to get another crack at her. And so, rather than grab another couple of beers, I'd grabbed my phone instead, and put it to good use.

The plan was as simple as it was ridiculous: get her hot, get her horny, get her here. This place was an hourly-rate motel, built strictly for fucking. Brick by brick, someone had constructed it for exactly the kind of situation that was unfolding right now.

Worst case scenario, she balked and went home. Hell, she already hated me. She'd hated me all her life. Then again, how much could you really hate someone you just drove clear across town for, in boots like these, dressed purely for sex?

That part confused me, just as it did Harper. We loved to hate each other, so maybe it stood to reason we hated to love each other, too. Fuck if I knew. All I was really sure of was these boots were *totally* fucking doing it for me.

Buried comfortably inside her, I leaned over her back

and put my lips against her ear. She was still busy with Preston. She didn't stop sucking him, or even miss a beat.

"I didn't realize you were this greedy," I whispered accusingly.

Harper moaned, then pulled my roommate from her lips with a wet pop.

"You called *me*, remember?"

"Yeah," I chuckled. "And you came."

Staring at me over her shoulder, Harper screwed her ass back into me even harder. Her smile was wicked.

"Not yet..."

My God, now she was fucking me with her eyes, too. Those jewel-like eyes were glazed over with lust, turning me that much more on as she went back to blowing my friend. I dug in and pumped her harder, drilling her faster, giving her exactly what she wanted. Her whimpers grew louder. Her moans turned to groans and then cries of pleasure, until she couldn't take it any longer.

Harper came like the end of the world, her insides surging around me as she pulled Preston from her throat with a desperate gasp. She gripped him with both hands as she came, contracting wildly, bucking against me and twisting her hips until I was in the exact spot she needed me to be.

I drilled her straight through her orgasm, and then right out the other side. The lust in her eyes turned to pure adoration. The usual sarcasm and hatred dropped away, at least for the moment, leaving her spent and dizzy and totally vulnerable.

In that one brief moment, I actually loved her.

Fuck!

And that scared me more than anything else in the whole fucking world.

"I... guess we gotta switch, then?" I finally murmured.

By now Preston was desperate. If he didn't get to fuck her soon, he might explode.

"Yes," Harper breathed, adding a nod.

"Tell us, then."

She moaned softly through another aftershock of her insane climax, but said nothing. Her eyes were half-closed. Her body was spent.

"Tell us to switch."

I needed to hear her to say it. I wanted her to own it, to give us full permission, to make this whole crazy experience as much hers as it was ours.

Besides, for some freaky reason, hearing her *tell* us to switch would seriously turn me on.

Harper's lips, swollen from kissing and sucking and everything else, could only barely form the words.

"Switch..."

I withdrew, and slid to the opposite side of the bed. Harper locked eyes with me as Preston eagerly took my place. She bit her lip as he pushed his way inside, and together they moaned with how amazingly good it felt. But her ice-blue eyes never left mine. Even as he began thrusting into her, she never once looked away.

Fuck, fuck, double-fuck.

The thoughts in my head were intrusive, but still there. Watching the two of them go at each other, right before my eyes, turned me on more than I'd been in my entire life.

"Jax…"

Harper's voice was softer than I'd ever heard it, especially toward me. She was still on all fours, screwing my roommate. Grinding her ass snugly against his rippled stomach, just as she'd done with me.

"C'mere."

Her head was tilted upward, her eyes still focused on mine. There was a new but distinct beauty in her face now. Beyond the sultriness, the sensuality, the raw, animalistic act of the sex itself, she was staring at me in a whole different way.

"Jax…" she breathed again.

Harper's lips were soft, plump, wet. Her eyes were pleading. They drew me inexorably downward, to her level, where her body rocked rhythmically back and forth.

When I finally took her face in my hands and kissed her, the whole rest of the world went away.

~ 29 ~

HARPER

The boys took me together… they took me alone. They took me from both ends, surging into my body, eliciting whimpers of joy and screams of pleasure that grew so loud at times they also took turns holding their hands over my mouth.

Physically they were almost the same; both strong, dark, and unreasonably well-muscled. But there was such a dichotomy too; a thousand differences between the two of them. I really liked Preston. I totally hated Jax. But did I *truly* hate him? Or did I hate the idea of the person I'd built up in my mind?

There were times, especially while I was kissing him, when I wasn't so sure.

I could dwell on that later, though. For now, I was happy to let myself go. I cleared my mind, and surrendered my body to the two incredible men who were making it feel so good right now. Men who brought me to the edge of a sheer cliff that overlooked paradise, before shoving me off and letting me fall…

I dropped into a sea of biceps and triceps and rippled

abdominals, rolling hotly against me. I was impaled upon spires of flesh that pierced me all the way to the core. They took turns kissing me, licking me, fucking me. Flipping me over and pulling me upward, downward, into them, *onto* them…

Each time they switched it made me that much hotter. Each time one would withdraw from my quivering wetness, I'd spread my legs even wider for the next. It left me dizzy and breathless, giving myself over to them. It turned me on in depraved and crazy ways I'd never imagined.

At one point Jax drilled me from behind so hard I thought I'd pass out, while Preston went to find much-needed water. He came back, we re-hydrated, and then next thing I knew we were back at it again. It seemed there was no limit to the positions three people could achieve, and we tried them all. I'd fantasized my whole life about this. I'd always wondered, secretly, if it would ever happen to me.

Right now I wondered how I could ever possibly stop.

Jax was the first to let go, roaring and grunting through gritted teeth as he exploded inside me. I hooked my ankles behind his back and milked him dry. Toward the end I was bucking and grinding my hips, while pulling his face against my chest so I could tell him how much I still hated him. By now though, I doubt if either of us actually believed it.

Jax assured me that he hated me too, and eventually rolled to one side. Not even a minute later I was gripping Preston's shoulders as he fucked me deeply, with my booted legs high over his shoulders. We shared a secret smile and an intimate series of smoldering kisses, while Jax went back to the vending machine for snacks.

"Sorry if we uhh… sprung this on you," he murmured against my lips.

He surged into me, and I couldn't help but chuckle. "More like sorry, not sorry?"

"Yeah," he admitted sheepishly. "That."

"It's okay," I breathed, staring into his soft brown eyes. "I'm not sorry either. I wanted this." I paused, making sure that his eyes found mind. "And I wanted *you*."

I kissed him again, deeply, soulfully, swirling my tongue through his mouth. Preston responded by shoving my thighs even further apart, then grinding his ass forward as he bottomed out inside me.

Fuuuuck!

I was delirious with ecstasy, lost on cloud nine. I'd wanted him again for so long. It seemed totally absurd that I'd denied myself the pleasure of this man, and for no good reason I could think of.

I was determined it wouldn't happen again.

"I gotta admit, Jax was right about these boots," Preston grinned, gripping my ankles. "They're totally amazing."

His arms were flexed, his eyes half-closed. I could tell he was getting dangerously close.

"The boots are part of my Harley Quinn cosplay," I smiled up at him.

Preston's head tilted curiously. I could feel his whole body stiffen.

"You should see the rest of the costume," I teased. "Fishnets. Bustier. Push-up bra." I shrugged, clawing at his tightly-coiled ass with my fingernails. "Maybe one day I'll wear it for you."

I glanced down to our physical connection, where his

deeply-tanned skin contrasted sharply against my pale complexion. Hovering above me, Preston's lips brushed gently against mine.

"You have a Harley Quinn costume?" he asked, incredulously.

I giggled and nodded.

"Marry me," he whispered, as he flooded me with his seed.

~ 30 ~

PRESTON

"So his features are exactly the same as yours? Right down to the hardware?"

Harper shrugged one delicate shoulder as she poured raspberry syrup over the top of her pancakes. It cascaded down the stack in five different directions, pooling on the plate in a near perfect circle.

"I really can't tell," she admitted. "I mean, he *mentions* a lot of the same features I have. He talks about the tactile functions. He goes into the response times. But it's always vague, and there are never any closeups. And there's never any hard data to back it up."

She looked bummed, and that bummed me out as well. Even the waitresses milling around us looked bummed, but then again we were at IHOP, so maybe they always looked that way.

"If you were the one putting out the YouTube video, would *you* show the data?"

Harper made a face. "Of course not. But I also wouldn't be putting my tech out there for the world to see. At least not until I had a buyer, first."

Her pretty face looked suddenly alarmed. Those eyebrows went up so quickly it broke my heart.

"Wait!" she cried fearfully. "Do you think he has a buyer *already?*"

"No."

"Why not?"

"Because if I were the one paying good money for that tech, I wouldn't want it out there until it was all ready to market. There'd be an iron-clad, nondisclosure clause in the contract."

Harper's whole body slumped in relief. She began cutting into her pancakes.

"Look, I haven't even seen the video yet," I told her. "Let me look into it first, and I'll tell you what I think."

She smiled, and together we tore into our breakfast. It was early, but not that early. Jax left the motel for home sometime around daybreak. He'd already be riding an ambulance by now. That left the two of us lying in bed, with a few more hours still on the room. I was proud to say, we'd put it to *very* good use.

"Is it weird?" she asked suddenly.

Using my fork, I smeared the whipped cream of my Rooty Tooty Fresh and Fruity. As an adult, the dish was getting much harder to order with a straight face.

"Is what weird?"

"This," Harper smiled sheepishly. "You know, just casually having breakfast together. After... well..."

"Double-teaming you all night in a cheap motel?"

She looked around conspiratorially, while shushing me with a finger against her lips.

"Yes!" she whispered.

"Nah," I chuckled, popping a cream-covered strawberry into my mouth. "It's not weird at all."

With Jax gone, she had to drive me home, of course. We stopped at her place first, so she could shower and change. I showered too. With her, in fact.

That little act of water conservation had led to another fifteen minutes of frantic fucking, with Harper's two-handed death-grip testing out the strength of her showerhead. Thankfully, it held.

"Is it weird for you?" I asked.

She shrugged again. "A little."

"Why?"

Her eyes searched upward for a moment, as if the answer was floating somewhere near the ceiling. Eventually, she shrugged.

"Probably because I liked it so much."

Her skin flushed, and her eyes flared wildly at the admission. She almost looked down, but didn't.

"I liked it too," I agreed, holding her gaze. "Way more than I realized I would."

My assertion seemed to put her somewhat at ease. As if her debaucherous confession was somehow a tiny bit more normal.

"Look," I grinned. "After missing out on you for so long, and then coming so close to having you again? I was willing to take you any way I could get you."

"Oh you took me, alright," she laughed. "More than a few times, too."

"I sure did," I agreed, searching her beautiful face. "And this time, I'm holding onto you."

Now she did look away, letting her eyes fall into her lap. Harper flushed even redder than before. Even so, she didn't refute me.

"I know Adrian's coming back tomorrow night," I said to her, "and you've got babies to watch. But if you're free in the afternoon, I'll stop in and check that subroutine that keeps locking up. You can show me the new patches. And we can talk more about your would-be competitor then, too."

Harper looked up again, gratefully. "I'd like that."

"Good. Everything needs to be perfect before you tie up your product, Harper. Then we can get you to market before anyone else."

She was beaming now, happier than ever. But the look she gave me as she pointed her fork was fun and mischievous.

"You help me tie things up like you said, and you can tie *me* up," she agreed. "Any way you want to."

My dick jumped.

"Promise?"

She winked. "Oh, I promise."

"Deal."

We went back to breakfast, which we both ate ravenously. I should've been tired — even exhausted — but somehow I wasn't, and I attributed that to Harper. Just being around her made me feel awake and alive. She was intelligent, funny, charmingly sarcastic, and had all the same interests I did.

We shared love for the same books, the same movies, the same hobbies and everything.

And on top of all that, she was a sexual match for my seemingly endless libido; beautiful, sensual, and explosive in bed. I wanted to grab her, hold her, pull her against me. I wanted to kiss her until she realized all the same things I did: that the two of us were meant to be together; that she was mine, and I was hers.

I'd stayed awake late the past few nights, kicking myself for not having looked harder for her. But yet here she was, sitting across from me. Smiling. Laughing. Chomping on bacon. Weighing the pros and cons of a Unix vs. Linux operating system, in terms of open-source code and commercially-available upgrades.

Shit, she may as well have been talking dirty to me.

No, now that we'd found each other again, there was no way I was *ever* letting go. She'd have to pry me away like a face-hugger from the *Alien* universe.

"Soo…" she said, casually sipping her coffee. "The demon queen was over at Adrian's the other night."

I let my eyes go comically wide. "Lolth?"

"No, not *that* demon queen," she chuckled, appreciating the Dungeons & Dragons reference. "Although that would be pretty fucking epic."

"It sure would," I agreed.

"I'm talking about Erika. Adrian's ex."

I nodded, finally pushing my plate away. "Oh, I know who you're talking about. You gonna eat that?"

Harper laughed and shook her head. I stole the rest of her side of hash browns.

"I heard she rattled you."

"A little," she said, toughening up. "But only because I wasn't expecting her. That won't happen again."

"I bet it won't," I smiled.

She looked abruptly introspective, like there was something more to say. I didn't press. Instead, I put my hand over hers.

"Hey…" I said gently. "We're wiped. The both of us."

"Yeah."

"What do you say when you drop me off, you come inside for a few hours? My bed is pretty nice."

"Oh, I already know," she laughed. "Remember?"

"Yeah, but you haven't really slept in it," I answered her with a wry smile. "And that's what I'm offering. You come in, we pull the curtains tight, get the room all nice and dark and warm… and then we strip down and snuggle up beneath the blankets."

"Uh huh."

"And then we sleep," I went on. "*Just* sleep. Holding each other."

Harper let out a dreamy sigh. "I gotta admit, that sounds nice."

"It does?"

"In theory, sure."

"What?" I grinned. "You don't think I can keep my hands off you?"

She returned my grin with a smirk. "It's not your

hands I'm worried about."

I shrugged, let go, and leaned back in my chair. Just then the waitress caught my eye. I made the universal chicken-scratch-in-the-air sign for the check.

"Alright," I shrugged. "Suit yoursel—"

"But let's do it anyway," said Harper, flashing her blue eyes my way. Her look was even flirtier than mine.

"What's the worst that could happen?"

~ 31 ~

HARPER

I had mixed emotions, walking the hall to Adrian's apartment. On one hand I was excited to see Brayden, and even more thrilled to see his father. He'd been torn away from me so quickly after we'd gotten together. I'd missed the *hell* out of him.

On the other hand, there were things I'd kept from him over the past week. Things I hadn't mentioned during any of our text messages and phone calls between New York and Australia.

It wasn't because I'd done anything wrong either, although sometimes it felt that way. This just wasn't something you brought up over the phone. It required facing the person. Telling them how it was. Trying to make them understand that, well, sometimes when you were on the other side of the world from each other... stuff just happened.

I knocked softly, and Adrian let me in. He greeted me in the doorway with the hottest open-mouthed kiss that left zero doubt as to his intentions. It was the kind of kiss you gave your lover after not having seen them for a week. I kissed him back with just as much heat and passion, dropping the

Fischer Price Xylophone I'd brought for Brayden to the floor with a cacophony of semi-musical noise.

This was going to be hard. Or easy. Or weird. Or—

"Wine?"

I shook my head, and looked around. I was babysitting tonight.

"Where's my little guy?"

Brayden, I realized, was nowhere to be found. My disappointment was quickly mounting.

"He'll be here in an hour or so," Adrian assured me. "Come. Sit down and relax."

I was relieved, and in more ways than one. I'd dreaded having to have this talk with Adrian in front of the baby. Even though the little boy probably wouldn't understand a word of it, it just didn't seem right.

"You look wound up," Adrian smiled. "You okay?"

The apartment smelled delicious again, but in a different way. Whatever Adrian was cooking this time around had my mouth literally watering.

"I'm fine. I've just been working a lot."

Damn, he looked good. I'd forgotten it was summer down in Australia, so of course he came back with a beautiful all-over tan. It contrasted nicely with his pristine white T-shirt. A pair of tight blue jeans hugged his perfect ass, as he led me into the kitchen. I couldn't pry my eyes from it.

I noticed eventually that Adrian had already set the table. Steam rose slowly from a pot simmering on the stove. A juicy-looking steak sat resting on his butcher block, all seared and herb-crusted and smelling absolutely delicious.

"Soo… what's been going on in the world of Harper Hayes?"

He poked the steak to check for doneness. When he popped his finger into his mouth, I just about lost it.

"I… I have to tell you something."

I couldn't hold it in any longer. I wanted to keep looking at him but I felt too guilty. I wanted to kiss him some more, but I knew I couldn't until—

"So what do you have to tell m—"

"I was with Jax," I blurted quickly.

I dropped the words like a bomb, waiting for it to explode. But Adrian's expression never changed. His face registered no response as he turned sideways, and began stirring what looked like mashed potatoes.

"And Preston," I added.

Still no response. Except that he turned the heat down on the stove top.

"At the same time," I finally sighed.

The series of admissions made me feel like I'd been exorcised of a giant demon. I sank dizzily into the nearest kitchen chair, my shoulders slumped.

"I know," Adrian said simply.

My head stopped spinning instantly. I nearly bit my tongue.

"You... you *know?*" I asked, utterly astonished.

Adrian added a dash of salt to the potatoes. "Uh huh."

"But how?"

"They told me."

A quick knock preceded the door opening, as Jax and Preston let themselves inside. It couldn't have been timed any more perfectly if they'd been sitting with their ear to the door, listening from outside.

"Is it dinner time yet?" Jax asked, rubbing his hands together.

"Sure is," Adrian declared. "Steak's rested. Grab the knife."

The men nodded as they passed me, then sprang into action. Preston grabbed a round of beers from the fridge. Jax dragged a finger through the potatoes, got punched in the back by Adrian, then slid a meat fork and knife from the block on the counter and began cutting up the steak.

Two minutes later, we were all seated around the table. That's when I realized it had been set for four.

"Jennifer's bringing Emma over with Brayden in a little while," said Jax, looking at me for the first time since the motel. "If that's okay."

I could barely speak. Barely breathe.

"Of course it's okay."

He helped himself to some mashed potatoes and passed me the bowl. I took it like a zombie. When we were done passing everything around and serving ourselves, Adrian poured me a glass of wine anyway. This time I did nothing to stop him.

"Here's to good friends, and good food," Adrian toasted. He winked at me and added in a quieter voice: "And honesty."

Three beer bottles clinked together merrily. My wine

glass followed more slowly, but it eventually got there. As everyone tilted their head back to drink, I eyed the boys one by one by one...

...and still didn't have a clue what the hell was going on.

~ 32 ~

HARPER

The food was delicious, the conversation light. The boys ate and drank and talked about anything and everything except the elephant in the room, which of course was all I could think about.

Finally I finished my wine, set the glass back on the table, and folded my hands in front of me.

"So you're not mad?" I asked Adrian, loud enough to cease all other conversation.

Jax and Preston looked at him for a moment, then all eyes drifted to me.

"Mad?" Adrian repeated. "Hell no. I'm happy, actually. You know how long I've been trying to get you to *like* Jax? Much less actually sleep with him."

He was smiling now. So were the others.

"But—"

"None of us are mad, Harper," Adrian went on. "And we're sorry if we overwhelmed you. It's not like we planned this. We all just kind of got into you at the same time."

"Some of us at the same *time,* time too," Jax winked.

I couldn't believe it. The three of them not only knew, they were somehow okay with it. I didn't know whether to be flattered or angry or—

"Anyway," Adrian went on, "we sat down together and talked it out. We're all *really* into you, Harper. Even Jax, although the asshole won't easily admit it."

Jax grumbled and drained the rest of his beer without saying a word. I expected no less.

"How can you *all* be into me?" I asked incredulously. "I mean, after, you know…"

"How can you be into all three of us?" Preston challenged.

I turned to look at him, and his smile was friendly. The question was valid.

"I just sort of, well…" I paused for a moment, searching my heart. Trying to find the most logical answer to such a complicated question.

"Well, Adrian and I *always* had a thing," I said. "Unfinished business that eventually got finished." I shrugged. "And Preston and I met randomly a year ago. It's just dumb luck he happens to be your roommate."

I was looking at Jax now, who was waiting patiently on his own answer.

"You and I…" I nodded toward him. "You know, we've always been frenemies."

"Frenemies?" he chuckled.

"Yes," I shot back. "Friends, but enemies. I've always fundamentally hated you, but at the same time, you were always around." I shrugged. "You hang around a frenemy for too long and, well…"

"You fuck them?" offered Adrian.

I looked over and found him smiling at me over his beer. Strangely enough, he was enjoying this thoroughly.

"More like hate-fuck," I answered truthfully. "But if you're attracted to them, sure."

"So you think I'm hot," Jax said glibly, leaning back. His conceited grin took a victory lap of its own.

"Oh, it could've been the wine," I said sardonically. "It could've been the uniform. It could've been I was horny and desperate, or it could've been nothing more than sheer curiosity."

"My money's on the wine," Preston laughed.

"It was probably a combination of all four," I shrugged. "Plus you being in the right place at the right time."

Adrian coughed through another grin, causing Jax to ball up his napkin and throw it at him. I couldn't believe how much of a kick he was getting out of this whole thing.

"Collectively, I haven't seen you guys for years," I finished up. "I've been lonely. Working like crazy. Honestly, I'm glad to be back in your lives again. The three of you mean a lot to me. Even this asshole."

I jerked a thumb at Jax. He curled his lip.

"So yeah, I guess all my past inhibitions were gone this time around." I finished by folding my arms. "But hey, no apologies on my end. In all three cases, I wanted it to happen."

I looked down at my hands, which had begun to fidget.

"I guess the bigger question is, what happens now?"

The boys looked at me thoughtfully, each lost in his own thoughts. Jax was leaning back in his chair. Adrian ran to the fridge and came back with more drinks; this time, a round of waters. It made sense, considering two out of three of them were leaving for work soon.

"What happens now is actually up to you, Harper," Adrian eventually said. "Whenever you're ready, that is."

"Me?"

"Yes."

"Whenever I'm ready?" I chuckled. "What the hell does that mean?"

"It means we've collectively decided to back off," said Preston, matter-of-factly. "With all due respect, we're going to give you some space."

My eyes narrowed. "Space?"

"That's right," Adrian agreed. "Space to decide. It's not fair to you if we're all rushing you together, like some busy fraternity. This is about what *you* want. Or don't want." He shrugged. "That part's up to you."

I wasn't sure I liked it, but I was slowly getting it.

"Soo… you want me to make a decision."

"Well, yes," said Preston. "But only if you *want* to. You could decide on none of us, and that's okay too. We understand that we put you in a tough position. And we acknowledge the whole thing is kinda crazy…"

"And if I picked one of you, then what?" I asked. "The rest of you are just going to be okay with it?"

They nodded, twisting the caps off their waters.

"That's what we agreed upon, yes."

"Seriously?"

"Yup," said Adrian. "The others will back off entirely. As difficult as that might be."

"Besides," Jax grumbled. "You obviously want one of us more than the others. That's human nature. And who wants a girl who wants someone else?"

Several beats of silence followed. For some reason, my heart sank.

"That's not fair," I told them.

The boys looked at each other in confusion. They seemed honestly surprised.

"Why? We thought it was the fairest way to—"

"You're making me choose between three men I've grown to care about very much," I cried. I pointed to Jax and Adrian. "You're asking me to come between lifelong childhood friends," I nodded toward Preston, "or to give up on someone who's so super-compatible to me, it's like he was molded specifically to be my boyfriend."

"Then choose him," Jax shrugged, as if he didn't care. "If that's what you want—"

"That's not what I want!" I shouted. "I— I wanted…"

My sentence trailed off awkwardly. There was no good way to finish it.

"What?" asked Adrian.

I sank my head into my hands. I should've used them to pull my foot from my mouth.

"She wanted all of us," Jax laughed gruffly. "*That's what she wanted.*"

Another span of silence followed, even more awkward than before. I could feel their eyes on me.

"Is that true?" asked Adrian. "Is that what you want?"

I didn't know what to say. All I could do was shrug.

"I don't know what the hell I want," I admitted finally. "I know I don't want to lose any of you, though. That's for sure."

"Unbelievable," Jax laughed.

I whipped my head up. The others were staring at him, angrily.

"Jax—"

"Greedy," Jax grunted. "Just as I said. Just like—"

The door to the apartment opened abruptly again, and our heads turned in time to catch Brayden and Emma. They flew inside happily, ahead of a smiling woman who could only be Jennifer, the sister of Jax's sister-in-law.

"Hi!" cried Jennifer. "Sorry if I'm a bit early, but…"

Brayden rushed to his father first, hugged him, then headed straight for me. Emma did the same with Jax. Both children reached me at about the same time, arms outstretched, as I struggled to pull each into my lap.

The life-changing double-hug they gave me drove every last worry from my conflicted head.

~ 33 ~

ADRIAN

Going a week without Harper sucked badly enough. But going another five days, afterward?

That drove me pretty much out of my mind.

She hadn't taken my calls. She hadn't answered my texts. As far as I knew she wasn't talking to Jax or Preston either, although she'd shown up to watch Emma on two separate occasions.

It wasn't until now that she'd finally contacted me, in a semi-cryptic text message that left my head spinning:

I need to see you tonight.

My first thought was that maybe she'd made her decision. The very thought of it threw my stomach in turmoil. It could be good news, or it could be bad. It could also be that she had a blown fuse or a clogged sink and she just needed someone to come over and fix it.

Sharing the Nanny

Or it could be the worst news in the world.

If Harper had chosen one of the others, I knew it would devastate me. I'd have to keep my feelings secret though, because I was already committed to our agreement. If she didn't choose me, I'd have to forget our time together and move on without her. Those were the rules.

The worst part though, would be knowing that I'd come so far. So achingly close to an actual relationship; with a woman, who I realized, perhaps too late, I'd truly loved all along.

I was more than nervous as I pulled up to her house and knocked gently. Harper let me in with warm hello. She embraced me, but didn't kiss me. There was inner turmoil and conflict in the way she carried herself. I knew her well enough to sense these things without so much as a word.

Maybe she hadn't made her decision yet at all.

"How've you been?" I asked.

"Busy," she answered.

I took one look around and let out a low whistle. "I can see that."

The house was a total disaster, as compared to the last time I'd seen it when I'd dropped Brayden off for a few hours. There were piles of electronic components, and spools of wires scattered throughout her living room. I stepped over scraps of black and red electrical tape, and around empty amazon boxes. I moved around a plethora of scattered tools and other assorted pieces of electronic equipment, only to nearly slip on one of the hundred pieces of bubble-wrap that littered the floor.

Her kitchen table had been dragged into the living area, and three different computers were now running on it, side by side. A fourth computer — this one a laptop — was open and also running. Entire rows of numbers and characters flashed by, so fast I could barely follow them. It reminded me of every computer hacking movie or TV show I'd ever seen.

"Please don't touch anything," she said needlessly.

"Oh, you don't have to worry about that," I said, putting both my hands up. "I'm afraid to even breathe."

Harper's face softened a little, and she even smiled. She slid deftly over to where I was standing, and took my hand in hers.

"Thanks for coming, Adrian."

"No problem," I told her. "I have to admit, I'm a little worried, though. When you stopped answering my—"

A knock at the door, much louder than mine, drew our attention away. She took her hand back.

"Who's that?" I asked.

"The others."

Harper crossed the room and opened the door. Jax and Preston stepped inside, accompanied by an intimidating blast of cold air. Their reactions to my presence told me they hadn't expected me to be here.

"I'm glad you're all here," she said, once the door was closed. "I've got kind of an emergency."

I stepped forward, suddenly concerned. The others did too.

"You got robbed, didn't you?" said Jax, looking around.

"No."

"Yeah, well it looks like the morning after *The Hangover* in here," he quipped. "Or someone threw a grenade through your window. Or maybe you hosted the Running of the Bulls this year."

"No parties. No bulls," said Harper. "I've been... working."

Preston's eyes crawled over the equipment more shrewdly than ours. I could tell he knew exactly what he was looking at.

"Harper, if you need help—"

"I'm not asking for help, either," she interjected. "Not right now. I'm this close to a breakthrough." She held up her thumb and forefinger, barely touching. "This close to figuring out the final pieces of this puzzle."

Preston smiled, nodding slowly. "Your eureka moment."

"Yes."

"So then what's the problem?" I asked, folding my arms.

She stood in the middle of the room now, in the middle of the mess. Her eyes shifted methodically from me, to Jax, then to Preston, all in the span of three or four seconds.

"The problem is *you.*"

A measure of silence followed, broken only by the wind howling outside. Everyone looked confused.

"Me?" Jax asked gruffly.

"All of you," declared Harper. "The three of you are keeping me from finishing... this."

She gestured around the room with extended arms.

The motion was a little frantic.

"Is someone not leaving you alone?" I asked, throwing suspicious glances at the others. "Because we all agreed on giving you—"

"I know what you agreed on," Harper cut me off. "You agreed on giving me space. And you have been. The only problem is, *I* didn't agree upon it. Shit, I wasn't even asked."

She stomped over, stepping delicately around every single piece of equipment like she'd memorized its position on the floor. Her blue eyes wide, and full of fire. It both frightened me and turned me on at the same time.

"Since the three of you asked me to make a choice, I've been totally useless," said Harper. "I can't sleep, I can't eat, I can't focus. Worst of all, I can't work."

I searched the others' expressions for help. Preston appeared as confused as I was. When I looked to Jax however, I saw his eyes narrow.

"What do you mean you can't—"

"I can't do anything!" Harper shouted, her arms still in the air. "All I can think about is losing one or more of you, after having just gotten you back in my life again. I keep going back to having to choose, and making the wrong choice terrifies me."

She was so animated she actually shook when she moved, her feminine parts bouncing mouthwateringly in her tight half-shirt and loose-fitting sweatpants. But Harper wasn't putting on a show. She was genuinely upset.

"So you know what?" she went on, just as one of us was about to say something. "Fuck choosing. I'm not choosing at all."

Preston looked utterly miserable now. Like he wanted to scoop her into his arms and console her, but totally knew better.

"So you're choosing nobody, then?" Jax asked, a little angry. "Is that it?"

Harper rolled her eyes in frustration. Her hands went to her hips.

"You'd rather be all alone," Jax went on snidely, "than to have to—"

"No."

I spoke the word loudly enough that everyone turned to face me at once. Even Harper.

"What she means is, she's not choosing at all."

I saw the tension slowly go out of her shoulders. With my understanding, the frustration melted away.

"She's saying she doesn't want things to change," I went on, still maintaining eye contact with her. "She wants them to stay exactly the same."

"The same?" Jax's brows scrunched together in confusion.

Preston was busy scratching at his jaw. He cleared his throat. "You mean the same as…"

"Yes."

His eyes went abruptly wide. "Oh."

Harper didn't move, or shrink away. She stood her ground, without flinching.

"You know what this means, don't you?" I asked her. "I'm certainly not going to stop. *They're* not going to stop, either."

I extended a finger, pointing at the others. They were already nodding.

"We're going to continue on with everything the way it was," I said. "No one's backing off. And no one's going to hide it now, either."

Harper swallowed. "I know."

"So are you sure this is what you want?"

She bit her lip and nodded, and the nod was adorable. "Yes," she said, a little more breathlessly. "I'm sure."

Her stress was gone now, having totally fled. Wicked confidence slid right into its place.

"In fact, let me show you *how* sure."

Harper grabbed me, pulled me in, and kissed me deeply… right in front of Jax and Preston. She didn't even hesitate. Not for a single minute.

Holy…

I melted into her hands, and those hands were now roaming my chest, my shoulders, the small of my back. Harper kissed me for another few seconds that felt like blissful eternity. Then she let go, and slid right up against Preston.

Holy fuck.

I watched her kiss him too, and a stab of jealousy tore through me. It didn't seem real. There was something crazy about seeing the girl you loved kissing someone else, yet still having to be okay with it.

But are *you okay with it?*

Oddly enough, I was. If it meant not letting her

down, I could cope with it. If it ensured I didn't lose her again like I had before, I was all in.

Harper finished kissing Preston and moved on to Jax. He was her frenemy. Her nemesis. For these reasons, I knew she'd chosen him last.

That, plus I'm sure she did it just in case it pissed him off.

Holy shit, look at them.

I watched, as my best female friend stood on her toes and locked lips with my oldest, closest friend in the world. Their kiss was fiery and passionate, full of sparks and chemistry that belied their love-hate relationship. Whatever bullshit facade these two had kept up all these years, I knew in that one kiss that it had all crumbled away. And it wasn't just one kiss, either, but a series of electrifying kisses that had Preston and I ready for a second and third turn.

Unfortunately, there were no other turns to be had. Harper stepped back, thoroughly satisfied with her handiwork. There was relief in her eyes. A new relaxation in her body language.

But there was lust there, too. I could see the goosebumps that had risen up on her arms. The deep pink hue her skin had taken on after kissing all three of us. It was in her eyes, her cheeks, the rapid rise and fall of her chest. She wasn't just relieved by not having to decide, although that was definitely a part of it.

No, Harper *wanted* this, and she wanted it badly. That much was obvious.

"So…" she said, stepping back. "Are we convinced?"

"I'm convinced you're bat-shit crazy," said Jax.

"I am," Harper admitted. "But are all three of you *good* with it?"

I glanced at Preston, then at Jax. Together, we gave the weirdest triple-shrug in the world.

"So you're going to be our girlfriend, then?" Preston asked. "All three of us?"

Harper paused, touching a finger to her lip in contemplation.

"Sure. I'm your girlfriend."

"A girlfriend comes with responsibilities," I offered.

"I know."

"And benefits," Jax growled.

Harper's faint smirk turned into a grin. "There had *better* be benefits," she agreed. "Otherwise, what's the point?"

Somewhere between my legs, something stirred. I had a good feeling I knew exactly what it was.

"So we're okay then?" she finally asked. "I can stop obsessing over this and get back to work?"

We looked at each other one last time.

"Sure," I told her. "We're golden."

"Good," smiled Harper, extending an arm toward the door. "Now please, and I mean this in the nicest possible way…" She smiled sweetly. "Get out."

~ 34 ~

HARPER

I worked continually for four straight days, then nannied for three nights. Aside from handing off the babies, I hardly even saw the guys. I barely saw my pillow, too.

But they were all still in, and that was all that mattered.

In the meantime, I got shit done. I worked out my last major programming bugs, as well as some of the minor ones, before moving onto the physical product. The new circuits I ordered came in, and they were working even better than expected. I made a shit-ton of wiring harnesses. Connected haptic patches to an actual, wearable suit. I sat in front of my soldering rig until my back locked up, then walked around the block to stretch it out and clear my mind.

It was during those crisp winter walks that I thought mostly about the guys. They sent me daily text messages of encouragement, offers of help, and individual promises to take me out on dates once I'd finished my beta testing. I got a few strategic pics of Adrian winking at me with his shirt off, some heavy nerd-flirting from Preston, and even a few lines of late-night dirty talk from what I suspected was a semi-drunk Jax.

As much as I loved all the attention, I loved even more that they were respecting my work. It helped that I was in the home stretch, of course. I'd made contacts within the major VR corporations, and some were already expecting my prototype. I gathered all the data I could, on every aspect of the product. I collated it all into neat folders, so I could work it into whatever final presentation I would ultimately be giving.

During my work stretches, I tried not to think about potential competitors. It was hard, though. Telengard sent me near-daily updates now on the YouTube channel, in which the kid was still traveling down many of the same development paths as me.

The closer I got to launch, the more nervous I knew I would get. And the knowledge of this made me even more anxious. More paranoid…

I needed a break.

I needed release.

Luckily, I knew where to get both.

~ 35 ~

HARPER

"Oh my God, he's *adorable!*"

The little dog ran straight through my legs, then circled back the other side. It was white and brown and looked like a baby beagle. Only it wasn't a beagle, it was a dachshund.

"I didn't know they even came in this color!" I cried.

"It's a double-dapple piebald," said Preston. "The color's caused by a recessive gene."

Adrian looked strangely at him, so he shrugged.

"That's what the shelter told me, anyway. So I looked it up."

I was down near the floor now, where the dog was busy sniffing and licking my face. Preston took our coats. He hung them next to one of Jax's many EMT jackets.

"Awww… what's your name, boy?" I asked the dog, while scratching its long, sleek sides. It immediately rolled over to give me access to its belly.

"His name is Guido."

Two little ears perked up instantly, at the sound of the dog's owner calling its name. Guido still didn't move though. He remained contentedly on his back while I ran my nails down both sides of his ribs.

"Guido…" I repeated, thinking aloud. My eyes shot up to meet Preston's. "As in Guido van Rossum?"

Preston's grin told me he was suitably impressed. "Holy shit, yes!"

"Who's Guido van Rossum?" asked Adrian.

"The Dutch programmer who created the Python programming language," I said nonchalantly. I kept scratching away, while shaking my head. "Unbelievable."

"What is?"

"This is the first time I met a wiener dog that wasn't named Nathan, or Frank."

"Or Sabrett," Adrian added with a smile.

Preston laughed along with us as he made his way to the kitchen. "Nah. Low-hanging fruit."

I heard the clink of glasses as he rummaged around in the kitchen. The three of us had been drinking wine all night. We'd already spent hours laughing and talking and picking on platters of tapas at a local Spanish restaurant. But right now I was ready for something *else*.

"Wait, when did you get a dog?" I asked, suddenly realizing Guido hadn't been here the last few times I'd been around.

"I've had him for years," Preston replied. "I uh… well, I sort of share custody."

"With an ex-girlfriend?" I mused.

He shrugged and smiled. "Guilty as charged."

Guido got bored once I stopped petting him, and went back to his comfy-looking dog bed at the opposite end of the room. Still, I couldn't help but chuckle out loud. Partly from the wine, but also because I found it interesting that all three men in my life were sharing custody of someone or some thing. Silently I wondered if that's what made them so okay with sharing. They were used to it.

Right now I was in the company of two out of three of those men, and only because Jax was working another marathon shift. When I called hoping one or more of them would take me out tonight, he'd let out a long, shocking string of scathing curse words. I promised him a raincheck, and to even cook him dinner. He promised me it would be a short dinner, and that he'd be eating dessert first.

He also left no doubt that *I* would be the dessert.

The whole conversation made me wet, but not nearly as wet as I'd been tonight at the restaurant. After waiting at the bar so we could get a booth near the back, the guys took turns flirting with me, feeding me, and then ultimately kissing me… right in full view of anyone who might be watching.

It started off subtle at first. Adrian would guide my mouth to his with a gentle hand, letting the kiss linger as our tongues explored for as long as they dared. A minute later I was kissing Preston, enjoying the two different hands roaming up and down my thighs beneath the table.

This went on for a while, happening intermittently and without prompting. I was left breathless as they passed my lips back and forth, kissing me like they owned me, none of us in any hurry to finish eating, drinking, or playing. Eventually though, the sense of urgency grew. With each passing hour I could feel the electricity between the three of us rising, until I was so slick I was literally sitting in a puddle of my own wetness.

As the waiter brought the check I had my hands safely under the table, working two very hard and uncoiling cocks beneath my eager palms. I squeezed them both through the fabric of their slacks, letting their owners know in no uncertain terms that the three of us *really* needed to get home soon.

And now here we were, one very brisk ten-minute walk later. The cold wind had invigorated me even further, charging me up for the welcome warmth of Preston's apartment, and the heat that would inevitably follow. We'd chosen Preston's place mainly because Adrian was completely out of wine. But also, I suspected, because he planned on doing something in Jax's bed.

And by something, I meant *me*.

The glasses were handed out, and this time we drank without toasting. In our defense, we'd been toasting all night. By now I was dizzy with Merlot, thrilled to be relaxing, and of course, giddy at the idea of finally getting laid.

"Got any music?"

At my request, Preston pulled out his phone and sent something remotely to some very expensive-sounding speakers. Whatever it was, it had a slow, beautiful rhythm that was perfect to sway my hips to. Which of course, I did.

"Nice. Dance with me?"

I breathed the words softly, seductively, while trailing my wine glass in one hand. I allowed the music to wash over me, guiding my movements, lifting me through the dimly-lit apartment as if floating on a cloud. No one joined me, although I could feel their eyes following me with every step.

"Fine," I chuckled. "You boys just watch, then."

I looked back to find the guys sprawled out in soft chairs, gazing at me intently. Their shirts were only half-buttoned. Their wine glasses, already half-empty. They looked dashingly handsome with their shoes and slacks still on, like real, true men and not the immature boys I'd been so used to dating. Their expressions were unapologetically lecherous, though. And that was just fine by me.

I kept dancing, swaying, moving before them. Then, piece by piece, I began removing my clothes. My dress came up, my bra came undone. I left my G-sting on, though. After all, a girl had to leave *something* to the imagination.

I was stripped bare before them in no time, my body undulating slowly to the haunting yet beautiful song. It felt absurdly normal, being naked and dancing before them both. I let my hands wander slowly up my hips, then over my breasts, then down across the flat of my stomach...

"So, it's like this, now?" Adrian asked casually.

Still moving with deliberate slowness, I sauntered over to him. Bracing a hand on one muscular thigh, I leaned in close enough that my lips brushed his ear.

"Yeah," I nodded sultrily. "It's like this."

I grabbed his cock, growing even wetter in anticipation. He didn't flinch.

"And this."

I turned around and grabbed Preston too. He didn't flinch either. To reach him, I had to bend at the hips, giving Adrian a full view of my G-string covered ass.

"And something like this."

I dropped to my knees and gave my full attention to Preston, flipping my hair forward, rubbing my face all over his lap. I could feel him stirring beneath the fabric. His manhood was straining against its cotton prison, struggling to break free.

"After all, you *did* agree to share me," I murmured softly. "Didn't you?"

I unbuckled him with a mischievous chuckle, then used my teeth to pull his zipper down. The whole time, I was putting on a show for Adrian. I shoved my ass high in the air and rolled it left and right for him, moving it like a cobra emerging from a snake charmer's basket.

"You wanted a girlfriend?" I teased Adrian, sultrily. "Well, this is girlfriend stuff."

It was threesome stuff too, of course. I knew that part might be new to him, and maybe a little strange. But it *was* what he'd signed up for. He needed to know that in not choosing any of them, I'd chosen them all.

Baptism by fire.

Preston's beautiful member popped free as I yanked his pants and boxers down. Just dragging it against my face made my mouth water. Before I closed my lips over it, I heard the familiar jangle of a belt buckle, followed by the sound of Adrian standing up. My stomach erupted in butterflies. This was all really happening.

A strong pair of hands went straight to my hips, and in no time Adrian was stretching my G-string to one side. He buried his face into me from behind, pressing his lips against my wetness, driving his tongue so deep I wanted to scream.

Then I did scream, and that felt even better.

He devoured me expertly, as I stroked Preston up and down. For a while I just coasted, rocking forward and back, floating through a warm haze of sex-saturated bliss. I could stay here pinned between them forever, and spend the rest of my days squirming against that model-handsome face...

Adrian had other ideas, though. Eventually he got up on his knees, and his hands went to my hips again. When he rubbed the bulbous head of his thick shaft through my already-drenched folds, I bit my lip and just about cried.

Girlfriend stuff is fucking awesome, I sighed to myself, as he sank right in.

~ 36 ~

HARPER

They took me on the floor, on the couch, up against the wall. They reveled in sharing me. Trading off on me. Using me like they'd been doing it all their lives, instead of the last thirty or forty glorious minutes.

At some point I was picked up and carried into the kitchen. Once there, Preston spread my legs and took me right on the empty counter, just next to the coffee machine. Not willing to be outdone, Adrian fucked me from behind, bent over the kitchen table. He railed me so hard we had to stop before the neighbors called the police; the banging noise was just too great. But not before Preston pushed him aside first, to make sure he had his turn, too.

"You boys wanna do this in a bed, maybe?" I quipped. "Or at least somewhere more comfortable?"

From there, things got hazy.

I remember being spread out on pillows and blankets and comforters, scattered over the living room floor. I was devoured and then plundered with my thighs spread wide, whimpering happily as they took turns sharing either side of me. My mouth was always busy kissing, licking, sucking… sometimes gasping, while clutching one lover tightly against me as the other waited his turn. But my favorite was when they *both* took me, surging into me from either side. Holding my hips and face steady as they fucked me from opposite ends, switching silently back and forth whenever they felt like it, or perhaps exchanged some secret signal.

Adrian adapted to the uniqueness of the situation almost immediately, and even took charge in the hottest of ways. He was always the one repositioning my body; shoving me down, pushing my head into a pillow so he could ram me from whatever angle pleased him at the time, or opening me up so his friend could do the same. Preston would pin my legs back so his friend could drive deeper inside me, then after a rapturous few minutes, Adrian would return the favor. Their team effort turned me on in new ways I couldn't fathom. There was just no way to describe how hot it was to feel four strong hands pinning you down. One lover keeping your body from moving as the other pistoned in and out of you, penetrating you mercilessly until you finally came, screaming all the way through your orgasm.

As the luckiest girl in the world, I was able to experience all of that and more. I forgot all about work, and stress, and everything else… everything except the feel of having these men inside me, sharing me, ravaging me over and over, until I was crying with tears of joy.

And now, here I was, in the penultimate moment: my hands on Adrian's chest. Hovering over his rock-hard erection. About to fulfill my dirtiest, wildest fantasy, if I could actually go through with it.

I sank down on him, impaling myself so fully and completely he was buried snugly against my womb. Our eyes locked and I squeezed him internally, my mouth breaking into a smile.

"You sure about this?" he asked, holding me by the hips.

I nodded, then blew an errant lock of hair from between my lips. Adrian reached up with one hand, to help pin it back behind my ear.

"I *want* this," I whispered huskily.

He smiled back as I leaned forward against his body, screwing my tits against his hard chest. Our lips hovered tantalizingly against one another's. His every breath was my breath.

"Just go slow," I called over my shoulder.

A second pair of hands went to my hips, as Preston guided himself home. He was well-lubricated. Rock-hard and glistening wet and ready for what just might be the greatest thing ever.

Or, it could be that it just hurt like hell.

Relax.

I tensed up a little as Preston pushed himself between my cheeks, then worked his way slowly into my ass. Inch by inch, millimeter by millimeter, I could feel him sliding inside.

You've got to relax.

I'd done this before, of course. An ex-boyfriend of mine had been somewhat of an ass-freak, and I'd always enjoyed it. But I'd never tried getting fucked in the ass while another man, a second, even bigger man, was already buried to the hilt inside me.

HOLY FUCK...

Getting filled like this felt nothing like it had before.

Instead, it felt so much fucking *better*. It was tighter and raunchier and ten times more exciting, with the additional thrill of four hands, two throbbing shafts, and the exquisite feeling of being sandwiched between two hard, beautiful bodies.

My pussy had never felt this full, and the feeling was indescribable. The worry dissolved away as I relaxed completely. Happiness and enjoyment filled the void where apprehension had been.

And then the boys started rocking me forward and back, thrusting slowly in and out of me. And my entire world changed for the better.

"OhmyGod, ohmyGod, ohmyGod…"

It was a mantra I repeated over and over, as it softly escaped my lips. I was fucking two guys. Two guys at *once!* They were both inside me together, double-penetrating me, filling me front and back.

I spread my fingers wide across the comforting warmth of Adrian's chest, bearing down on him as I rode them both into sweet oblivion. I felt incredibly lucky. I'd been somewhat apprehensive in bringing it up — maybe even a little embarrassed — but the guys had been sweet and accepting and even excited by the idea of fulfilling my fantasy. They were as adventurous and crazy as I was. Totally sexually compatible.

Just another good reason why choosing only one of them seemed foolish.

You're a greedy girl, Harper, the little voice in my head sang smugly. *Jax was right.*

The Jax being right part made me frown. Even if the voice wasn't exactly wrong.

Maybe, I sighed to myself, as we picked up speed and rhythm.

And so what if I am?

After initially letting me move at my own pace, the guys had seized back some control. Adrian was clenching and unclenching his perfect ass, thrusting wondrously into me from below. And Preston's hands were in full command of my hips now, giving him even more leverage as he plunged in and out of my tight little ass.

Unfuckingreal.

I surrendered completely to the heat of the moment, giving myself to their every whim. Eventually Preston's hands slid down to my wrists and seized them tight. I was alarmed at first when he began pulling my arms back, forcing my body to arch backward, my breasts pointing upward. By then I was grunting like a whore, making obscene, guttural noises as my hair spilled all the way down my naked back. I could feel it bouncing against the top of my ass — the same ass Preston was so thoroughly and expertly fucking — as Adrian continued bucking upward, drilling me so deep I was ready to lose my mind.

My whimpers eventually turned into moans, and the moans into cries of pleasure that rode the razor-sharp edge between pleasure and pain. The pleasure was so total, so magnificent, it always won out. Everything below my waist was so wet, so swollen, so incredibly hot, all I could do was continue in my compliance, surrendering my body wholly and completely as nothing more than a tool my magnificent lovers could use to get themselves off.

And when they finally started coming inside me… pulsing and throbbing and filling me in two places at once…

I came too.

~ 37 ~

JAX

"Oh my God Jax, I can't believe you're letting her do this!"

Harper's mouth hung open, the straw from her vanilla shake hanging off her plump bottom lip. Her eyes tracked upward, to where Emma had just disappeared into an overhead tube. I could see the tube vibrating as she crawled through it. She came out the other side and waved to us through the Plexiglass porthole.

"You do realize we're gonna need a steam hose and six gallons of bleach to disinfect her, right?" she added dramatically.

I laughed.

"Seriously, Jax! A McDonalds indoor Playplace?" She pointed again. "There have to be at least a half-billion different colonies of germs and viruses living in there. And she's *crawling* through it."

I tore into Emma's hamburger, which of course she had no intention of ever finishing. The second she saw the colorful ball-pit and the slide that fed into it, all interest in food went right out the window.

"Look, kids need germs," I told her with a smirk. "They keep the immune system healthy. Besides, our parents' generation let us run rampant through places like this, and even worse."

"Maybe, but…"

"And just look how great I turned out?"

Harper rolled her eyes and made a face, so I made one back. Hers was better though.

"Give her a few minutes," I said. "She'll make a friend or two, like last time. And if she doesn't, we'll crawl up there ourselves."

At that, my 'date' laughed. "Speak for yourself!" she said. "And I hate to break it to you, but you're not gonna fit up there."

"Oh no? Watch me."

I moved to stand up, but Harper pulled me playfully back down. I fell heavily into the tiny molded seat, spilling french fries everywhere.

"This place isn't made for guys your size," she chuckled.

"Yeah, well it should be," I countered, still keeping an eye glued on Emma. "Guys my size have kids too, you know. Take Jason for example. He was bigger than me, and well…"

Harper's whole expression softened. I realized too late I'd been talking about my brother.

"Anyway," I sighed, "maybe it's better off I wasn't there the other night. You and Preston getting together is like hanging out with the Geek Squad. Adrian must've been going out of his mind with—"

"It's okay, Jax," she said gently. "You don't have to change the subject. You *can* talk about him."

"What subject?" I balked. "Talk about who?"

"Jason," she murmured. "Your brother."

My face twisted into a frown. Instinctively I turned my full attention back to Emma, and for a few seconds she let me. Eventually though, her fingers found my cheek.

"I need you to know how sorry I am about what happened," she reiterated, guiding me back to those striking blue eyes. "I never got the chance to fully tell you."

"You weren't there, so why should you be sorry?" I shrugged. "It's in the past now. I don't need a pity party every time someone realizes—"

"I'm not throwing you a pity party," she interjected angrily. "Jax, I've known you forever, and I knew Jason too. A tragedy like that is obviously horrific, and I can't even begin to imagine your pain. But the way you handled it was inspiring. I'm in awe at how incredible you are, for stepping up and taking on Emma as your own."

I didn't expect the hurt in her eyes. But it was there, and it was genuine, and it certainly wasn't pity.

All of sudden I felt foolish.

"There's nothing incredible about it," I finally countered. "I did what anyone—"

"Jax, you and Jennifer took on a *daughter,*" Harper asserted. "You made her your own. The two of you did it when no one else would, and at a time in your life when things are at the absolute busiest. But you did it anyway, and you didn't hesitate. That makes you amazing."

I looked away again, if for no other reason than there was suddenly a knot in my throat. Emma had moved to a different tube, now. I could still see her through the Plexiglass, laughing away with some little boy in blue overalls.

She called you amazing.

My mind spun through a storm of conflicting thoughts. Harper and I weren't supposed to talk like this. We should be in some shitty bar insulting each other, like always. We weren't supposed to be out on a date, much less a play date complete with a toddler, vanilla shakes, and deep conversation.

And yet somehow, I didn't mind it. Somehow it seemed... right.

I turned back to look at her, silhouetted so prettily against the snowy bank of windows. Yet this was *Harper*. She wasn't pretty, she was an asshole. Or maybe I was the asshole. Either way, she wasn't loving, she totally hated me. Right?

Wrong.

I'd been incredibly jealous of Adrian and Preston the other night, getting to be with her when I wasn't available. Enjoying her in ways that I so desperately wanted to. And yet, as much as they'd so thoroughly *had* her, she was also still mine. I didn't begrudge them for wanting her, or for taking her, or even for Preston's smug announcement that as far as the battle for sexual bed-supremacy went, he and I were now 'even Steven.'

No, somehow I was okay with all that. In fact, on some deep, perverted level I still had yet to fully explore, it actually turned me the fuck on. It made me want her *more*. It made me want to possess her, to reclaim her. To nudge those beautiful thighs apart and take her back as my own, all while kissing her until she was whimpering those sexy little noises into my open mouth.

I could do all that and more, later on, after we'd dropped Emma off at Jennifer's. But right now…

Right now I was still exploring the crazy idea that Harper and I actually enjoyed each other's company.

"Trust me, I'm far from amazing," I told her flatly. "I'm kind of a dickhead, actually."

Harper's smirk came back so fast it made me love her even more.

"Oh, no one's arguing *that*."

"But I'm an amazing dickhead?" I countered. "Is that it?"

She shrugged. "Better than average. As far as dickheads go, anyway."

I tried to keep a straight face as my eyes continued tracking Emma. She'd come down the tube slide, finally. The smile on her face as she sank happily into the ball-pit was something that couldn't be bought.

"Speaking of dickheads," I continued, "Preston told me you gave him a world-class blowjob the other night."

"Really?" Harper replied casually.

"In my *bed*."

Tucking the straw between her lips again, she shrugged innocently. "Maybe."

"Maybe?" I balked. "Fuck maybe! I need to *know* these things. Did he leave a mess? Did he floss his ass with my pillows? Exactly how much bedding do I have to wash?"

Harper began laughing so hard she almost spit up her shake. Personally, I didn't see what was so funny.

"Do I have to go out and buy a blacklight today, or —"

"You really want details?" she asked coyly.

I thought about it for a butterfly-inducing moment. "Yeah, sure. Give me details."

She took the straw from her mouth again, looked over both shoulders, then leaned in close. So close I could smell the vanilla on her breath.

"You don't need a blacklight," she whispered huskily, "because I didn't miss a drop."

There it was again — that surge of adrenaline, tinged with jealousy. It was followed immediately by a distinct physical movement, somewhere down in my boxers.

And for some reason, I loved it.

"I still mostly hate you, you know," I told her.

"No you don't."

Harper laughed, leaned in, and kissed me. It was a sweet kiss. A sexy kiss.

"At least three-quarters," I murmured against her lips.

"Nope."

"Definitely halfway?" I sighed.

"Nah-uh."

She kissed me again, this time more deeply. Her tongue was pleasantly cold, and tasted like vanilla.

"At least a little, then," I offered.

"Fine," Harper agreed, "Maybe a tiny bit, sure."

Before I could do anything else, she bit my lower lip

playfully between her teeth. Forehead to forehead our eyes locked, and she chuckled into my mouth.

"But I think that's the part I like the most."

~ 38 ~

HARPER

I'd been on dates that were fun and exciting, and dates that unequivocally sucked. Dates that brought me to places that were pretty or romantic or outright beautiful, and one date that took place on the trash-strewn cement dock of a garbage compactor, replete with the accompanying smell.

But I'd never had a date on a thousand-foot cliff overlooking the ocean at sunset, while walking through a field of beautiful wildflowers, bordered by a thick green forest. Gorgeous, multicolored butterflies surrounded us, and the distant sounds of buzzing cicadas along with the crickets provided a rhythmic background hum.

Until now.

"This is the most beautiful thing I've ever seen."

I turned my head to smile at Preston, who was still open-mouthed and gaping in awe. He had been since we'd gotten here, only a few minutes ago.

I reached out and slid my hand into his. Preston squeezed my fingers gently, sending a tingle of excitement up along my arm all the way to my shoulder. I even slid closer to him, and I could actually *feel* his presence. It was warm and comforting and reassuring.

The best part of all though, was that Preston wasn't there. Not even close.

Preston was standing in the living room of his apartment, miles away. Dressed head to toe in one of my haptics suit prototypes.

I was at home, wearing the other one.

"Harper... just... *wow*."

He led me forward, toward the edge of the cliff. He did it slowly, trepidatiously. Watching his expression with calculated interest, I could read the fear in his avatar's eyes.

"You don't have to be afraid," I told him. "You can't fall."

"Bullshit," he answered nervously.

"I mean, you *could* fall if it were part of the program," I continued. "But we could also jump off that cliff and fly if we wanted to."

I felt him tense up. The micro mnemonic adapters in our hands reacted to each other, sending packets of data back and forth with near-instantaneous speed.

"We won't jump," I chuckled. "I promise."

He relaxed, and I felt that too. Yet the thing I felt most was pride. The beautiful vistas and sunset skies were only partially mine; most of them belonged to a VR scenery program I'd bastardized long ago. But the important thing was that my haptics were working. And not just working, but operating at even better than expected levels.

For example, we could feel the heat of the sun on one

side of our bodies, and the cool of the wind on the other. It was in the vibration of our footsteps, the interactions within our environment. Most of all, we could sense the newly-developed haptic surges against the surface of our skin. The subtle force feedback system I'd developed was responding to our physical nerve endings, registering every movement, every caress, every touch.

"This is incredible," Preston breathed, still looking in every direction.

"No. This is only pretty," I told him.

Reaching out with my free hand, I snapped my fingers and the scenery disappeared. The field of flowers dropped away, and the surface of an alien planet rushed up to meet us. The ground was lush with thriving, glowing plant life, unlike anything that existed on Earth. The sunset disappeared, replaced by an inky black sky that wasn't a sky at all.

"Now *this* is incredible," I declared proudly.

Preston gasped, reflexively letting go of my hand. We were in outer space, now. Ringed planets hovered above us, so big and bright they were borderline terrifying. I could see asteroid belts in the distance. Comets soaring, trailing dust. In every direction we looked, the sky exploded with a billion, trillion stars.

"Holy shit…" Preston choked.

I let him wander for a moment, touching things, stepping past flora and fauna that made no sense except to the programmers like me who imagined it in their minds. Eventually he turned around to face me.

"Harper…"

I responded by reaching out and running a finger down the length of his arm. He shivered, involuntarily. I both saw it *and* felt it, because I'd programmed my suit to deliver some of his own experiences.

This is insane.

I reached out and touched his chest. His stomach. The small of his back. The eyes of Preston's avatar mirrored his own, growing larger and more saucer-shaped with every passing second. Eventually I slid a hand down his leg. Reversing the movement, I dragged the tips of my fingers up along the inside of his thigh..

"Eventually there will be haptics here too," I said, gliding my hand over his crotch. Mechanically, I gave a light squeeze right where his balls would be.

"But… but I can *feel it!*" Preston gasped.

"That's because I temporarily added some," I told him. "You get *some* sensation, and your brain fills in the rest. I can't bring it to market like this, though. Too much liability. That, plus I haven't gotten all the bugs worked out."

Preston stiffened again.

"So you're saying I've got the alpha version of an electrically-dangerous haptic system somewhere down near my balls."

I laughed. "Not dangerous, just experimental." I stepped closer and squeezed again, this time a little less gently. A thrill of accomplishment shot through me, as his body reacted instantly to my touch.

"Why?" I whispered sultrily, sliding my face alongside his. At this proximity, my voice would register into his right ear only. "Don't you like?"

"Oh… I *like.*"

"It'll be much better than this, eventually," I promised.

"I just need to figure out a few more things."

As I watched, Preston's avatar shook its head slowly in disbelief.

"You get those things figured out, and people will never leave the house."

I laughed again, this time longer and louder than before. Using my left hand, I toggled my index finger a few times to increase my height, growing me just tall enough so that I didn't have to stand on my toes to face him. Eventually, we were eye to eye.

"Wow," said Preston. "That's a neat trick."

"Sure is. It helps with *this*..."

I could tell by the appearance of his avatar that Preston was wearing the full headgear I'd sent him back with, including the facial mask. And so was I.

Just as in real life, I leaned in and kissed him.

Holy shit...

My kissing software kicked in instantly, the delicate receptors around my mouth causing my lips to tingle. I could sense Preston's were too. We could *feel* each other — actually feel each other! Each subtle movement of the mouth. Each tiny muscle, quivering with desire.

"We're the first ones to do this," I murmured softly against his virtual lips. "Not just with my system, but maybe ever. The first in the whole world."

It was surreal. Unbelievable. Especially standing on the surface of an alien planet, surrounded by mountains, beneath an outer-space, star-filled sky.

We kissed and touched and the whole alien world

began spinning away beneath us. We kissed through the heat, the thirst, the longing. Through whole different levels of want and desire.

We kissed until we were dizzy, and vertigo threatened to take over.

And then we kissed some more...

Eventually our bodies parted, and together we stepped away. My avatar shrank back to its normal, non-matching height.

I looked to him for a reaction, but Preston's avatar was stone-faced and still. I could tell solely by his body language, he just couldn't believe it.

"You're going to make a zillion, billion dollars," he breathed, totally dumbstruck.

"Yeah, right."

"You're gonna be the next Jeff Bezos," he swore softly. "The next Elon Musk."

"I doubt that," I chuckled.

"You're going to have a super-yacht, and maybe a beach house on Mars," he went on. "You're going to sprout wings and fly away from Buffalo. You're never going to talk to us again."

"Oh, stop it!"

"And that's going to be sad too," he said. "Because... well because..."

His voice trailed off, as his gaze shifted upward. Somewhere over his head, a meteor exploded spectacularly in the sky.

"Because what?" I pushed.

Preston stepped in again. He reached out and set his hands on my hips. From the point where he touched me, electric shivers shot down my legs.

"Because I think I love you."

His words shattered everything around us, as my breath caught in my throat. I was shocked. Dismayed. Secretly thrilled and abruptly guilty and a hundred other sensations, all at the same time.

Because of the conflict, I just didn't know what to say.

"Scratch that," he corrected himself, before leaning in to kiss me some more.

"I *know* I love you."

~ 39 ~

HARPER

"Fuck. This."

Sophia flopped back on my couch, blinking her eyes rapidly. She had a stitching needle in one hand, and the sleeve of my custom VR suit in the other. As she tilted her chin toward the ceiling, I giggled.

"Too much?"

"Why'd you have to make these so ridiculously *small?*" she whined. "I'm not kidding, Harper. Keeping up with these stitches is nuts."

"Go ahead and take your fifteen-minute break, then," I teased.

My friend sighed into her mostly-empty glass as she tilted it back, then drained it. She set it down and began working again.

"We're almost out of wine, you know."

I stopped sewing. "Wait. Really?"

"Yeah! We've been at this for hours. I'm dizzy. Plus, I

think I might've stitched one of these sleeves to the pocket of my jeans." She hissed a stream of hot air through clenched teeth. "I guess we'll find out when I get up."

I looked over in admiration at all the work my friend was doing to help me out. She'd volunteered, of course. As long as I bought her dinner, which I had, and kept her plied with wine.

"We're getting there though," Sophia said, a little more cheerfully. "So there's that."

The past week had been a busy one, in both my work and personal life. I'd spent it fine-tuning the physical connections of my haptic receptors, as well as upgrading the overall appearance of the suit itself. I didn't see why this was even necessary, because the suit wasn't even close to an actual finished product. Whoever bought my tech would design their own suit, so the present look of it was meaningless in the grand scheme of things.

But, as Sophia kept pointing out: 'first impressions matter.'

I hadn't thought about it initially, but I would need something to present potential investors that didn't look like a patchwork of rags and wires. And so here we were, pouring over my prototypes with needle and thread. Sophia was surprisingly good at stitching things tight, and tucking wires into seams. Almost better than me.

"Pass me those scissors?"

I leaned forward to toss the tiny scissors onto the blanket covering her legs. They flashed momentarily silver in the firelight from my open stove.

"You're not supposed to throw scissors," my friend teased.

"Sue me."

I picked up my phone, punched through a few screens, then dropped it back on the coffee table. That done, I went back to work. With all the cosplay I'd done over the years, I had some *serious* sewing chops. I'd made a six-layered steampunk costume from scratch. I'd cut and stitched four different Marvel outfits, three from the DC Universe, and more Disney villains than princesses, including a Maleficent gown with four-foot silk wings that took six solid weeks to put together.

Right now, my haptics system was working great. Once I got it looking great, it was time to make some calls.

"So... how are things with your big beautiful man?"

"Which one?" I asked, then immediately stopped myself.

Oh shit. Did I actually say that?

"There's more than *one?*" asked Sophia.

I paused, just a little too long to make up a lie. By then it was too late.

"It's Jax, isn't it?" she pressed. "The friend who hates you!"

Again, my silence became my undoing. Sophia's eyes shot all the way open.

"Holy shit, you dirty bitch!" she screamed. "You're screwing his *friend?*"

"No!" I cried defensively. "I mean... well..."

"You are!" She dropped everything. "Holy—"

"It's not like you think," I cut her off. "It... well, the way it happened was—"

"I'm not judging, mind you," Sophia interjected quickly. "I'm just surprised, that's all. It's not like the two of you are committed or anything. But... his friend?"

I let out an exasperated sigh. How could I possibly explain this? The answer was, I couldn't.

"It's... complicated."

"Again?" she laughed. "*More* complications?"

"Look—"

"I thought you said you loved Adrian?"

I paused for a moment, then shrugged. "I do."

"And does he love you?"

"Yes," I said without hesitation. "He always has."

"Then what's the problem?" Sophia pressed. "Is he icing you out? Doesn't want to commit?"

"No. It's not that."

"Then what would make you—"

"He *knows* about Jax," I blurted in frustration.

I hadn't meant to put it exactly like that. But there, the cat was out of the bag. Sort of.

"Actually," I added, "Jax and I slept together before Adrian and I did."

Sophia's expression was caught between shock and admiration. On pure reflex she reached for her wine, realized the glass was empty, then stopped.

"So how did Adrian find out?" she asked.

"Jax told him."

She balked. "Holy shit, was he angry?"

"Actually, he wasn't."

"Jealous, then?" asked Sophia. "He *had* to be jealous."

"No."

"No?" she repeated. "Seriously?"

Setting aside the suit I was working on, I took my own wine glass and poured half of what I had into her empty one. Then I took a long, emboldening sip.

"Look, it's a weird situation. A unique situation. But yes, I'm sleeping with both of them. And yes, they know about each other."

Sophia's mouth turned upward, but only in my defense. "So they're using you."

"No!" I cried quickly. "No, not at all."

My friend appeared thoroughly confused. "You're using *them?*"

"No," I repeated again. "We're all… sort of in a relationship together."

I stopped.

"Wait, that sounds weirder than it actually is," I explained. "I mean it's still true, don't get me wrong. But it's not something we planned on. It just sort of… happened."

"Happened," Sophia repeated skeptically.

"Yes."

"You're in a relationship with both of these guys — best friends, no less — and they're totally okay with it."

"Yes."

Sophia rubbed at her eyes with both hands. When I was still there, and hadn't faded away like a mirage, she squinted back at me.

"How the *fuck* did you arrange that?"

"I didn't," I admitted. "Like I said, we just sort of—"

"I mean, what universe did these guys come from?" cried Sophia. "And how do I get there?"

"Only in a very special spaceship," I quipped.

"And how do two different guys share the same girlfriend, anyway?" she asked. "Do they take odd and even days? Do they split the weekends? What the hell is the sex like?" She shook her head in disbelief. "Is there a sex schedule that's independent of the rest of the schedule, or do they tag in and out like a wrestling team?" She paused to catch her breath. "So many questions!"

I let her spin herself out, like a spent yo-yo dangling helplessly from the end of its string. When she finally stopped moving, and talking, I looked her in the eyes.

"Are you done?"

Sophia merely shrugged and drained her wine again. "For now."

I stared back at my friend, as I debated how much to actually reveal to her. Would she be shocked to know I'd spent the night with both those men, twice this week alone? Or that I'd shoved them down and taken my time riding each of them, side by side, until they'd both exploded inside me?

And my God, how could I even *begin* to tell her about Jax and Adrian, without mentioning Preston?

How could I explain to Sophia that I'd met a *third* man, every bit as gorgeous as the other two, who was absolutely perfect for me in every way? Would she understand how Preston and I held hands on an alien planet, flanked by comets and asteroids and untold galaxies, and that it was probably the most romantic moment of my life?

No. She really won't.

I mean, how could Sophia possibly comprehend what it was like to kiss him there, as he stared into my eyes and told me he loved me?

Or that, not-so-deep down inside, I'd wanted to tell him the same thing?

"Well this sucks," Sophia lamented, leaning back.

"What does?"

"First, running out of wine," Sophia complained. "But even worse, you finally get a sex life that totally dwarfs mine, and you're keeping all the juiciest details to yourself!"

I laughed again, but my laughter only deepened her frown. Sophia was a good friend, and one who historically kept her mouth shut. She kept secrets, and without passing judgment.

"What if I told you there's two more bottles of wine on the way here, right now, even as we speak?" I asked with a grin.

It was like a switch got flipped in her brain. Sophia's entire demeanor changed.

"You're shitting me!" she gasped.

"I shit you not. I already Doordashed it."

"I knew there was a reason I loved you so much!"

I chuckled some more. "And hey, what if I told you that once the wine got here, I'd probably go into some of the juicier details about what it's like to have two boyfriends?"

Now I had her full, undivided attention. "You would?"

"Probably, yeah," I teased.

I got up, picked out another piece of wood, and laid it carefully onto the fire. The embers blazed bright orange under the new weight.

"And depending upon how *much* wine we drink," I added slowly. "I might even tell you why none of us ever worry about a 'sex schedule…'"

~ 40 ~

HARPER

I watched Adrian from the heated comfort of the back seat as he drove us home. His long arms were extended, casually turning the wheel left and right through a series of snow-choked streets. My mind wandered to fun places, as my eyes fixated lazily on the handsome fingers gripping the leather-stitched steering wheel.

God, even his hands were sexy.

"You wouldn't believe what Brayden said to me the other night," he smiled at me in the rear-view mirror.

I settled even further into the soft warmth of the luxury sedan. I was pleasantly buzzed. Contented and happy. Especially with Preston's thigh resting against mine, and his strong arm around me.

"What did he say?"

"He flung his peas onto the floor, and told me *you* would eat them."

My mouth dropped open in disbelief.

"He's not wrong," Preston needled me. "She probably

would eat them."

The car erupted in laughter, at my expense. Rolling with it, I elbowed him playfully.

"I've seen her eat lots of things," Jax winked.

There were a lot of advantages to dating three men at once, including some I hadn't thought of until I was in the thick of it. First, you had three times as many things to do. You had three times the ideas, three times the cool places to go, and three times the access to fun stuff and hobbies.

And for the *really* ambitious girlfriend, three times the number of dates all week long.

Two months.

I seriously couldn't believe it. I'd been seeing three men for two straight months, while working, nannying, and getting my end product ready for market. Yet somehow, through all the chaos and craziness, things had only gotten better between us.

Each of my boyfriends was unique in his own way, and I enjoyed spending one-on-one time with them. Still, I loved when they doubled up on dating me even more. Not just for the obvious sexual benefits either, but for the extra boost of laughter and camaraderie that came with having three people instead of two. Those kind of dates were still cozy, still intimate, still romantic. Yet with an extra person, they were always more fun.

Finally, there were amazing dates like the one I was on tonight, where all three men showed up to take me out together. Getting all four of our schedules to line up was like stumbling upon some rare planetary alignment. It was beautiful when and if it happened, but so special that you *really* wanted to take the time to enjoy it.

That was the case tonight, believe it or not. Brayden and Emma were with their other parents for the evening, leaving the four of us totally unhindered. We had time, we had each other, and now we had a night spread wide with a thousand open-ended possibilities.

We used the first portion of the night to head downtown, get outside, and work off some steam. So far we'd walked at least twelve city blocks, stopping at two craft breweries for flights of beer. As darkness fell we found ourselves clear on the other side of the town, gathered around a tiny Formica table, sharing a spicy pepperoni pizza at Carbone's.

Eventually we made our way back to Adrian's car. By then we were cold and shivering, but also invigorated and looking forward to his warm apartment. We had plans there for the night, and big plans at that.

But first, we had to stop at my place.

"Emma thought the moon was following us the other night," said Jax, with a gruff chuckle. "Jennifer and I took her out for ice cream, then stopped at a Starbucks drive-thru, and the whole time she kept staring at it through the car window."

Just the visual of her chubby little face pressed up against the glass made me laugh. "So what'd you tell her?"

"Well, when we got home the moon was in the exact same place in the sky," Jax reasoned. "I told her there's no way it could've moved, so she must've seen the moon's evil twin."

"You're such an asshole," I smirked.

"Oh, he tells her stuff like that all the time," Preston spoke up. "Last week he told her there were tiny people living in stoplights that turn them red and green."

"You did not!"

"And that chocolate milk comes from brown cows," Preston went on.

"I also heard him tell her that whenever she wasn't around, her dolls threw parties without her," Adrian added. "And they had milk and cookies and everything."

His hands firmly on the wheel, Adrian looked back over his shoulder at his friend. "Sorry man, but that one's kinda fucked up."

"Yeah, well she's gonna remember all this," I poked him. "And she's gonna kill you when she grows up."

"That's fine, because she's never growing up," Jax shot back. "I'm not giving her permission to get any bigger."

He was dead serious of course, but that didn't stop my smile. All three of my men had amazing fatherly instincts, but as a dad, Jax could be unintentionally adorable. He loved Emma so much it made my heart sing.

"Alright, here we are," said Adrian, finally pulling up to my place. He winked at me. "Make it fast. My couch is waiting."

"Don't worry," I assured him with a sly, promising grin. "This little pit stop will be *well* worth your while."

Jax had already popped the passenger door, and in no time he was opening mine as well. I teased him with something about chivalry. He sneered and told me he was merely following me in to make sure I didn't spend a half-hour in there doing 'women's stuff.'

"Whatever," I rolled my eyes. "C'mon."

I *did* need some women's stuff, to be honest. There was makeup I needed, and a few other toiletries as well. I'd been using Adrian and Preston's deodorant for the better part of a week now. I wanted a new toothbrush too.

But the real reason I'd stopped over, was because I'd promised the boys a night of 'depravity and debauchery'. And this included dressing up like a dirty harlot, dancing provocatively before them, and then letting them have me in any way that they wanted.

I knew exactly the outfit I wanted too, constructed piecemeal from some of the more sexy cosplays I'd done over the years. I'd take the corset from little red riding hood, and the legwraps from Poison Ivy. I wanted the heels from Jessica Rabbit. The mask from when I was a flirty jester. I also had a Sailor Moon skirt that was too short for anything but the bedroom. I'd never worn it out because it barely came down past my asscheeks, but it was perfect for a scenario such as tonight.

Earlier in the week, I'd promised to dress all the way up, sit the boys on Adrian's couch, and grind myself into their laps until all three of them were ready to go. I had an entire dance routine of sexy moves planned. A song by AC/DC, all picked out. The whole thing would be perfect. I'd have them rock-hard in no time flat.

And once my end of the bargain had been fulfilled, the boys promised to carry me into the bedroom and totally *demolish* me.

That one little word had me wet all week, just thinking about it. Their proposition was exciting. Scary. Totally fucking thrilling.

I couldn't wait to take them up on it.

Somehow, Jax and I made it to my front door without slipping on ice, and I drew out my key. Buffalo was bitterly cold still, even with spring approaching. Something about the groundhog, and his shadow, and—

"What the…"

I couldn't put my key into the door, because the doorknob was completely gone. Only a hole existed, where the knob used to be.

"Jax!"

"Get behind me."

It wasn't like I really had a choice. I half-fell, was half-shoved backward as Jax shouldered the door. Without a lock it opened easily, and a moment later we were both inside.

"OH MY GOD!"

The whole inside of the house was an absolute wreck. Furniture was turned over, shelves removed and upended. Electronic parts and pieces were strewn everywhere, including two monitors that lay face-down in the middle of the living room.

They were monitors that had previously been in my bedroom.

Oh no…

Jax was still determining whether or not intruders were still in the house when I pushed past him. He reached for me feebly, but I was too fast.

"Harper, wait!'

Into the bedroom I ran, at nearly a full sprint. I tripped over something unknown, pinwheeled for a split-second, then went crashing into a pile of clothing that had been torn from my closet.

I looked up, fearfully, and my worst nightmare came true.

Everything was gone.

"NO!"

My computers, my laptops, the mini-rack of servers I'd once been working on as a freelance project for a difficult client. Everything was missing. Only dangling wires remained.

"Shit…"

Jax was in the doorway. He was flanked by Adrian and Preston, who'd apparently heard my screams.

Preston's eyes were especially wide.

"Holy shit, Harper did they—"

I twisted sideways, leapt to my feet, and flew into the closet. It looked like a bomb went off — everything was tossed. Nothing was in its proper place…

… including the air-gapped machine where I kept all of my haptic development files.

Nooo!

My research. My development. All the hard work I'd put in, over the past several months and years.

Everything, all of it…

Gone.

My legs buckled helplessly as I sank to my knees and cried.

~ 41 ~

HARPER

"It's over! That's it!"

I was shaking, head to toe. Nauseous to the point where I wanted to vomit. Adrian reached out to comfort me, but I shied away. When Jax did the same, I ducked backward, tears streaming.

"It can't be *all* gone," Adrian reasoned. "I'm sure you have backups, or copies, or—"

"No, it's gone!" I shouted. "Everything!"

"What about the cloud?" Jax offered helpfully.

He was being genuine, of course. But the look the others gave him shut him up completely.

"Should I call the police?" Adrian asked, his phone already in hand.

I shook my head at him miserably. "No. Not yet."

Timidly they began sifting through the wreckage of my house, picking things up, trying to put them back where they figured they belonged. Adrian actually started sweeping, but I couldn't have cared less. They could set a match to the place at this point, and I'd be fine with it.

"They took it all?" Preston asked gently. "The haptic prototypes, the suits, everything?"

I nodded, sniffed, then collapsed miserably onto the couch. The blanket draped over the back cushions was too far away, otherwise I'd have pulled it over myself like an invisibility cloak.

"Well then we'll just have to get it back."

His words snapped me from my pity-party, stirring me to abrupt and sudden action.

"Really?"

"Yeah," Adrian agreed. "Of course."

"And how are we going to—"

"Do you have a ring camera?"

Despair settled over me again. I shook my head.

"Maybe your neighbors do," Preston offered hopefully.

"No," I sighed despondently. "The woman across the street is ninety-five years old. The only camera she owns still uses flash-powder."

None of them dared to laugh. I couldn't believe I was making jokes, anyway. I wanted to slap myself in the face.

"They took your computers, but not your monitors," said Preston off-handedly. "That's weird."

"Why is that weird?"

"Because if you're a thief, you'd want them both," Jax finished for him. "You'd sell them as a pair. You can't use one without the other."

Adrian shrugged. "Makes sense, I guess. But they left your televisions too. Do you know how light these things are, nowadays? Stealing them would be easy. You could carry them out, one under one arm."

I rubbed at my eyes. I still didn't know what they were driving at.

"I saw money on your dresser too," said Preston. "At least sixty or eighty bucks. Why they hell would they leave that?"

I sniffed. "Maybe they didn't see it?"

"Or maybe they weren't *after* it."

Preston's words were followed by a long, uncomfortable beat of silence. I perked up again.

"Who wouldn't be after money, though?" Jax scoffed. "Especially money laying there in plain sight?"

"The same people who wanted her computers, but not her monitors," said Preston. He dipped into my bedroom again, but came right back out. "The kind of people who ransacked her whole closet, but didn't take any of her Coach bags."

He held them up. Dangling from his fingers were two of the only designer bags I ever owned.

"They took her prototypes on purpose," Adrian realized. "They wanted her machines. Her designs."

"As well as her servers, her thumb drives, and all her test data," Preston nodded.

His eyes shifted to mine, just as an icy feeling stole over my still-trembling body.

"They *knew*," I swore.

Adrian dropped the broom he was holding. It clattered to the kitchen floor, as Jax's hands balled into fists.

"Who else knew what you were doing?" Jax demanded angrily. "Besides us?"

"I... I don't think many people, really," I breathed.

"Think hard."

In my devastated state, I wracked my brain. "Well, Sophia, for one. But she knew very little, and she'd never—"

"Who else?"

I thought some more. "Obviously I've been on message boards," I told them. "I brainstormed with other programmers about certain *parts* of my overall system, but I was always anonymous. And I was careful to never mention anything specific."

"What about that YouTube channel you've been following?" Preston asked. "The kid who was doing a lot of the same things you were."

"What about him?"

"Well, you were worried he was maybe stealing your designs." He squinted thoughtfully. "Think there was some way he could've been?"

"I don't see how," I shrugged. "My machine was never connected to the internet, not even once. It's always been air-gapped. There's not even a network card."

Everyone's gaze slowly dropped, and my dread deepened. Everything I'd worked for; tens of thousands of hours of blood, sweat and tears. All of it — gone, in the time it took for me to go out for dinner and drinks.

FUCK!

I could rebuild the prototypes in a quarter of the time it took to do them originally, maybe even less. Rewriting the code would take much longer. In my heart, I knew I didn't have it in me to do either. Especially with the looming deadlines I'd set, in the form of meetings with SONY in San Mateo, and Valve just outside of Seattle. Shit, I already had plane tickets.

But no, it's not that I couldn't rebuild everything, I just wouldn't. Especially since the people who'd taken my work most likely knew exactly what it was, and therefore, planned on taking it to market way before I ever could.

"Holy shit," Preston said suddenly. "It's gone."

His words came out sort of strange. I looked up to find him staring into his phone.

"What's gone?"

"The whole channel!" he exclaimed. "That YouTube kid you showed me, who was doing the haptics stuff."

He reached out and handed me his phone. Sure enough, the entire channel had been deleted.

"What does that mean?" asked Adrian.

"It means he's involved at the very least," said Preston.

"Good," said Adrian.

"Good?" My brow furrowed. "How can this possibly be good?"

"Because a minute ago we had nothing," Adrian explained. "And now, at least, we have a place to start."

He slipped the phone from his pocket and began tapping away. As Preston did the same, the roller coaster in my stomach began its uphill climb again. Just over the rise, far off in the distance, I thought I could see something: the faintest glimmer of hope.

A heavy hand slipped over my shoulder. I looked down the massive arm that hand belonged to, and found Jax was actually grinning.

"What the hell are you smiling at?" I challenged him. "How can you be—"

"Because we're going to fix this," he said, his voice full of confidence. "I already know it."

His smile felt abruptly reassuring, and I could feel my blood pressure coming down a bit. Like Fox Mulder from the X-Files, I wanted to believe.

"Look, you nerds are great at computer stuff, but when it comes to breaking and entering?" Jax gestured around. "Sloppy. Very sloppy."

"Sloppy…" I repeated.

He nodded. "I'll bet there are a dozen ways we can figure out who did this. And when we do?"

Extending his arms, Jax interlaced his fingers and cracked his knuckles.

"Someone's getting their ass kicked in."

~ 42 ~

PRESTON

"Uhhh... thanks," I said, accepting the food being slid across my desk. "I think."

I stopped analyzing the nine different monitors on my screen for only a split-second, just long enough to glance down. A sandwich rested on a paper plate, next to a pile of ridged potato chips. The bread *looked* stale, and that's because I knew it was stale. After all, I'd bought it almost two weeks ago.

"Tuna fish?"

"Yes," Harper answered.

"Did you make this from a can in our cabinet?"

She hesitated. "Yes, why?"

"Then I don't even want to know the expiration date," I replied glumly.

"Funny," said Harper, "Jax said the same thing before he left."

I grabbed it anyway and took a bite. It wasn't bad. It wasn't good. But it was food, and that was something.

"Have you found anything?" she asked for the tenth or twelfth time.

I didn't answer immediately. My eyes were still locked on a black-and-white monitor in the third row, second column. Nothing had happened on that monitor yet. But if and when it did, I needed to know about it.

"I'll let you know," I said again. "But as I told you, it's better if you're not in here. You're not seeing *any* of this, remember?"

"Yeah," Harper replied. "Sure."

The need for plausible deniability was for her benefit, of course. I'd taken my machine to some extremely illegal places over the past sixteen hours, including a few that could send some very high-level officials' panties scurrying up their tightly-clenched asscracks. Some of *those* could even bring a SWAT team down on our apartment, if I wasn't diligent with the VPN program that covered my tracks. But that Rubicon had already been crossed.

The little glowing rectangle of night vision stared back at me, unchanged, as I realized Harper was still in the room. Without looking away, I turned to speak to her over my shoulder.

"Why don't you go call and check on the others?" I suggested. "See if they—"

"I've checked on them enough," she said bitterly. "They're big boys. Let them do their thing."

Her words came with a scraping sound, as she dragged one of the chairs in from the kitchen. As she sat down beside me, the intensity of her body language alone stopped whatever objection I was about to make.

"Yeah, I know, I shouldn't be here," she said evenly.

"So let's agree that I'm *not* here, but you could use another pair of eyes, and there's no way I'm sitting on my hands in the fucking living room."

She was right about the second pair of eyes. And her tone told me there wasn't going to be a debate about this.

"Alright then," I said, my voice going lower for no good reason. "This is a recording of last night's—"

"City cameras, from NITTEC's Traffic Operations Center," she finished for me. "Niagara International Transportation Technology Coalition."

I turned to look at her incredulously, but Harper just waved her hand.

"I figured that out hours ago," she said, dismissively, "and I don't even want to *know* how you did it."

"No," I agreed. "No, you don't."

"That's fine," she nodded. "So now what are we looking for?"

There was no time to be duly impressed, though I thoroughly was. Instead, I pointed to the monitors on my left and right.

"There's a traffic camera at either end of your block," I explained. "None that capture your house or anything, but I've been monitoring all the cars and trucks that drove on and off your street during the time you weren't home yesterday."

She nodded, peering into the screen. "There had to be a lot of them, no?"

"There were," I agreed. "But then I used Google Earth to compile a list of vehicles that *belong* on your block, in driveways and such, and I eliminated all of those. I also eliminated delivery trucks, postal vehicles, the cable company…"

"Okay, I get it," she interjected. "That's smart."

"Yeah. Thanks."

"So what's this?"

Harper pointed to the grid on my central monitor. The one that showed nine other cameras pointed at various roads and businesses.

"This camera right here," I pointed to the top left, "is a license-plate reader. It gathers the driver information of everyone who passes through this intersection."

"Shit," Harper swore under her breath, as she shook her head. "Privacy really *is* dead, isn't it?"

"Oh, that shit's dead and buried," I agreed. "Decades ago, in fact. But we may as well use it to our advantage."

I punched up a few other screens, and spent half a minute flipping through them. Some were from the afternoon, while others were traffic feeds from the evening, and into the night. There was a distinct progression of darkness, as the cameras switched from day to night vision. A few, like the license-plate scanner, were better and higher-resolution than others. Most however, installed long ago, just plain sucked.

"Anyway, I followed any vehicle that had been on your block and cross-referenced it with the plate-reader," I told her. "I looked for out-of-state plates first, just because I figured they stick out. But there were none."

Harper nodded, still staring into the screen. Like mine, her eyes were tired. But at least they were no longer puffy from when she'd been crying.

"So right here," I said, punching the keys necessary to split the left screen into four quadrants, "is a list of drivers who were on your block last night. Name, address, ID numbers... and of course, photos."

I clicked the mouse a few times, then swiveled my chair to look at her as the screen filled with people.

"Do you recognize anyone?" I asked hopefully.

Harper's blue eyes darted left and right as she scanned carefully through the grid of driver's license photos. I got lost in those eyes, thinking about how much she meant to me. I wasn't just falling for her, I was already in love with her. And I was being honest with myself... I was pretty sure we all were.

There was no way in the world we weren't fixing this for her.

No matter what the cost.

"I don't see anybody I know," she said finally. Her voice was tinged with frustration. "Names, faces, addresses... none of it rings a bell."

"I didn't see the kid either," I told her. "The one from the YouTube videos."

"Yeah, well he looks barely old enough to drive."

"True."

I thought about Adrian and Jax, and whether or not they were having any luck. They'd canvassed the neighborhood twice already, but no one had claimed to see anything out of the ordinary. At the moment, they were expanding their search to a few of the outside blocks.

"What's that?" Harper asked.

She was pointing to a different screen, on the other monitor. I punched it up and enlarged it.

"Those are just the license plate scans," I told her. "I

already cross-referenced them. You wouldn't believe how easy it was to access the personal data of millions of drivers," I added bitterly. "They leave this stuff on servers with almost zero security—"

"THAT ONE!"

Harper shouted so loudly I almost fell out of my chair! She was pointing at a particular part of the screen. I clicked to make it even bigger.

"TLNGRD," I repeated, letter by letter. "What's it—"

"Telengard!" she screamed. "It's *Telengard!*"

Harper leapt from her chair and began pacing the room in a tight circle. She looked frantic and euphoric yet also vehemently angry, somehow simultaneously.

"Holy fucking shit it's *HIM!*" she cried. "It's been him the whole time!"

"Who?"

"Telengard!" she repeated again. "He's this guy... this other programmer, who's always helped me! He's been my friend, my mentor, my sounding board. I've known him for like... like..."

"Since you started on your project?" I theorized.

She reached out and shoved the chair over. Her hands were fists.

"YES!"

My fingers flew wildly over the keyboard. In no time at all, I had the driver's license associated with the license plate filling the screen.

"Bennett M. Papas," I read aloud. "Bay Ridge, Brooklyn."

A man stared back at us from the monitor, his face frozen impassively in usual driver's license fashion. He was middle-aged and slightly overweight, with a full head of spiky white hair and wire-rimmed glasses.

In truth, he looked very plain. Like an accountant, or a math teacher, or maybe a—

"Oh my God, I'm such an IDIOT!" Harper screamed. She had both hands on the side of her head now, buried in her hair. "How could I be this stupid!? How could I be so blind?"

"Hey," I interjected. "Come on, now…"

"He knows *everything!*" she went on. "The concepts, the coding, the prototype design. I showed him so much of the project, whenever I was stuck. He even sent me some of the haptics!"

She threw back her head and roared. I grabbed hold of her shoulders.

"Harper, we know who he is, now!" I said, forcing her to look at me. "We know *where* he is!"

Her face was bright red. Her eyes burned with rage.

"You need to get it together. Brooklyn's ten hours away, and he's got almost a day's head start."

The anger stayed, but reason slowly returned. Harper glanced back at the screen, at the man in the driver's license photo. She glared at him with such intensity it made my blood run cold.

"Let's go then," she seethed. "We're wasting time."

I grabbed for my phone. There were a million things to do and not much time to get them done.

But first, I had to get the others back here.

~ 43 ~

HARPER

It felt like Jax drove a thousand miles an hour, and even then it didn't feel fast enough. He got pulled over twice for speeding. Both times he produced his EMT badge, and was let go with a warning. Both times he slowed down for just two or three miles, then floored it right back to maximum speed again.

Route 390 stretched out before us like an endless road. I cursed every mile of bleak, featureless pavement as I fought to keep my stomach from rolling over. My head was a storm of miserable, sickening thoughts.

Telengard…

The internet handle was utterly meaningless now. Yet I'd once held the name in such high regard.

How the hell could I have trusted him?

The remaining pieces of the puzzle came together during the long ride down. Telengard hadn't just stolen my project, he'd done even better than that: he'd waited patiently for me to finish it. He'd recognized the initial innovation, encouraged my ideas, and mentored me through the design process. Knowing of course, the entire time, that one day he'd drive up and steal the finished product.

Motherfucker!

Telengard had been with me the whole ride, without really being with me at all. And when the vehicle that was my brain would get stuck from time to time? Telengard would get out and help push. He always provided precisely the help I needed, or somehow produced the resources I was missing to get back on track. He wasn't just riding my coattails, he was shadowing me the whole time.

"I still can't believe I didn't suspect him," I mumbled aloud, from the back seat of Jax's truck. "Of all the people who could've done this, I should've known it *had* to be him."

"Look, you said it yourself: he was a mentor," Adrian said consolingly. The hand resting on my knee gave a reassuring squeeze. "So you confided in him. That's the kind of person you are, Harper. It's nothing to be—"

"It's stupid, that's what it is," I growled. "Naive. Idiotic. Gullible."

"Trusting, not gullible," Preston called back from the passenger seat. "Generous, not idiotic."

"But he was pushing me the whole time," I protested. "Guiding me to finish this thing so he could steal it."

"That doesn't make you stupid," said Adrian. "It only makes him a thief."

The truck rolled on, devouring the road. Either we'd find the things this man had stolen from me, or we wouldn't. But I was more certain than ever; we would find *him*.

The idea of that was of course satisfying, but also scary. Telengard was resourceful. It was obvious now that he'd created the fake YouTube channel to light a fire under my ass, hiring some kid to mimic my system, my designs, my original ideas. He made me believe I had direct competition. That I had to rush to get things finished.

I had to admit, it *did* keep me motived.

The scary part was I didn't know what would happen when we inevitably found him. The guys could easily do something rash. Jax, in particular, looked ready to take my ex-mentor's head off. He'd barely said three words during the long drive down, other than to call Jennifer, who'd unselfishly dropped everything to take care of both Emma and Brayden.

There were some pieces of the puzzle still missing, of course. I didn't know how Telengard — or Bennett M. Papas — or whoever the fuck he was managed to find me in the first place, but for someone as computer savvy as him, it probably wasn't too hard. And once the connection was made, I'd been the idiot who'd given him my full address and personal information. He's snuck in here like a thief in the night, not caring I might eventually suspect him, or learn who he was.

Or maybe, I hoped, he just didn't think I'd figure him out until it was too late.

The thin-lipped face on that driver's license was still burned into my mind. I could picture him driving all the way up here, on this very same road, ready and willing to steal my work. Thinking about our online friendship disgusted me now. I'd been so happy and grateful to him, too. So willfully blind.

But as the miles between us and New York City bled away, I realized that my anger and disappointment would only hold me back.

Hold us back. Remember?

Of course I did. I wasn't alone, I had three incredible

men with me. *My* men. Men determined to not only follow this through to the end, but to make me whole in every single way.

The plan was still sketchy, and I didn't fully understand it. But these were men who'd dropped everything in their lives to take care of me. Men I trusted.

Men I *loved*.

That part I knew now more than ever before. In fact, I was sure of it, and I couldn't wait to tell them. Adrian. Jax. Preston…

I loved these men with all my heart, every bit as they loved me. No matter what happened next in my life, I had that going. Unlike that which had been stolen from me, I would never, ever lose it.

And with each passing moment, *that* seemed more important than anything else.

~ 44 ~

HARPER

The restaurant was mostly empty, except for the bar. It made blending in a little harder, but really, I was the only one who needed to blend in. The man I knew as Telengard knew what I looked like, I was sure of it. But not the others.

"Be back in a minute," said Jax, sliding off the stool beside me. He jerked his head in the direction of the men's room.

I nodded, surprised at how incomplete I felt when he suddenly wasn't there. Adrian was just outside, checking things out, and Preston was several blocks away, doing something else entirely. The presence of any one of them was extremely reassuring, even in a place this crowded, this safe.

That's when I realized I trusted these men in every way.

The bartender swiped my empty glass, so I ordered another beer even though my stomach was in knots. I hadn't drank the first one, I'd poured it into Jax's glass. More than four hours ago we'd checked into a hotel in lower Manhattan, just to regroup, splash water on our faces, and feel human again. But we took that time because, thankfully, Adrian had a friend already parked in front of Telengard's tiny brick house in Bay Ridge, watching that his car never left the driveway.

We ended up with a high floor suite, overlooking the city. The room was beautiful, as well as a place Adrian had stayed often. He met with one of his colleagues in the lobby, who'd already checked us in. But the more important favor he'd cashed in had been with another friend and colleague he'd known for years now, a man by the name of Angel Rivera.

We'd met the man briefly, when we'd dropped Preston off with him. Angel Rivera looked every bit the beautiful male model with smooth brown skin, a chiseled jaw, and a flawless white smile. He looked even more amazing for a guy who spent half the day parked against a curb, crammed into his own car. But that part was over now. Angel had called less than thirty minutes ago, and Telengard was finally on his way here.

The thought of it being *this* close to getting my work back made me want to throw up.

The four of us had thrown around a lot of plans on the way down from Buffalo. Adrian suggested working with the police, but I knew they'd never enforce property rights. Besides, there was no real way to prove anything was mine. At best they'd fill out a report, and the civil court system *might* deal with it months or even years from now. The police were a total dead end.

Jax had wanted to storm straight in, and I was behind him on that. But Preston had other plans. Better plans.

He'd disappeared into one of the suite's bedrooms for over an hour, with nothing but his laptop. When he emerged staring into a strange new cellphone, he looked hurried and triumphant.

"Bring the truck around," he'd told us. "He's moving, and I know exactly where he's going."

I couldn't even begin to imagine the level of hacking it took to clone a phone remotely, but I was sure that's exactly what'd he'd done. A few minutes later we were racing through the Battery Tunnel, formulating a plan. It involved splitting up, and I wasn't crazy about that. But as long as I got to face the asshole who'd stolen my work, I didn't care about very much else.

I barely nodded as the bartender slid me a new beer. Right now I was dividing my attention between the front door and the bathroom hallway. Maybe that's why I didn't notice the woman who'd hopped up on the stool, right beside me.

"Umm... there's someone sitting there," I told her.

She laughed glibly. "There sure is."

The woman didn't even look my way. She gave me her back and began talking with her friend.

"Alright," I shrugged, and this time I did take a sip of my beer. "It's your funeral."

Jax returned not half a minute later. He tapped the sassy little brunette on the shoulder.

"Sorry, but this is my seat."

"Then your ass would be in it," the woman shot back with a smirk. "Wouldn't it?"

She went back to talking with her friend like nothing happened. In the meantime, I was literally choking on my beer.

Holy shit...

Sixteen different looks crossed Jax's face, in the span of two seconds. None of them were good. Somehow though, and only in the interest of staying low key, he managed to keep his composure.

"Look," Jax said diplomatically. "For the sake of civility—"

"Ugh," the brunette cut him off. She stuck up her palm dismissively, in a 'talk to the hand' type gesture, while making a gross-out face. "Stop talking! I'm not going to sit here and worry about what you think—"

"Don't worry about me. Worry about your eyebrows."

I could see the confidence drop away, the haughtiness dissolve. The woman reached up to touch an eyebrow, then snapped her hand back as she quickly realized what she'd done.

By then, it was too late. Between that and Jax's shit-eating grin, he already had her.

"Whatever," she barked at us both.

Her friend — a shorter, even bitchier-looking brunette — took her hand from her cosmopolitan just long enough to flip us off. I smiled at her sweetly.

"Honey, you have something on your chin."

The friend frowned, and made the mistake of touching her chin.

"No, the third one down."

Jax threw back his head and laughed at my insult. He laughed so long and hard that both women grabbed their drinks and stepped away from us.

"Let's go," the first brunette told her friend. "This bar sucks ass anyway."

"Maybe *you* suck ass, and the bar is fine," I quipped. "Ever consider that?"

They left in a huff. I turned back to Jax, who was still

grinning as he took his seat back.

"That was fun, actually," I admitted.

He grabbed his beer and toasted me. "See? Come to the dark side."

I chuckled. "Well, it was only fun because they deserved it."

Mid-gulp, Jax shook his head at me. "Trust me," he said, wiping his mouth with one big forearm. "Everyone deserves it."

"But—"

I stopped mid-sentence and turned, as his steel-blue eyes shifted abruptly over my shoulder. There, just inside the front door, was the man from the driver's license photo. Telengard looked shorter than I'd always pictured him in my mind, but just as intelligent and calculating. Just as capable.

My pulse quickened, but even more concerning to me was a deep, rising anger. My rage was more powerful than I thought it would be, especially now that he was here. It would be a lot harder to keep in check.

"Speaking of deserving it…" Jax muttered, cracking his knuckles again.

~ 45 ~

HARPER

I walked behind Jax at first, letting his massiveness shield me from our target's view. Preston had lured him here by using the spoofed phone to text message him as a friend. And so Telengard stood there for several moments, scanning the crowd.

Eventually the hostess sat him down at an empty table. Telengard took off his jacket, and draped it over the back of his chair. By the time he pulled out his phone to check on his friend, we were already there.

"Hi," Jax said cheerfully.

He led the way, dropping into the chair right beside him. The man couldn't have looked more surprised.

"Uhh... hi," he said awkwardly. "I umm, I'm sort of waiting for—"

His words died as I slid into the chair directly opposite him. By now my heart was thundering away in my chest. I could feel the blood in my face. It was everything I could do to keep from scratching his eyes out.

"Oh," Telengard said, his face breaking into a friendly smile. "Hello, Harper."

He actually had the balls to extend an arm, as if to shake my hand. A quick glance at Jax told me he was only waiting for the signal, and he would snap that arm clean off and give it to me as a souvenir.

"You have no idea how amazing it is to finally meet you," he said, eventually putting his hand down. His voice was so genuinely cheerful it only deepened my rage. "You're an absolute genius, you know. Someone I look up to and admire, very muc—"

"Give me one good reason why I shouldn't kick your balls straight up your ass right now," I seethed.

The man sitting across from me leaned back and chuckled. "Interesting visual."

"Answer the question."

He shrugged. "Honestly, I can't think of a single reason why you shouldn't."

"Glad we agree on that," Jax growled.

"However," Telengard added calmly, "I have much better things to do with my day, so…"

He went to stand, but two giant hands on his shoulders forced him back down. Telengard looked up, straight into the face of Adrian. His face registered momentary alarm.

"Relax," said Adrian. "Stay a while."

In one smooth motion, Adrian whipped the man's coat from the back of his chair and tossed it to the person directly behind him. I recognized that person instantly as Adrian's friend; the one who'd checked us into the hotel. In a flash of movement, he disappeared through the front door.

Telengard grunted, trying to look more annoyed at the situation than alarmed, as Adrian took the seat on the other side of him. When he moved to stand up a second time, he found that Jax had pinned his wrist to the table.

"Let me go."

"Go where?" asked Adrian, innocently.

Telengard said nothing as his eyes shifted to each of us in turn. He was exploring his options, I knew. Trying to gauge whether he could talk his way out of this situation, or if he needed to call for help.

"He can leave anytime he wants to," Jax said casually. "But his arm is staying here."

"You owe this woman an apology," Adrian nodded in my direction.

"Fuck his apology," I growled. "And he owes me a lot more than just that."

Telengard looked away. Moving with the speed of a striking viper, Jax slapped him in the face, forcing him to look at me again.

"Why?" I asked simply, forcing my rage down. "Why the *hell* would you do this?"

Telengard paused, then relaxed a little as he let out a sigh. "For the same reason you did it. Money. Patent rights. Prestige." He shrugged. "I could even do without the prestige, if we're being honest. As long I got paid."

"I thought you were a friend," I said. "A fellow programmer."

"I was," he said simply. "I am."

"You're nothing but a thief!"

"Thief?" he cried loudly, in mock surprise. "I beg your pardon, but I don't know what you're talking about."

Telengard leaned back, and the smile returned to his face. I expected Jax to slap it right off, but he didn't.

"Look," he said, in a lower tone, "if you're expecting me to admit to anything, you're wasting your time."

I wanted to slap him across the face, the way Jax had. I wanted it so badly I could physically taste it! But here in full view of the public restaurant, I knew there were limits.

"What, you don't think I know you're recording every word of this?" Telengard said smugly. "Please."

"I'm not here for—"

"Where's the camera?" he challenged, cutting me off. "Is it under the table? In your purse?"

With his free hand, he reached out and tapped Adrian's phone, which happened to be next to him.

"Is it right here, running a recording app? Or—"

"Reach over here again and I'll break your fingers," Adrian growled, flicking his hand away.

Telengard looked pleased with himself. "Hope you got *that* on tape," he said loudly, leaning slightly in the phone's direction. "Physical threats. Possible kidnapping. Keeping me here, when I clearly want to—"

Just then, Adrian's friend returned. He handed him the coat, as well as a set of car keys.

"It's clean," the man muttered. "Front, back, trunk… there's nothing in it."

Adrian nodded, and the man left again. When Telengard reached out to snatch his coat back, he didn't stop him.

"Did you really think I'd be dumb enough to be driving around with it?" he swore, his voice going so low I could barely hear it. Telengard shook his head in disappointment. "C'mon Harper. You're smarter than *that*."

I found myself staring at him, wondering when it all went south. Did he always plan on this? Or had he realized at some point along the line that I had something special, something marketable, something he could actually make money on?

"And I thought you were the real deal," I replied, my voice full of my own brand of disappointment. "But it turns out you're just code-savvy. You're a gifted programmer, I'll give you that, but these days gifted programmers are a dime a dozen. You have no vision, no creativity, no drive. No ambition to breathe life into or follow through on your own ideas, because you *have* no ideas of your own."

If my words were getting through to him, I couldn't tell. Telengard was sitting calmly, enduring my rant. I gave him a tiny bit of credit for still holding my gaze; for actually facing me instead of looking away this time. But not much.

"How pathetic does it make you feel?" I asked rhetorically. "To be so lame and uninspired, that you have to stoop to stealing the ideas of others?"

Telengard yawned. Gathering his coat in his lap, he looked back at the front door. "Are you done?"

Adrian and Jax leaned in menacingly. At this point they were even angrier than I was. They looked ready to break him in half.

"You're nothing more than a grifter," I told him. "And not even a smart one at that."

"Smart enough, apparently," he smirked. "Wasn't I?"

He settled back in his chair, looking more comfortable than he really should. Jax, unable to help himself, grunted threateningly. Beneath the table, I dropped a restraining hand on his knee.

"Can I give you a bit of advice, Harper?" Telengard asked abruptly.

I leaned forward, my eyes burning fiercely into his. Somewhere through my haze of disgust, I eventually nodded.

"In life, you're either the hammer or the anvil," he said. "This time around, I'm the hammer. You're the anvil. That's just how it played out."

His smug sense of self-righteousness was overwhelming. I could tell this stream of utter bullshit was ingrained in him. He'd bought into it long ago.

"Don't hate me for it," Telengard shrugged, nonchalantly. "I didn't make the rules, I only follow them. But you should take this loss as a learning opportunity," he went on. "Next time, *you* be the hammer. And don't let yourself be the anvil, ever again."

His smile reminded me of the Grinch's, now. It grew wider and wider until it was interrupted by the distinct chime of a smartphone.

Adrian reached out, picked up his phone, and glanced at the screen. Then he looked at us and nodded.

"It's done."

My heart soared, as relief flooded through me! My whole body felt electrically charged, as my skin broke out in goosebumps.

Adrian's boyish grin was so handsome, I wanted to kiss

him all over his face. On the other side of me, Jax released our guest's arm with a smirk of his own.

"W—What's done?" Telengard stumbled, rubbing his wrist.

I shrugged and looked back at him. "You."

He glanced back at Adrian's phone again. To my surprise, he slid it across the table to him.

"Here."

Telengard's expression changed from impassivity to horror as he looked into the screen.

"Go on," said Adrian. "Scroll left."

The man sitting across from me no longer looked so intelligent, crafty, or smart. Or smug either, for that matter.

Telengard scrolled. His mouth dropped open even further.

"What *is* this?" he demanded.

"It's a series of photos of the front of your house," said Adrian. "The driveway, the street, the—"

"I know what it is!" he shouted. "But what... what are they—"

"You're having an impromptu garage sale!" Adrian said with an excited grin. "It's marked as an estate sale, actually. Everything must go."

Telengard leapt to his feet so fast his chair nearly tipped over. "B—But that's my stuff!"

"Maybe," Adrian shrugged. "By now though, maybe not. Everything's been marked at a deep discount, with five and ten-dollar price tags. And these photos are at least a few minutes old."

Terror crossed the face of the man standing at the other end of the table. I almost felt bad for him.

Almost.

"That's my couch, my furniture, my stuff!" he screamed.

Telengard was utterly frantic now. I grabbed the phone and pulled it to my side of the table.

"Look," I smiled, pointing. "Your bed too!"

I passed the phone to Jax, who could barely control his laughter. He scrolled quickly through a few of the pics.

"I think that's just the headboard," Jax said, squinting. "The mattress is gone already. It's hard to tell, what with all the people milling around." He slid the phone back in Adrian's direction. "I mean, just look at the size of the crowd."

"I know, right?" Adrian piled on. "And they didn't even advertise. Just the signs in the driveway—"

"Well if I know Preston, he probably tweeted the sale on multiple websites," I cut in. "Garage sale people are tech-savvy these days. And with prices like these—"

The phone chimed again. Adrian read the newest message and looked up.

"You'd better hurry home," he advised, holding up another photo. "Half the stuff in those other pics is already gone."

Telengard was trembling now, all over. He backed away slowly, his coat dangling from one limp arm.

"And look," Adrian pointed. "The street's backed all the way up to the end of the block with a whole line of cars and trucks and—"

He took off, flying straight through the front door. It happened so fast, he almost knocked over the waitress who'd been waiting to approach our table.

"Well shit," Adrian quipped, holding up a set of car keys. "You'd think he might need these."

~ 46 ~

HARPER

We found him exactly where we expected to, in the back end of the parking lot. Telengard — at least the person I knew him as — was dead. Bennett M. Papas was still very much alive, though, and sitting miserably on the *very* low front end of his now useless car.

And that's because all four tires were utterly flat.

"What the hell happened?" Jax asked facetiously.

The man didn't have the strength to answer. He barely even flinched when we walked up to him.

"I think I know," I offered.

Bennett still refused to look up. Not that I blamed him.

"Today you were the anvil," I said, matter-of-factly. "And someone else was the hammer."

Adrian tossed him his car keys, but Bennett made no move to catch them. They skittered across the hood of his car, before landing in the gravel-strewn parking lot.

"You should try to be the hammer," Jax said, rubbing salt in the wound. "I heard it's better than being the anvil."

"Or you could just stop ripping people off entirely," Adrian added with a shrug. "And then nobody has to drive four-hundred fucking miles just to get their own property back."

Bennett sank his face into his hands. Resting his elbows on his knees, he shook his head back and forth for what seemed like a long time.

"Enough," I said finally. "Let's go."

We turned and left him there, alone and helpless. The man looked utterly defeated, not even interested in calling for a tow-truck, or at least an Uber so he could get back to his house and put a stop to the carnage there.

Just before we hopped into our own truck however, Jax and Adrian marched back over. I feared for the worst. Even though I hung back, I could hear every word that was said.

"Don't ever forget that we know who you are," Jax growled, "and we know *where* you are."

Adrian nodded pointedly. "If you go a single mile north of Westchester County, we'll already know it," I heard him warn. "And if you come *anywhere* near Buffalo, ever again…"

The two of them shrugged, not-so-innocently.

"Things will end a *lot* differently than they did today."

~ 47 ~

HARPER

The elevator up to the hotel suite was a butterfly-filled rocket ship. I stood there flanked by Adrian and Jax, still shaking from adrenaline levels that hadn't subsided at all. My heart was hammering away, pumping the drug to every last corner of my trembling body.

Then the door to our room opened, and I saw Preston standing there holding one of my haptics suits.

Crying, I flung myself straight into his arms.

"Thank you!"

The tears flowed as he hugged me back. The others closed in, and soon I was hugging them all.

"Thank you all so much…"

Eventually my tears subsided, and I scanned eagerly around the hotel suite. I saw my machines, my laptops, my servers, as well as the other haptic prototype. Even the thumb drives were there, lined up neatly on one of the fancy mahogany tables.

Then I saw the air-gapped computer that had *everything*

on it, and my tears started flowing all over again.

"How much of this asshole's stuff did you actually sell?" Jax asked Preston.

"A *lot* of it," Preston said with a whistle. "At first I thought Angel and I would only carry a few things out. You know, just to make a point. But then Angel's friends showed up. *Six* of them, in fact. And then, well…" he shrugged and sighed. "It was kind of like having a moving company."

"And you really made everything five and ten dollars?" asked Adrian.

"That was Angel's idea," said Preston. "But holy shit, yes. Everyone started fighting over stuff, so we made them do rock paper scissors. Cars were piling up everywhere. People drove off in pickup trucks, packed so full they were overflowing."

"Damn," Jax swore. "Sounds like a clusterfuck."

Preston nodded. "Trust me, the neighbors were getting pissed."

"You're lucky you got out of there before the police showed up," said Adrian.

"Only barely, yeah," Preston agreed. "By the time we'd recovered Harper's work and stripped out that asshole's own machines, more than half of his stuff was already gone."

"Wait," I interjected. "What machines?"

"Those," Preston pointed.

I turned my attention to the other end of the hotel suite. Lined up against the opposite wall was a whole array of strange computers, laptops, and other electronic equipment. I gasped, involuntarily.

"You mean…"

"We took everything he had," said Preston. "Shut down his whole operation. Just look at all that stuff," he pointed. "Some of those newer machines are cutting edge. Expensive as hell."

I had my hand over my mouth. I couldn't help it.

"Are those *Bitcoin rigs?*" I choked.

"Down at the end there, yeah. He had a whole mining operation going on," explained Preston. "But not anymore."

Open-ended wires stuck out in every direction, making the whole mess look a lot crazier than it actually was. But wow, it looked like Preston and Angel had taken *everything*. They'd left him with nothing, just like the Grinch's storybook.

Not even a crumb too small for a mouse.

"I don't think he even got to turn your machines on, much less figure out your passcodes and transfer your files onto his own computer," said Preston. "But we figured, why risk it?"

"Yeah. Makes sense."

"While his friends were running the yard sale, Angel and I went into the basement and physically tore out his fiber-optics, too. It'll take days to fix. He even had a T-1 line down there as a backup, if you can believe it."

"Had?" asked Adrian.

"Oh yeah," Preston swore. "Very much *had.*"

Jax shook his head and scratched at his stubble. "I dunno… this sounds like some real savage geek shit."

"Trust me. It is."

"Well it's not like he didn't deserve it," Adrian jumped in. "He stole Harper's work. Betrayed her trust, and took everything she had. Now that we've done the same, I don't feel the least bit bad for him. Do you?"

Preston shook his head solemnly. So did Jax.

"Nah," Jax growled. "He messed with our girl."

He reached out, slid an arm around me, and pulled me close. Holding my face in his hands, Jax gave me a slow, deep kiss that sent my already spinning head sailing through a universe of stars.

"And *nobody* fucks with our girl," he growled sexily, into my mouth. His hand slid to my ass and squeezed hard. It felt amazingly possessive. "Nobody except *us*."

More hands found my body. They slid down the outsides of my thighs, and up along my ribcage, and all the different places hands could go. I was kissing Preston, then Adrian, then Preston again. Jax undid my bra, straight through my shirt, while explosively kissing my neck. The familiar release of pressure felt wonderful, as another pair of hands slid up under my shirt to cup both breasts.

"You boys *love* me," I breathed, matter-of-factly. "You know that, right? All three of you."

They didn't answer. They were too busy kissing me all over.

"Nobody would've done the things you've done for me, unless…" I sighed momentarily as a hand slipped past my waistband. "Unless—"

Fingers plunged downward, curling against my sex, causing me to jump and whimper in the middle of my sentence. I was so wet it was ridiculous. It happened so fast.

"You know how I feel," Adrian murmured, his lips teasing the outer edge of my ear. "I've *always* loved you. Throughout all these years, I never stopped."

I curled involuntarily into his hot breath. Gooseflesh exploded everywhere.

"I loved you even before I saw your cosplay collection," Preston sighed, his face buried between my breasts. Jax had already helped him pull my shirt off. At the moment, he was lost happily in a valley of warmth and flesh.

"But yes," Preston breathed, coming up for air just long enough to look into my eyes. "I knew it the moment I saw you. I love everything about you, Harper. You're pure fucking amazing."

Tears filled my eyes. I grabbed him and kissed him and pulled him into me.

"I love you too," I cried against his lips. "*All* of you. It's crazy and it's stupid and it might even be impossible. But I don't care. It's just… it's just too—"

"Impossible?"

The word came from Jax, who embraced me from behind. He had both arms wrapped around my body now, with one hand curled inward, buried between my legs.

"You think this is impossible?" he breathed into my opposite ear. At the same time, he slid three very wet fingers downward, gliding them along my sex.

"I… I just…"

"Because it could be," Jax murmured, applying pressure. "We could easily stop. Tell ourselves something like this would never work…"

His fingers glided further downward, his thumb now

hovering against my clit. When he curled it toward him I jumped and gasped.

"Or you could choose one of us," Jax said aloud. "Make the others go away…"

I tried to swallow, but my throat was too dry. I shook my head vigorously.

"Make a run at a traditional relationship," Jax went on. "Try and forget this ever happened."

"No…"

"Think you could do all that, Harper?" Adrian whispered, following his friend's lead. His breath was still hot against my other ear. "Think you could go all the way back to the way it—"

"NO."

I reached back with both hands, pulling them in, trying to get them as close as physically possible. My arms went tight. I had a beautiful vision of the four of us just melting together.

"I *won't* go back," I said, spinning to face them. "I'm yours, for as long as you'll have me. I'll be your lover, your girlfriend, your wife. I'll be the mother of your children. I'll… Ill be—"

Adrian kissed me, crushing his lips against mine, as my adrenaline-fueled senses overloaded my brain. I couldn't believe the things I was saying! I was talking, babbling, making zero sense. Or maybe, on some level, I was making all the sense in the world. Maybe this was just my way of opening my heart, and speaking the bare naked truth. Making myself fully and gloriously vulnerable. Spewing out anything and everything I ever wanted when it came to these amazing men, including a future I now totally knew I desired.

"Even *I* love you," I heard Jax say. "And I've hated you since the moment you first showed up."

He pulled my mouth from Adrian's and brought it to his. I found myself giggling against his lips.

"I've hated you too," I cried, with a smile so big it felt like my face would break. "I still hate you so fucking much..."

I kissed him hard, grabbing his ass. Pulling him in every bit as roughly and possessively as he pulled me.

"Thank fucking God," Jax murmured, as the they crushed me from all sides.

~ 48 ~

ADRIAN

The city was breathtaking at night, especially through the floor-to-ceiling windows of our sky suite. We were a thousand feet in the air. The lights of New York lay spread out far beneath us, like a sea of glimmering, twinkling jewels.

At the moment though, I didn't care about any of that. And that's because Harper was kneeling before the three of us, on her hands and knees. Taking turns crawling over to each of us in turn… before lowering her mouth tantalizingly downward, until we were buried all the way deep in her hot, eager throat.

She wore nothing but a pure white thong, which bisected her hot, rounded ass. As she bent low to blow Preston, relaxing comfortably in the chair across from me, I thought I could barely make out the shape of her pussy. The swollen mound peeked back at me, glistening with wetness. Winking at me from the shadows of the dimly-lit suite.

Holy fuck.

Even now, I still couldn't believe it was actually her. Harper, my neighbor, the quintessential embodiment of the girl next door. I'd loved her so much growing up, even if I didn't fully realize it. Now, I loved her even more. She was the one who'd almost gotten away but returned, storming back into my life as a strong but beautiful woman to give love a second chance.

Even if that love had to be shared.

I settled back into my chair to enjoy the show. Harper's head moved in a slow, circular motion as it bobbed rhythmically up and down. I knew that motion well, just as I knew how it felt to sink my hands into her soft hair, playing with it as it cascaded downward, spilling over my naked thighs. Just as it was spilling over Preston's, now.

I should've been jealous, but I wasn't. It should've made me sick to my stomach, watching the girl I loved go down on another man, just a few feet away, giving him every last ounce of her boundless sexual energy and attention.

Instead, it only served to turn me on.

I looked briefly at Jax, who was watching from his own chair as well. His eyes were glued to the same scene mine were, glazed with the same lust-filled look of pure sexual addiction. It was so fucking *hot,* sharing the same woman. So mind-numbingly twisted, but in the most amazing, sensual way.

Of course she was physically gorgeous, inside and out, but it was Harper's intelligence and ambition that drove us crazy with the need to have her. She was sarcastic, yet loving. Smarter than perhaps all of us — Preston included — but also humble in the sweetest, most self-effacing ways.

She'd shown that she loved us, but ever more, she loved our children. Brayden and Emma both worshiped her, and Harper absolutely adored them as if they were her very own. We'd proven that we'd fight for her, that we'd do absolutely anything for her. And after sitting down together, and discussing it at length? The three of us had decided to make her the center of our world.

The decision was surprisingly easy. Preston was head over his nerdy fucking heels for her, and Jax's love-hate relationship with Harper had already been taken to all new points of no return. As for me, I certainly wasn't letting go of her. Not now, or ever again. And this left us with only one option:

Sharing her equally… for as long as she'd have us.

My more complicated thoughts drifted away, as Harper switched from Preston and crawled over to Jax. She pushed his knees apart, stopping to plant a whole series of hot kisses along the insides of his thighs. Then she turned, winked at me playfully, and swallowed him whole.

Damn.

Harper was ours now, and she was enjoying every moment. We were going to keep her, love her, protect her. Give her anything and everything she ever needed. Between the three of us, she would continue to thrive and succeed, and we'd give her everything we possibly could. She'd be our girl, our lover, our wife even, if that's what she wanted.

And she would never, ever be lonely.

Right now, there was little doubt as to Harper's present intentions. She'd turned her ass strategically in my direction, and had begun swaying it back and forth enticingly. Her face was buried deep in Jax's lap, and the pumping, swirling movements of her head were certainly for him. The soft, sexy moans escaping her lips however, which were still wrapped wetly around him, seemed to be entirely for my benefit.

Fuck.

The dilemma was real. Half of me wanted to sit there

watching that beautiful ass, waiting patiently for my turn. But the other half...

Harper's moans grew louder, and then suddenly she made the decision easy for me. She reached back, pulled her thong to one side, and dragged three delicate fingers up and down through that perfect, pink wetness.

"Mmmmm..." she moaned.

Those fingers disappeared, momentarily plunging inside her. They glided in and out a few times... then came back coated in so much sticky wetness I was on the floor kneeling behind her in three seconds flat.

Harper's hips slid into my hands, as much from her thrusting backward as from me reaching out for them. They locked right into my palms, as perfectly as if they were made to go there. The two globes of her naked ass rolled enticingly against my boxers, rubbing me through the fabric, seemingly begging my cock to come out and play. I wasn't going to deny either of them the pleasure.

Pulling them down, I guided the head of my steel-like shaft right up against that warm, molten entrance, which was already saturated with Harper's own excitement.

She did the rest.

~ 49 ~

HARPER

The past few dozen hours had been a roller-coaster of emotions. I'd gone from extreme lows to extreme highs. From fear and hopelessness to anger and frustration, and ultimately, sweet revenge.

The influx of adrenaline was finally waning, and the lack of rest was catching up. Right now though, I wasn't sleepy. I was loopy, yes. Physically drained, but emotionally high as a kite on all the love and adoration I had for my three awesome, incredible boyfriends.

And before I let sleep take me… I needed *all of them*, simultaneously.

All of them at once.

My eyes rolled back as Adrian filled me from behind, drilling me to the core. He felt magnificent as he began pumping away, squeezing my hips in his powerful hands as his best friend, who happened to be my sworn enemy, rolled the fingers he had embedded into my hair into a tightly-clenched fist.

Oh, hell yes.

I felt Jax's arm flex tight, as he began fucking my face. The hand buried in my hair forced him even deeper down my throat, in perfect rhythm to his friend's equally-deep thrusts. I turned me on because it felt wholly amazing, but it made me even more excited to know how good it must feel on their end. I wanted them to enjoy me, first and foremost. I wanted to please them, to make them happy, to show how much I not only loved and cared for them, but how grateful I was for how they'd gone above and beyond, to save my life's work.

On top of it all, it just felt incredible to be so thoroughly and completely *fucked*. To be seized hold of; taken by force and thrown down and flipped over in all manner of dirty, wonderful things. These were my men, my boyfriends, my lovers. Any of them could use me, any way they wanted. I needed them to know I belonged to all of them, one-hundred percent. Together, or alone.

"Fuck…"

Jax grunted a curse and pulled my hair back, forcing me to face him. I knew he'd stopped because he was *this* close to losing it. I could feel it in how tightly his body was coiled, like a panther about to spring.

"You love this, don't you?" he growled.

My blue eyes flared, burning into his own. They said everything I needed to say, no words needed.

"You love *us*, don't you?"

I kissed him in response, crashing my lips against his. Our tongues danced. Our mouths churned, devouring each other desperately, through breathless whimpers and moans.

"I love you," I whispered truthfully; against his lips. "All of you."

I kissed him again, then bit his lip. As he pulled back

to look at me, I grinned.

"And yes. I know that makes me greedy."

Jax's eyes burned into mine. In that moment we forged another connection, on an even deeper level.

"And I don't care," I murmured against his mouth.

In the meantime Adrian was behind me, still plowing away. The obscene sounds of our bodies crashing together was so hot, so unmistakably sexual, it shattered the silence of the hotel suite. He moved over, and Preston took his place. He pushed straight inside me with a different thickness, a different length, fucking me from a slightly different angle. His hands roamed my ass, instead of my hips. The speed and depth of his strokes was different too.

Three boyfriends... I thought to myself.

The benefits were limitless. I wanted these men physically, sexually, even emotionally, in every which way. I wanted to take them one by one, or two at a time, or three of them inside at once.

Was that even possible?

I didn't care. I craved it. I *needed* it. There was no limit to what I would do for them, and they for me. I bucked back into Preston, rolling my ass, willing him to finish inside me, even though I knew that moment was still very far off. When it came, I would relish it. I'd grind him like a greedy bitch until his balls were empty, and then I'd shove Adrian down and ride him reverse cowgirl, so he could watch his friend's hot load seeping out of me as he fucked me to oblivion.

The vision of all this drove me over the edge. I came so incredibly fucking hard, squeezing Preston's thrusting member so tightly inside me it felt like I could take him with me. And then I *did* take him with me, because he couldn't help himself. He bucked and grunted and buried himself as deep as he could, ramming his body into mine and then holding it there complete and utterly still, except for his thumping, throbbing shaft that was filling my insides with his molten, musky seed.

"FUCK!" he cried, in a mixture of both elation and frustration. "I couldn't—"

Adrian lifted me up, pulling me from Jax, and guided me on shaky legs to the window. Once there, he raised my arms high overhead, interlaced his fingers with mine, and pressed his body against me from behind.

"How's the view?" he whispered.

Still dizzy from my own orgasm, I looked down. I saw streetlamps. City streets. The red and white lights of traffic, flowing through veins and arteries of New York City. But the real view was down between my legs, as Adrian guided himself back inside my come-filled womb. My dripping folds swallowed him instantly. I felt the shudder of pleasure that wracked his body, as he pinned me to the window and began thrusting away.

Oh my God…

It felt incredibly sexy and dangerous, getting fucked with the world at my feet. The city began spinning beneath me, as I squeezed Adrian's fingers between mine. Soon I was bucking back to meet his thrusts. Surrendering the rest of my body completely, as he fucked me wildly, and without reservation. I thought about how long I'd wanted this, and how crazy it was that I could've missed it. I didn't just love this man, I absolutely adored him. I knew now that he was my world, my everything, my soul mate. He always had been.

"Hey…" a voice called impatiently. "We're sharing her, remember?"

Adrian reluctantly withdrew, and Jax filled the void he left. It happened effortlessly, like they'd practiced the move. Like they'd been trading me back and forth their whole lives, sharing my body like two brothers taking turns with the same toy.

And they were exactly like brothers, I knew. I was lucky enough to have not come between them, or cause any jealousy, but at the same time I craved being sandwiched between them.

Jax's lips closed over my shoulder, and he began kissing up and down my neck. The shivers from these kisses plunged me into a whole new universe of tingles, until every inch of my exposed skin was a bundle of nerve endings waiting to be caressed and touched. His hands slid up my sides, then over my breasts. He squeezed them firmly enough that I gasped, but the feel of his palms dragging over my nipples felt totally fucking amazing.

This is more than just a fantasy, I told myself, as he drilled me even deeper.

This is your reality, now.

Pressed so close to the glass, so many floors up, I should've felt frightened and exposed. Instead, I felt safer than I ever had. These men loved me more than I knew — maybe even more than they knew, also. They were focused on me, committed to me, hellbent on making a run at a real, genuine relationship. I was their woman now, and there was nothing in the world I wanted more.

In having them, I had an instant family. I had love. Children. Hope. A future that involved laughter and excitement and unlimited possibilities, instead of the lonely, empty home I lived in now. The change would be radical, that much I knew. But I wasn't just ready for it, I was thrilled at the prospect of sharing my life with them.

I reached back to grab Jax's head, begging him to go deeper. He responded by wrapping an arm around my waist, squeezing me tight, grinding harder and closer than ever. I craned my neck to kiss him over my shoulder, then whispered something dirty and nasty into his ear. I exaggerated my whimpers a little, for his benefit, but I didn't have to exaggerate them much.

A minute later his eyes screwed shut, and he was emptying himself inside me.

Ohhhhhhh....

It could've been the begging that got to him, or the angle, or the incredible view outside. But I was betting it was the heat, the wetness, the hot load Preston had already deposited, deep inside me.

Or, it could've been the last thing I said to him. Because after the dirty talk, after describing all the filthy, twisted things I intended upon doing with them when we got home…

I'd told him how much I loved him.

Jax's hands guided me as I staggered backwards, into the arms of the others. Adrian lifted me into his arms. He wasted no time in carrying me to one of the suite's bedrooms, throwing me down, and pushing his way back between my trembling legs.

I couldn't spread my thighs wide enough for him.

"You boys are impatient tonight," I chuckled as he slid inside me. We both looked down, as he pierced me like a hot knife through warm butter.

"Might as well get the first one out of the way," Adrian grunted against my lips

"First one, huh?"

He nodded. "First of many."

I sighed contentedly, even as my stomach began tying itself in knots. There were a few dozen places the boys could fuck me in this giant hotel suite, if they used a little imagination. And I had no doubt we'd explore most, if not all of them, at one point or another.

With that in mind, I kicked things into overdrive. I clawed at his ass, and kicked my heels into the small of his back. Having a mattress beneath me gave me the leverage to rock back against him. Adrian's eyes changed, his head rolled back, and he began grunting in a deep, primal way.

"It's okay, baby," I murmured sweetly. "Let it go"

His tortured expression changed to one of sweet relief. Adrian looked down at me, his chiseled face so exquisitely handsome I wanted to pinch myself to make sure I wasn't dreaming.

"*Come* in me," I urged, letting my voice go wicked.

It was all it took. His grunts became cries, and then a drawn-out roar as Adrian climaxed into me. His whole body went rigid as it surged forward, his face turning dreamy and very far away as his thrusts eventually slowed down. He was in heaven, I knew. I watched every moment of it. The first thing he saw when he opened his eyes was my smiling, happy face, as he floated back down. Still half-drenched in his own euphoria, I reached out gently to cradle his cheek.

"Welcome back," I giggled, and then kissed him.

Adrian stepped away to recover. Behind him, the others stepped forward to surround me on the bed. I could see they weren't empty-handed. They'd carried in extra pillows from the other bedroom, a stack of towels, and several bottles of water.

"So it's going to be one of *those* nights," I teased, "hmmm?"

Letting my legs flop even wider, I slid a palm down through the glistening valley between my thighs. Everything was already so wet, my fingers were disappearing.

"Yes," Preston said confidently. "It sure is."

I let out a long, heated breath as I squirmed into the softness of the blankets. They felt warm and amazing against my naked back.

"Good, because I need the three of you together tonight," I told them, sighing as I said the words. "*Together*, together," I added with a purr. "Somehow. If you can figure that out."

The three of them glanced at each other, but only for a moment.

"Oh, we'll figure it out."

As they dropped to the bed on all sides of me, I realized how incredibly lucky I was. How outrageously happy and sated I would be by the end of the evening, and not just *this* evening, but every evening from here through the immediate and distant future.

And I had zero doubt in my mind that the boys would 'figure it out.'

Epilogue

HARPER

"This is incredible," Adrian gawked, walking in a circle. "Unbelievable. I mean, this isn't even *camping* anymore!"

He put his arms straight out, and still couldn't touch any of the walls. I couldn't help but notice those arms looked especially tanned and amazing in his sleeveless leather shirt. But for once, that wasn't the amazing part.

"He's right," Jax agreed. "I wouldn't call this camping. This is some real next-level shit."

The title of the YouTube video had been innocuous enough: 'The Largest Inflatable Tent on Amazon.' It led us down a rabbit hole of other impulse purchases like sleeping bags, inflatable beds, portable grills… even an indoor, solar-powered air-conditioning unit.

The tent was so big it had it's own furniture. Chairs. A table. We could set up a television in here if we wanted to, but we decided the experience would be more enjoyable without it. There were doors, windows, skylights. I had to agree, it was kind of nuts.

Even so, I was grateful that the whole thing went up in only five minutes with just a plug-in blower. And that's because we'd spent the last eight hours walking the entire New York Renaissance Fair, catching just about every single show and exhibit. By the time we retreated to our designated spot in the adjacent camping area of Sterling Forest, we were utterly and completely exhausted.

"So… when are we eating?" Jax said for the twentieth time, rubbing his hands together.

"Once you start the grill," Adrian poked him.

"Are you serious? But I put up the tent!"

"Yeah, and that must've been brutal," laughed Preston. "You flipped a switch and the tent inflated itself!"

"Not *all* by itself," Jax protested. "I had to run the extension cord between the blower and the truck."

I smiled and watched them fall into their usual banter, while carrying in the rest of our supplies. Two full days and nights away, just the four of us. It wasn't much of a vacation, but I was happy to take it. And considering the whirlwind of non-stop work I'd been exposed to since taking my haptic system to market, it was going to be absolutely magical.

"Did you bring the radio?" asked Jax.

Adrian shrugged. "I didn't. I thought *you* had it covered."

"How can we listen to the game without a radio?" Jax seethed. "It's opening week, for fuck's sake!"

"When the game comes on, go sit in the truck. Turn it on in there."

"The hell with that," Jax spat. "Preston?"

He turned, and Preston was already smiling. "Don't worry," he grinned. "I'll pick it up on an internet station. We can stream it through my phone, cast it to the portable speaker, and…"

His voice faded as I wandered back to the truck. There was a lot to carry. Like everything else we did, even in camping we liked to go big.

A year and a half!

I still couldn't believe it had been that long. It seemed like only yesterday I was presenting to Oculus, and then SONY, and then back to San Francisco to pitch Meta. These companies didn't just like my tech, they went totally bonkers over it. I ended up spending weeks traveling from meeting to meeting, and being presented with contract after contract.

Unlike my men however, who were happy to share me, none of these companies wanted to let me go. Soon they were all pitching me, instead of the other way around. They offered me dizzying advances that were in the millions of dollars, to license my hardware, my software, and a contract to keep me on as program and design support.

I almost signed three times, until Valve sent a jet for me. I spent a week at their headquarters in Bellevue Washington, and came back with a licensing agreement for one of their products, too.

The strangest part about the whole thing wasn't the sudden influx of money. For everything I'd sacrificed, and prepared for, I expected that. No, the most unexpected aspect of my success was the continued work. Instead of selling my design and walking off into the sunset, I'd licensed it to multiple companies who hired me on as a consultant. That is, after paying me ridiculous sums of money for rights to the initial software, that is.

I opened the truck, saw my phone, and picked it up. Before I could turn it over to check the messages however…

"And just what the hell do you think you're doing?"

An iron-like hand clapped over my wrist.

"What?"

"You're breaking the rules!" Adrian admonished. Reaching out with his free hand, he deftly plucked the phone from my fingers.

"I— I was checking to see if there were any messages from the kids!" I pleaded. "What if they needed something?"

"And what if Oculus needed something?" Adrian countered. "Or SONY wanted a Zoom call. Or Meta needed to fly you across the country last minute again, to explain something to a panel of programmers, or Valve had a question about—"

"Alright, alright," I conceded. "I get it."

"Remember our rule? One weekend away, just the four of us. No business. All pleasure."

He placed my phone back in the truck and closed the door.

"But if what if Brayden or Emma misses me?" I asked. "What if they need to say goodnight?"

"The kids are just fine with Jennifer," he went on. "They'll call to say goodnight in a little while. On Jax's phone, or my phone, maybe. But even she knows… *your* phone is off-limits."

I set my hand on my hip and sighed, then gave him the once-over. Adrian had dressed like a warrior for the Renaissance Fair, complete with faux leather boots, a plastic helmet, and a double-bladed broadaxe hanging from his very medieval-looking belt. None of his costume was period, like Preston's archer cosplay for example. And this was a fact that some of the more experienced festival-workers had even pointed out.

Still, he looked pretty damned hot. Almost like a sexy Viking chieftain, with the longish hair and big golden beard he'd been growing for the past two months. I'd enjoyed that beard more than I thought I would, over the last several weeks. Even though it tickled the insides of my thighs; whenever he—

"Did you catch her trying to check her phone again?"

Preston stomped over, looking accusatory. Adrian shrugged and nodded.

"Unbelievable."

Preston's costume was a direct compliment of mine. He was a ranger, a tracker, and an all-around badass. Every part of his cosplay was not only historically accurate, it was handmade and hand-stitched, mostly by him. Right down to the quiver of arrows and maple longbow slung over his shoulder.

"I should shoot an apple off your head," he wagged a finger at me.

"You can try it, but I shoot back."

I slapped him playfully on the cheek three times, then stood on my toes to give him a kiss.

"Besides, there are much better things to do with me later," I promised slyly. "Once we get the tent all set up."

Each of us grabbed something from the truck, then headed back to our camping spot. We'd managed to score one of the more remote sites, although there were still other fairgoers camping all around us. Most of them, however, had the foresight to set up in the morning, rather than at the end of the day when exhaustion was setting in.

I intentionally lagged on the way back, so I could check the guys out from behind. It was an old trick I'd learned from them, of course. Besides the obvious benefits, it gave my mind a place to happily wander.

A lot had happened for my men also, in the past nineteen months. Not only had we moved in together, and into a much bigger place, but Adrian's budding new project had turned into a full-fledged photography agency. At first he was flying out to photo-shoots, but things had gotten so lucrative that models were flying into Buffalo, too. He'd rented space downtown, and had contacts all over the world. Many of them were friends he'd made along the way, but he was picking up new connections so fast he could barely keep up.

Preston, on the other hand, had joined forces with me. He'd given up freelancing altogether in order to work on tweaking my VR software, and by now he was almost as familiar with the code as I was. On top of that we were developing a radical new project, even though we'd only scratched the surface on it. We knew one day, when the contracts were up and our licensing agreements had expired, we'd need something fresh and exciting to devote our efforts to.

We'd even sent back the computers we'd taken from Telengard, but not before checking all the machines for anything to do with my work. Fortunately, he hadn't had a chance to move any files. Preston and I used formatting software to data-wipe the drives completely, overwriting every last bit and byte before packing them up and shipping them off.

"Where the *hell* have you slackers been?"

Jax's voice carried from inside the tent. We found him sitting in one of the fold-out chairs, eating goldfish by the handful out of a Costco-sized box.

"You stole those from Emma, didn't you!" I laughed.

"No," he answered defensively. "I mean, well, it depends on your definition of stole. If I'm the one who *bought* the goldfish, I can't really steal them, can I?"

"Picture that little girl right now, sitting at home with tears in her eyes," I chastised. "Not a single goldfish in the whole cabinet, because her father greedily took the entire box."

"Greedily, huh?" he asked, popping another few into his already-orange mouth.

"Yeah," I stared down at him. "Greedy."

"Takes one to know one," Jax countered.

If Adrian's costume fell a little short, Jax's was outright ridiculous. He had a plastic breastplate, a plastic sword, and a matching plastic shield with a cheesy-looking dragon on it. The whole set looked like something you'd find in the toy section of a five-and-dime shop, only this was an adult-sized version. Because, well… Amazon.

"Are you *finally* going to take that ridiculous armor off?" Preston sighed. Embarrassed to sit next to him during any of the shows, he'd been begging Jax to do it all day.

"Maybe," Jax crunched away. "Why, is it still pissing you off?"

Adrian laughed. "You *know* it is."

"Then maybe not," Jax winked.

I smiled at the most child-like of my three boyfriends.

Out of all four of us, Jax had most recently been the busiest of all. He'd taken up medical classes at the University at Buffalo, while still somehow keeping on as an Erie County paramedic. His days were no longer days. They were blocks of hours now, each of them dedicated to working, studying, and preparing for his upcoming residency.

For all of these reasons, plus taking care of the children? The four of us slipping away for just two days was a titanic effort.

"Got the air-conditioning hooked up yet?" Adrian asked him.

"Not even out of the box," Jax said proudly. "I'm on strike until we eat something."

"You are eating something," Preston pointed out.

"You mean this?" he shook the box of Goldfish. "Please."

The summer had been a hot one for us. Now, a week into September, the cooler weather was just starting to roll in. I was looking forward to sweaters, and pumpkin spice lattes. To Halloween costumes, apples, and the crisp fall air.

And eventually, even to snow.

"So what did you think of your first Rennfest?" asked Preston, leaning his bow and quiver in the corner of the tent.

Adrian and Jax looked at each other.

"Not bad," said Adrian. "I expected more swordfighting to break out, though. Seemed kinda tame."

"The food was good," said Jax. "I never ate some of that stuff before."

"Yeah, well now you've had *all* of it," Preston laughed.

"In fact, I think you ate everything they had."

"Not the fried Oreos," Jax disagreed. He wrinkled his nose. "They looked gross."

"I'm pretty sure they weren't period, either," Adrian smirked.

"I liked the wenches too," Jax said, turning to wink at me. "They seemed very… well…"

"Bosomy?"

"Yeah. That."

I reached down and pushed my tits up with a smile. "This better?" I asked him. "I don't have a corset laced up so tight I can't even breathe, like some of those gals. But I can always give you a temporary show."

All around me, the guys sank into their camping chairs. No one was setting up the grill, or unfolding the solar panels, or doing any of the things we needed to do. We were just too tired. Too weary from walking the entirety of the fairgrounds.

Instead of mounting a protest, I just smiled and sank into my own chair.

"Maybe tonight we just chill, and set all those things up tomorrow," I suggested.

Jax looked alarmed. "But what about—"

"I think there's a Burger King about a mile and a half from here," I cut him off with a shrug. "It's not exactly period or anything…"

My suggestion was met with a round of smiles, all around.

"We could pretend they were dragon burgers, and eat them anyway," Preston offered.

"Could we get enough french fries to fill a backpack?" asked Jax.

"Shit yes."

He jumped up so fast, his plastic breastplate flopped against his chest. "Then what the hell are we waiting for? Let's go."

I was laughing so hard I couldn't get out of my chair — or maybe it was just that my ass wouldn't let me. Eventually it was Adrian and Preston who stepped in. They offered me two strong helping hands, and brought me back to my tired feet.

As we filed out of our giant, inflatable palace, I went over it all in my head. I had a life full of promise, and a future filled of love. I had the adoration of three incredible men, and two beautiful adopted babies. Together we made up a whole new family, and we were far from finished.

These men had promised to marry me, as soon as they could figure out where and when. We'd always be together, even when life set us temporarily apart. I would love them, cherish them, hopefully bear children by each of them. These were just some of the long-term crazy plans we had, including finding the perfect location to build the dream mansion we'd always agreed we could live in forever.

But as far as I was concerned, right now there was no rush, no big hurry. Everything would fall into its proper place in due time. In the meantime, I was going to enjoy it to the fullest. I intended upon making many happy memories, and relishing every single minute of this long, beautiful ride.

Most of all, I was thankful for how lucky I was to *find* these men again, during the course of my life. They were second chances, all of them. Second chances, in a world where some people don't even get a first.

"Think they still have Shamrock shakes?" I heard Jax asking.

"Still?" swore Adrian, incredulously. "St. Patrick's Day was six months ago!"

"But I *like* Shamrock shakes," Jax lamented.

"Don't they taste the same, anyway?" asked Preston. "I mean, isn't it just a vanilla shake dyed green, or—"

"Blasphemy!" Jax shouted lustily. "Shamrock shakes are minty, and creamy, and they're absolutely delicious!"

"Not to mention they're from McDonald's," I chimed in from behind them. "Not Burger King."

The others laughed, while Jax's look of utter dismay made me chuckle. I stuck my tongue out at him. He flipped me off.

"Still hate you," he told me, but not without adding a wink.

"Right back at you, big boy."

Yeah, I thought to myself as we reached the truck. *Second chances pretty much rock.*

That said, I had so very many first chances to look forward to.

Bonus Epilogue

* * *

Wanna read the ULTRA-HEA, sugary-sweet, super-sexy, flash-forward BONUS EPILOGUE?

Of course you do!

TAP RIGHT HERE TO SIGN UP!

Or enter this link into your browser:

https://mailchi.mp/kristawolfbooks.com/bonus-epilogue-stn

to have it INSTANTLY delivered to your inbox.

Need more Reverse Harem?

Thanks for checking out *Sharing the Nanny*. Here's hoping it knocked your socks off!

And for even *more* sweltering reverse harem heat? Check out: The Auction. Below you'll find a preview of the sexy, sizzling cover, plus the first several chapters so you can see for yourself:

* * *

AMAZON AWARD-WINNING AUTHOR
KRISTA WOLF

THE AUCTION
A Reverse Harem Romance

~ 1 ~

AUTUMN

Putting yourself up for a singles charity auction wasn't something you aspired to, it was more like something that just happened. And it didn't seem real, to be honest. More like the type of thing that only occurred in sappy rom-coms, developed in the cheesiest parts of Hollywood.

Only right now I actually *was* in Hollywood.

And I was actually going through with it.

"One hundred dollars?" the voice beside me called into the microphone. "Anyone?"

The auctioneer smiled weakly, his hawk-like eyes scanning the well-dressed crowd. Forty-five minutes ago his voice had been cheery and boisterous. But now, with mine being the last date auctioned off, he just sounded tired.

"Ninety perhaps?"

I grinned through clenched teeth, trying to look pretty while silently cursing my lifelong best friend. Kinsley had ushered me up here spur of the moment, or at least it seemed that way. Right now she grinned supportively from the crowd just below the stage, sipping on her fourth glass of champagne and intermittently clapping to encourage more men to bid me up.

Only nobody was bidding.

"Seventy-five then," the auctioneer conceded, wincing a little as he said it. The mustached man in the thousand-dollar suit cast me a nervous glance. "I mean gentlemen, just look at her. She's lovely. And in fact—"

"I *am* lovely," I spoke loudly, deftly swiping the microphone from his tired hand. "*Very* lovely, and you'd be lucky to have me. But seventy-five dollars isn't going to cut it, gentlemen. Charity or no charity, this New York girl knows her worth."

The crowd that had been so attentive at the beginning of the auction had devolved into milling around, talking amongst themselves. But now a hush settled over them again. Apparently something interesting had happened.

"I'll bid on myself if I have to," I said, stepping forward to the edge of the makeshift stage. "After all, this *is* for a fantastic cause. The animal shelter needs every penny it can get. The poor dogs and cats still looking for homes are depending on you."

I shot a quick glance downward, at my friend. Kinsley's whole face had lit up. The bubbly brunette was smiling ear to ear, giving me the 'OK' sign with her free hand.

"Kinsley is my best friend," I went on, "and as you know, she's the manager of the place. The building is run down. The roof is leaking. There are too many animals, and not enough space. It needs our help."

I turned sideways in my borrowed red dress, showing myself off. Letting the men in the crowd know what they were about to miss out on.

"You all came here to support Cozy Noses," I said admonishingly, "or at least I thought you did. Back on the east coast there would already be a bidding war for this." I slapped a playful hand on my hip and angled it their way. "Apparently though, none of you sun-kissed valley guys can handle a date with me."

There was some intermittent laughter in the crowd, even scattered applause. I smiled back at them and winked.

"Which is why I'm bidding five-hundred dollars for a date with myself," I finished glibly. "And when I win, I'll take my *own* ass out to a nice dinner."

With that, I thrust the microphone back into the auctioneer's hand. There were looks of shock and surprise from the women in the audience, but from the men in the crowd, it was mostly comical appreciation and excited chatter. Apparently they weren't used to someone talking this bluntly. And if my New York accent hadn't slapped them in the face, my heavy Long Island accent had nearly bludgeoned them to death.

That said, the applause I received afterward was equivalent to a good mic drop.

"Holy *shit!*" Kinsley hissed, from somewhere just beneath me. She was clapping her hands together, her champagne forgotten. "Autumn, that was amazing! YOU were amazing! I can't believe you—"

"GENTLEMEN!" the auctioneer called loudly into the microphone, silencing the chattering crowd. He was finally awake and alive again. "You all heard the lady! The bid right now is five-hundred dollars!"

I spun around slowly, holding my hand out like a game

show hostess. The fund-raising event my friend dragged me to had been mostly dull, if I were being honest. But playing the crowd was suddenly fun.

"Will you let this gorgeous woman *shame* you into taking herself out to dinner?" the auctioneer teased, grinning. "Or will one of you step up and—"

"A thousand dollars!"

All heads turned, including mine. A blond-haired man with striking green eyes stood with one hand raised. And those piercing emerald eyes were locked on me.

Now we're talking.

"One thousand dollars!" the auctioneer repeated, as the crowd erupted in applause. "For a date with this strikingly beautiful and *vociferous* woman," he shot me a sideways glance, "who is apparently from New York."

It was already more than most of the other women — and men, of course — had gone for. And to think I'd almost balked when Kinsley suggested I get up here to help out the shelter. Right now I was smiling at the selfish notion they'd saved the best for last.

"This 'vociferous' girl thanks you very much for your generosity," I curtsied, leaning into the microphone this time without taking it from the auctioneer's hand. I made sure to stare directly at the hot, green-eyed stranger who'd just bought himself a date with me. "I'm sure you and I will have an excellent time tomorrow night, before I have to fly—"

"TWO thousand dollars."

Another voice, this one deeper and more resonant, echoed loudly above the noise of the crowd. I turned my attention to the opposite side of the room, where an exceptionally tall man stood a full head and shoulders above everyone else.

"Two *thousand!*" the auctioneer swore. He raised an eyebrow. "Seriously?"

The tall man nodded slowly. He was impeccably dressed, with model good looks and thick acres of gorgeous dark hair. His expression was stoic, but with a hint of mischief. Best of all his handsome face was shrouded in sexy dark stubble; the kind that I was always a sucker for, whether or not it was good for me.

And historically, it wasn't.

"Two thousand dollars then, for a hot date with the beautiful girl from New York!" the auctioneer shouted. "Thank you sir!"

Hot date? I repeated silently, mouthing the words to the auctioneer. The man only laughed and shrugged.

"Hey, you wanted to help the shelter, right?" he asked, covering the mic with one meaty hand.

"Yeah, sure. But—"

"Two thousand going once!" he stepped forward, ignoring me completely. "Two thousand going twice…"

"Twenty-five hundred!" another voice called out.

Everyone whirled their attention back to the original bidder. Only it wasn't the original bidder. It was the man standing *next* to him.

What the—

The new bidder's arm was still raised, much to the dismay of what apparently looked to be his blond friend with the green eyes. He had beautifully-tanned skin. Chocolate brown eyes. And of course, as fate would have it, even more sexy stubble.

"You really struck a nerve with these guys," the auctioneer swore under his breath.

"I… I didn't—"

"TWENTY-FIVE HUNDRED!" he boomed. "A most generous donation, for a very lovely—"

"Three thousand."

The tall man's voice was so naturally strong and commanding, it drowned out the excited murmurs of more than two hundred other people, even from the back end of the room. The crowd gasped. Kinsley choked. The auctioneer swung his arm left, pointing back at the new highest bidder. Before he could open his mouth, however:

"Thirty-five hundred!"

The blond man's hand was raised again. I noticed it was tattooed. He looked lean and strong, with an intensity about him that seemed oddly dangerous. But only to his enemies. Never to friends.

How the hell I knew all this without knowing anything about him was a complete mystery.

"FOUR."

The tall man bid again, directing everyone's attention back on the two apparent friends. The men conferred with one another, and their exchange got quickly heated. A moment later, the Italian-looking man elbowed his friend.

"Five thousand!" he shouted, before his friend could recover.

The auctioneer glanced at Kinsley. She nodded in shock.

"FIVE THOUSAND DOLLARS" the man shouted into the mic, "is the maximum bid allowed! Therefore sir, I declare you the winner of—"

"BULLSHIT."

The tall man near the back of the room took several steps forward, the crowd parting as he made his way to the stage. He had an undeniable aura about him. A raw charisma I could feel from up here.

"You never said there was a maximum," the man declared as he got closer. "I'd have bid five thousand right from the jump."

The auctioneer looked abruptly panicked. He lowered the mic.

"I'm sorry sir, but—"

"And I would've done the same," the blond man interrupted. He appeared beside the stage so suddenly, he might as well have teleported. "You should've told us about the limit from the beginning," he seethed. "What kind of auction has a maximum bid, anyway?"

"The kind that can only accept individual donations in certain amounts," Kinsley stepped in. My friend's eyes blazed with a defensive fierceness I knew well. "If you really wanted a date with her, you would've outbid your friend over there. But you didn't. And so…"

She paused mid-sentence, her shrewd eyes scanning away for a moment as an idea suddenly occurred to her. Just another one of her mannerisms I knew especially well.

"Wait," said Kinsley. "What if you *all* took her out?"

By now even the winner of the auction had made his way over. The three men looked at each other in confusion, then back at Kinsley.

"What do you mean?"

"I mean technically you could *all* be the highest bidder," my friend went on. "Three of you, three dates, three separate bids. Fifteen thousand dollars for Cozy Noses. Everyone wins."

Still standing over all of them, my mouth dropped open. "Wait a second…"

"Done," said the tattooed blond. "Count me in."

"That works for me also," the tall man nodded. He scanned me, top to bottom, beneath a pair of heavy, dark brows. "As long as I get my date."

All eyes fell on me. I was still in shock.

"Umm… would you *do* that?" the auctioneer asked hopefully. "Would you go on three separate dates?"

I was totally on the spot. I shrugged.

"Yes, but—"

"Then it's settled!" he smiled, uncovering the mic with his hand once more. "I'll declare all of you as winners, and—"

"Did you forget I'm *leaving* the day after tomorrow?" I nudged Kinsley. "I can't go on three dates!"

My friend frowned. So did the others.

"My flight back to New York leaves in thirty-six hours," I reiterated. "I'll go out on a date tomorrow night for sure, if it helps out the shelter. But after that—"

"What about a triple date?"

Kinsley's eyes flared as she blurted the words. She still hadn't worked out the details yet, that much was obvious. My friend's brain was always working its ass off to keep up with her mouth.

"What are you talking about?"

"I mean all three of you should take her out," she said, matter-of-factly. "Autumn and I were supposed to hang out together before she left, but I can give that up. You can have the whole day with her."

Once again the men glanced at each other, unsure of what to say. None of them were willing to show weakness, however. Not one of them wanted to give in.

"C'mon," Kinsley urged. "What do you say? It's just a *charity* date, really — you know, to support the shelter. That's why you all placed bids in the first place, isn't it?"

Two of the men — the sexily stubbled ones — scratched at their chins. Begrudgingly, they nodded.

"It's not like it's a 'date' date," Kinsley went on. She paused awkwardly. "Unless you *want* it to be. Or one of you happens to hit it off with her." She grinned up at me and winked. "I mean, my friend *is* pretty awesome. The three of you would be crazy not to jump at the chance to—"

"Okay."

The answer came from my handsome blond savior; the one who'd bid on me in the first place. He cleared his throat and said it again. "Alright, I'm in."

"Sure," his friend added immediately. "Me too."

The dark-haired giant paused for a moment, as if weighing his options. I could tell he was calculating everything at once; me, Kinsley, his apparent rivals. The incredible amount of money the shelter would receive. In the end he reached up and loosened his tie, which had been fixed in a Windsor knot, and not the easier, 'even your wife could tie it' version.

"Fine," he said at last. "We'll all take her out tomorrow. But I pick the restaurant. And also—"

"Done!" Kinsley said, clapping her hands.

The auctioneer's smile returned. He lifted the microphone again, apparently to announce all three extremely generous donations to the very patient crowd. As he did, Kinsley motioned me down to her level with a frantic hand.

"Autumn!" she hissed excitedly. I could tell by her expression how much this meant to her. "You *are* okay with this, aren't you?"

I laughed bitterly. "You're asking me *now?*"

"No!" said Kinsley. "Well, I mean yes, but not really. I mean—"

My expression softened as my best friend damn near bit her tongue off trying to make everything right again. I let her off the hook with a smile.

"Yeah, sure," I conceded. "It'll be fun, right? Just like you said?"

"Three times the fun," Kinsley winked again.

It was that wink that always got us in trouble. That same wink that had started entire *wars* back in New York, while the two of us were growing up.

"Besides," she added, just before the crowd's applause drowned out everything else. "You're going home the day after tomorrow, anyway. How much could possibly happen?"

~ 2 ~

AUTUMN

I couldn't remember the last time my best friend had brushed my hair, but that was exactly what was happening. It had to be high school at the very least. I was probably getting ready for a date back then, too.

"You *sure* you don't think this dress is a little too much?"

As with the rest of her wardrobe, the studded black dress Kinsley lent me walked the tightrope between slutty and sexy. It fit well though, and hugged my curves in all the right places. Maybe a bit too much.

"Are you kidding?" my friend laughed. "They're going to eat you up!"

"I'm doing this for the shelter!" I frowned at her in the mirror. "I am *not* going to get eaten up."

My friend chuckled mischievously. "You don't know that."

She continued brushing, and after a short but lingering stare I continued applying my makeup. There was limited time before my dates arrived, and we'd always been good at killing two birds with one stone. Plus, Kinsley had a date of her own. She claimed it was someone 'casual', which I knew to be pretty standard for her. But after almost a week catching up with her on the west coast, I suspected she liked this mystery guy more than she let on.

"I still can't believe I'm going out on a date with *three* guys," I bit my lip.

"Why?"

I half-whirled. "Are you serious?"

"If anyone can juggle three men at once its you," Kinsley said casually. "Besides, you're bringing in fifteen *thousand* dollars for Cozy Noses! Do you have any idea what that means for us?"

In fact, I did. Two years ago my friend had abruptly quit veterinary school, taken a defibrillator to a dying animal shelter, and somehow managed to bring it back from the brink of physical and financial collapse. Even now, Cozy Noses was running on fumes. But it was still running. And with each passing month, things were getting a little bit easier.

"You know I'm happy to do it," I said again, letting the warmth of doing a good thing push the nervousness away.

"Besides, is there really anything to complain about?" Kinsley smirked. "You get to go out, have fun, and sit down to a nice dinner with three very generous — not to mention yummy-looking — men." Her smirk widened as she slowly pulled the brush through my hair. "Who knows? Maybe you'll even get your clock cleaned."

My mouth dropped open. "I will NOT get my clock

cleaned!"

"And why not?" my friend protested. "*Someone's* gotta brush the cobwebs out of that thing," Kinsley winked. "You're flying back to Long Island tomorrow, anyway. Where's the harm in a last-minute California fling?"

I rolled my eyes, and she laughed some more. Kinsley had been teasing me mercilessly, ever since we arrived back at her place last night. She wouldn't stop asking if I liked any of the guys, or which of them I thought I could hit it off with.

"I don't even know anything about them," I'd told her.

"Well, that tall drink of water is Christian Gardner, a local lawyer and a ruthless one at that," she'd told me. "I can't believe you pulled him! Much less for five thousand dollars."

"And the others?"

My friend had only shrugged.

"I never saw them until last night, but before we left I asked around. Turns out they're contractors, and also friends."

"Friends?" I'd squinted. It seemed strange to me that two friends would try to outbid each other.

"Ex-military, too," Kinsley had nodded. "I think they served together. They run their own outfit now, and build houses all over the Valley. Someone said they'd be bigger if they put the profits back into the company."

"But they don't?"

"Not so much, no," Kinsley had told me. "Apparently they use those profits to build free homes for veterans."

If the guys seemed attractive before, their philanthropy made them damn near perfect, now. Kinsley's explanation certainly solved the mystery of why they'd been so generous. It also left me thinking a lot about them, as I drifted off to sleep.

The sound of my friend's doorbell snapped me back to the present. Kinsley stepped back, dropped the brush, and grinned excitedly.

"Oh my God they're here."

My friend was giddy with excitement, like some kind of proud parent. All of a sudden I felt like a senior on prom night.

"Are you coming or what?"

Kinsley's passion for anything new had always been infectious. Maybe that's why, right after graduation, she ended up at UCLA — clear on the other side of the country.

"What if I'm having a shit time?" I asked suddenly. "Is there some sort of secret code I should text you, or…"

"You put all that negativity out of your head right now," my friend admonished me harshly. Just as quickly, she smiled and kissed me on the cheek. "Now shut up and enjoy your last night in paradise."

She flung the front door open recklessly; a metaphor for Kinsley's life in general. Standing on the other side were two of the men who'd bid on me — the friends and contractors.

And holy shit, they were *gorgeous*.

Both men were tall, topping out at an inch or two over six feet, with smooth, sun-bronzed skin that made it easy to believe they worked outside. Their bodies were strong and lean, their physiques forged from what had to be long years of manual labor. But those years had been good to them. Very, *very* good indeed.

"Hey," the blond said simply. He was staring over

Kinsley's shoulder, directly at me. "Autumn, right?"

There was a pickup truck parked out on the street that wasn't there before. Big and blue and near-vintage old, it undoubtedly belonged to them.

"Right," I smiled, noticing that his sexy smirk came with even sexier dimples. "And you are…"

"I'm Shane," he said, flashing an effortless yet still panty-melting grin. Those emerald eyes that had locked on mine from across the auction floor were now right here, in all their glory. It was everything I could do not to get lost in them.

"And this here is Darius."

Shane nodded left, but Darius was already stepping forward to greet me warmly. He slipped past Kinsley and took my hand, his long arms dangling from a pair of impossibly broad shoulders

"Nice to meet you, Autumn."

His strong hands were absolutely enormous. And calloused. And enormous. And did I mention enormous?

"You boys are early," Kinsley stated flatly.

"Damn right we are," said Shane. "We were hoping to get here before he did."

"Who?"

"The other guy," said Darius. "The guy in the suit."

Kinsley had been standing against the open door, her arms behind her. But now she folded them over her chest.

"You mean Christian?"

"The tall guy, yeah," shrugged Shane. "We planned on sneaking you out of here before he showed up. Trust me, our date's going to be a lot more interesting if he's not—"

"Too late."

I smiled at the both of them, then pointed outside. Parked just in front of their truck, a long black sedan was now idling curbside. The vehicle was sleek and dark, with smooth yet wicked curves, and a logo I'd never seen before.

Leaning against it, equally sleek and sexy in his immaculate suit, was my third and final date.

"You were saying?" smiled Christian, crossing his arms.

~ 3 ~

CHRISTIAN

She was strikingly beautiful up close. An absolute vision whose shimmering blonde hair framed a girl-next-door face I could stare at for hours. On top of that she was bitingly sardonic, yet blind to her own unjaded heart. I'd bid on her. I'd won her. I was sitting right across from her…

But on my left and right, I unfortunately had Patrick and Spongebob.

"Really, this is it?" Shane scoffed again. "*This* is place you insisted on picking for dinner?"

He was louder than his friend, but no less disdainful. The two of them, I could tell, had been around each other for a long time. They'd probably settled into some sort of ranked hierarchy, one where Shane still believed he was in command. Either that, or Darius — the more calculating one, in my opinion — had allowed him to think that way.

"And what's wrong with this place?" asked Autumn, before chomping down on her burger again. She was really digging into it, too. A woman after my own heart.

"It's just funny, that's all," Shane shrugged. He jerked a thumb at me. "This guy is fancy. A lawyer in a thousand-dollar suit. He forces us into a four-way date, then insists on picking the restaurant. And of all places, he brings us here?"

"And what's your definition of a good restaurant?" I asked casually.

He looked down at the table for a moment. "One without paper napkins, for starters."

I stifled a laugh. So did Autumn. I couldn't tell if she did it for my benefit, or if she didn't want to give too much away. Her smile was worth it, either way.

"Forget about what he says," Darius chimed in. "These french fries alone are worth the trip."

He held one up to me. I toasted him with nod. Regardless of what anyone thought of the place, all of us had eaten our fill. It made sense that we were famished. We'd been out for hours now, walking the streets of Los Angeles and stopping for drinks, sights, and shows by street performers. The three of us had entertained Autumn's every last touristy wish; from stopping to check out celebrity footprints at the Mann Theater, to finding various stars on the Hollywood Boulevard. We'd even taken her dancing, which outside of weddings or holiday parties was something I never, ever did.

But this woman was worth it. I knew it the moment she'd stepped in front of the auctioneer last night, taking the microphone and taking control. She was smart. Sassy. Heartbreakingly beautiful. Her 'zero fucks given' attitude made her refreshingly raw and real, in all the ways the more plastic people around here could never hope to understand.

And so here I was, driving Ren and Stimpy around

town while they sat in the back, flirting with Autumn. Sure, they'd tried bumping me out of our shared date, but it's not like I couldn't blame them. I'd shown up early for exactly the same reason. Ten minutes sooner and I would've stolen her away myself, even if it meant paying off their bids to help out the shelter.

Of course I'd had them thoroughly checked out — that much was a given. Competition aside, they weren't bad guys. Shane Lockhart and Darius Knight had honorable discharges from a pretty serious unit of the United States Army. They'd started their own company from scratch. They gave back to the community. They worked out, ate their vegetables, and took the skin off chicken. I couldn't find a damn thing wrong with them, which was kind of frustrating.

But I knew nothing about *her*.

Looking up Autumn Holloway from Suffolk County, New York might've been easy, but for some reason I resisted the temptation. I wanted to go into this with no knowledge, no history, no preconceived notions. If the feelings that had driven me to do something as uncharacteristic as bid on a charity singles auction were real, it wasn't something I wanted to mess with. I needed our date to be organic. Or at least, as organic as possible when splitting it three ways.

"Excuse me while I powder my nose," Autumn said, sliding backwards. "And by powder my nose, I mean make myself smell a little less like ketchup and mayo."

"Same here," I said quickly, and stood up.

I followed her around the bar and into the narrow hallway where the restrooms were located. Before ducking into the ladies room however, she smiled and turned to face me.

"You used to come here as a kid, didn't you?"

I couldn't hide my shock, much less how impressed I was.

"How do you know?"

"You've been looking around all night," Autumn replied. "Scanning the place. Seeing things that are no longer there."

I nodded appreciatively. "My parents used to take me and my sister here, when we were young. It was a much different place, back then."

"How so?"

"Well for one, they served free peanuts at every table. And you were allowed — no, encouraged — to throw the shells right on the floor."

Autumn chuckled. "Every little kid's dream."

I nodded. "That other dining room over there was a little arcade area. They had a foosball table and a Battlezone machine. There were a couple of old coin-operated horses, too. My father would give my sister a handful of change, and she'd ride the unicorn until she ran out of quarters."

"So you come here for the nostalgia, then."

"That, plus you won't find a better hamburger in all of LA."

I wanted to tell her so much more; that simple nostalgia didn't even scratch the surface. I came to this restaurant because it was one of the last remaining connections to a happy past. I needed this place to exist, so I could keep a memory alive.

A trio of people came down the corridor, which was already tight. Autumn stepped into me without hesitation to let them pass, pressing parts of her body against mine. It was a level of intimacy we'd already shared in the club, dancing close together. Considering we knew each other for only a few hours, it still felt oddly natural.

"What are the chances of you and I slipping away from Joey and Chandler?" I murmured, inhaling her scent. "There's a side door right there. I already paid the bill."

She laughed, and her laughter was lilting and beautiful. But it was still laughter.

"What's so funny?"

"Joey and Chandler tried the same thing, back at the nightclub."

I raised an eyebrow. "Did they?"

"When you went for drinks, they tried pulling me out the back door."

Although the people in the hall had passed us, I noticed she still hadn't stepped back to her side of the corridor. My head was tilted down, and our faces were dangerously close together now. Our lips, hovering two or three inches from sweet oblivion.

It might as well have been miles.

"I can't just ditch them," she said, her voice cracking a little. "Any more that I could ditch you."

"I get it."

"I mean—"

"No," I said softly. "It's cool. I admire the loyalty to your commitment."

God, she was beautiful. I'd been fascinated by her all night, too. So much in fact, that I hadn't checked my phone even once throughout the evening. I hadn't read a single text-message. I hadn't answered a single email.

Those things alone were huge indications as to how much she'd affected me. Normally I wasn't one for instant connections. But this, I quickly realized, was on a whole different level.

"Wait, what was I saying?" I blinked.

Autumn grinned. "You were telling me how much you admire me."

Her skin was flush and pink, as our eyes searched each other's in the dim light. I could smell vanilla on her skin, now. The whole sensory experience was driving me wild.

"Tonight can't be the end of this," I told her flatly. "I know you're leaving, but I'd love to see you tomorrow."

"Maybe you *will* see me tomorrow," Autumn countered. She held up her phone. "See?"

I squinted at the glowing screen in the darkened hallway. There was a text-message from her friend, Kinsley. Something about getting together, followed by an address.

"There's a Midnight Mischief party, back in the Valley," she said. "A whole bunch of Kinsley's friends, plus some of the people from the fundraiser. She's asking us to swing by."

"What's a Midnight Mischief party?"

Autumn shrugged. "Fuck if I know."

If her New York accent was already sharp, it was a razor when she cursed. I don't know why I liked it, but I did.

"Wanna go? We need to head back toward Encino, anyway."

"Sure."

"And then it'll be after midnight," she smiled. "And so you'll see me tomorrow. Technically."

"Who's seeing *who* tomorrow?"

I didn't even have to turn to know Shane was standing there. Darius too. Their expressions were sour, like someone had just pissed in their beer.

"Making plans without us?" Darius folded his arms.

"Well the original plan was to sneak her out the side door while the two of you finished your fries," I said, without a hint of apology. "Similar to the plan you came up with back at the club, only my plan was better." I jerked a thumb. "I already parked on this side of the building."

"Thinking ahead," smirked Shane.

"Always."

"Almost as if—"

"Sorry," Autumn interjected loudly, "but all three of you are stuck with me for the duration of the night. And each other."

Diplomatically, she positioned herself between us.

"Great," Shane grumbled.

"Now, do either of you know what a Midnight Mischief party is?" she asked.

The guys looked at each other in confusion for a moment, then shook their heads.

"No," they said in unison.

"Perfect," our date winked, before finally ducking into the ladies room. "Then we're all gonna find out together."

~ 4 ~

AUTUMN

The place was beyond stunning, with sharp, contemporary architecture that molded it right into the side of the mountain it was built on. There was plenty of glass, complemented by more glass, complemented by beautifully-designed and expensive-looking furniture. And of course, like every other house on this hill, the back opened up into an unobstructed view of the valley. Stadium seating, for the rich and famous.

"Holy shit."

I breathed the words, more than actually said them. The galaxy of twinkling lights in the valley beneath us were astonishingly beautiful. My trio of dates flanked me as we stepped onto the immaculate back patio, which was little more than a frame of priceless-looking stonework surrounding a glowing blue swimming pool. Standing around it were fifteen or twenty people, sipping drinks. Half of them wearing... get this... *pajamas*.

"Oh my God, you came!"

Kinsley rushed me from the side, nearly knocking me over with her very enthusiastic and unquestionably tipsy hug. She wore only two things: a silky, sexy-looking green kimono, and the slippers that I'd gotten her for Christmas two years ago.

"I'm so happy!" she grinned. She stepped back and let her eyes flit from Christian to Shane to Darius. "Wow. I can't believe you're actually here!"

"Well, you *did* invite us."

"I sure did," Kinsley giggled into her wine glass. "And wait until you—"

"We do seem a bit overdressed, though."

My friend laughed again, then shook her head. "Nonsense. Look over there." She pointed at another couple, who were dressed like we were. "They showed up here from a different party. And there's another guy too — a basketball player, I think. He came in a hoodie, so no one would recognize him. And then there's—"

"Kinsley what *is* this?"

I looked around some more. Most of the guests were wearing pajamas, but many of them were in various states of undress. There were people swimming in the pool, too. Half of them were fully clothed, and the other half were skinny dipping. There was no in between.

It should've been awkward, but somehow it wasn't. The light coming from the pool was soft and subdued, and people were speaking in low but happy tones. Soothing music played from strategically-hidden speakers, so distant you could barely hear it. The whole vibe was very relaxed.

A beautiful woman with a spectacular figure walked by, wearing only a thong. She carried two drinks in each hand, and blew Kinsley a kiss as she passed.

My eyes narrowed. "Is this some sort of..." I struggled for the words. "I mean, is this like..."

"A swinger's party?" Darius blurted bluntly.

Kinsley touched my date's chest and laughed. "No, silly."

"So it's perfectly normal to just show up in practically nothing, or—"

"Maybe I should explain."

The new voice was attached to someone tall, dark, and very sexily bald. Wearing silk boxers and a plain white T-shirt, he slid a long arm very casually around my friend's waist. I knew immediately this was Kinsley's mystery man.

"It's a Midnight Mischief party," the man explained. "The party doesn't start until midnight, and everyone leaves for breakfast at dawn. When you come, you're supposed to be wearing whatever it is that you sleep in." He paused to take a pull from the beer he was holding, then pointed the neck of the bottle our way. "Or in your case, whatever you happen to be wearing at midnight."

I looked around some more. It was starting to make a little more sense.

"Autumn, this is Eric," Kinsley grinned. "Eric, this is Autumn... and Christian, and Shane, and Darius. She's *theirs* for the night, so..."

"No, not theirs," I corrected her.

"Well they *won* you," my friend corrected herself. "Fair and square. And they helped out Cozy Noses immensely," Kinsley winked, "so for the sake of the shelter, I hope you've been showing them a good time tonight."

Shane bumped my hip playfully.

"Yeah," he teased. "Where the hell's our good time?"

I smirked back at them. "I thought you boys were taking *me* out on a date."

"Actually, it wasn't specified," Christian teased back. "The event said 'win a date with a beautiful single.' But it never said who was taking whom out."

I thought he might bump me the way Shane did, this immaculately-dressed lawyer who'd only just loosened his tie. He surprised me by stepping even closer, and setting his hands on my hips.

"I *did* win you, though," he murmured huskily into my ear. "For the night, anyway."

His breath was hot on my neck, either intentionally or unintentionally. It made the little hairs stand up there, and sent shivers rocketing down both sides of my body.

"Anyway, go ahead and walk around," said Eric. "Everyone here is super nice, super chill. Get some drinks, and midnight snacks from the kitchen, and whatever else." He pointed to a bowl on the outdoor bar, filled with colorful packets of something that were unmistakably adult-level gummies. "Enjoy yourselves."

"And before you leave," added Kinsley, "go check out the pool house." She tilted her head toward the rear of the property, where an enormous structure looked almost like a second house. I couldn't help but notice it was the direction from which she came.

"What's in the pool house?" asked Darius.

Kinsley's smile was wider than I'd ever seen it before, and that was saying something. She shrugged coyly.

"Games and stuff."

With that she kissed me on the cheek and led Eric away by the hand. The two of them disappeared into the house, leaving us surrounded by glowing blue strangers.

"So that's the friend you've been visiting?" asked Darius. "The one from back home?"

Kinsley's Long Island accent, which was even thicker than mine, should've been confirmation enough. I nodded anyway.

"We played soccer together and ran track all through high school," I said. "Kinsley bolted out of New York the first chance she got though, and ended up at UCLA. She fell in love with California, and the rest is history."

"It's not too hard to fall for this place," Shane agreed, scratching the back of his head with a tattooed hand. "It's pretty. It's seductive. And it's a *lot* crazier than Montana."

"Montana's just as beautiful, though," I guessed. "No?"

"You bet your ass it is," he confirmed with a grin.

By now it was late, well past midnight. On any other night I would've been running out of gas. But there was something in the air here: an electrical charge that kept the night going. An energy of pure intimacy, fed perhaps by my three delicious-looking dates, and the casual connections we'd developed over the course of the evening.

"You wanna walk around a little?" suggested Darius. "Or..."

"Let's get drinks first," I suggested. "I'm thirsty."

Ten minutes later we were touring the house, weaving our way past small groups of soft-spoken adults in various stages of relaxation and undress.

"Is all of southern California like this?" I chuckled.

"You mean this movie-grade over the top?"

"Yeah."

Shane shrugged. "Depends on where you go. The Valley obviously does things differently."

"The richer you get, the more time you have for stuff like this," Darius added, gesturing around. "Not too many of these people are getting up to drive a bus or run a skid-loader tomorrow morning."

"Or to stand before a judge and litigate," Shane finished, jerking a thumb at Christian. "Like this psycho."

I glanced at the tallest of my three dates; who, as usual, had taken the joke in stride. Christian had undone his tie altogether, along with the top two buttons of his shirt. His double whiskey was nothing more than an empty glass now, dangling from the thick fingers of one big hand.

"I don't have court in the morning," he said. "At least not tomorrow."

My eyes flirted with his. "So you cleared your schedule for me?"

"Sure did."

We finished our tour of the house, exiting the master bedroom which had been occupied by two smiling couples sitting on the bed in pajamas. A pair of French doors spat us onto the back patio again, this time in a different spot.

"Sorry about Kinsley," I said, apologizing to my would-be suitors. "She's flaky, but harmless. Still, I had no idea what kind of party this would be. When she said we should stop by, I just figured—"

"Why don't we check out the pool house?"

The question had come from Christian, surprisingly enough. Glowing blue waves of light and shadow danced across his handsome face, reflected up from pool.

"I'm in," shrugged Shane. "Darius too."

"I am, huh?" asked Darius, glibly.

Without realizing it the guys had formed a little circle, surrounding me on the patio. For maybe the first time in my life, I welcomed the lack of personal space. We'd been together for hours, and I found myself enjoying the intimacy. The heat and closeness of their bodies had become strangely reassuring.

In my peripheral vision, I also noticed we were getting looks from all around.

"We're all in," I declared, pulling them toward the back of the yard. "No stragglers."

~ 5 ~

AUTUMN

Stepping into the strange new world of the pool house, I felt warm and loose. Sexy in my dress. Happily buzzed and oddly relaxed among a whole slew of other emotions, all of which happened to be good.

It occurred to me that this was the last day of my sorely-needed vacation. I'd spent the whole week exactly as I planned: soaking up the sun and reliving past glories with my best friend. Kinsley had always been (and still was) a complete wild child; a bit slutty at times maybe, but always in a sweet and somehow innocent way. If she could've fixed me up with any one of the sun-bronzed California studs she was always bragging about while I was here, I would've certainly gone for it. And if my blind date was even remotely good-looking, there was a fantastic chance I'd already be in bed with him.

Hell, I needed a win. I needed a fling. I was even willing to admit that I needed my clock cleaned.

Instead I was surrounded by three dates and not one. Which unfortunately meant my clock had to stay dirty, at least for now.

I turned to look back at them, even as I kept on walking. Shane's face was painted with a swashbuckler's smile. Between those green eyes and tattoos and bad boy swagger, he was everything I needed right now. Darius looked so good I could eat him alive, but it was even more fun to imagine him eating me. And Christian; well, I could imagine what it would be like to take him into my bed. To spread my legs wide for that big, beautiful frame. To bite my lip as he crawled between my thighs and pushed forward, surging into me for the very first time…

"Ummm… are you coming?"

I blinked back to reality only to find Christian staring at me expectantly. Back at the restaurant, I'd come achingly close to tasting those lips for real. The same went for Darius, actually. Shane too. Our bodies had writhed so closely together while dancing at the nightclub, the desires I sensed were a two-way street.

If only it wasn't my last day here. If only I'd had more time. If only—

"Is she wearing *handcuffs?*"

The question was entirely rhetorical. Of course the woman in the flimsy black negligee was wearing handcuffs, and furry red ones at that. You could plainly see them attached to the metal rung of the shelf just above her, as she smiled back at us.

"What time is it exactly?" she asked, as casually as if we were all standing in an elevator.

"One-seventeen," Christian shot back.

"Oh good," she sighed in relief. "I've only got three minutes left."

Bizarrely we continued forward, to where the enormous pool house opened up into two distinct areas. One was occupied with a hot tub, wall to wall, and that hot tub was packed with people. The other was exactly as Kinsley had described it would be: filled with people playing games.

Adult games.

"Wow."

I counted over a dozen party-goers in various types of pajamas, from cozy-looking flannel to more daring and sexier outfits, like the woman in handcuffs. There was a man blindfolded in a chair, while two women took turns kissing his neck. They were doing it slowly, silently, trying not giggle or give away who was who, because apparently he was supposed to guess.

Another foursome was gathered around the board of another adult-themed game. We stood and watched a round or two, only to learn it was like a kinky truth or dare, but with dice. On one turn someone dared a pretty redhead to kiss another guy in the room, while her partner watched. After circling the room for a minute she chose someone from another game entirely. Immediately afterward, her partner was dared to kiss a girl from the hot tub, too.

"This is crazy," I murmured, but only half-heartedly. In reality, the casual wantonness of the whole scene had me strangely turned on.

"You ever see anything like this back in New York?" asked Darius.

I shook my head. I hadn't.

"Well I'll tell you one thing," laughed Shane. "Strip poker is dead and buried."

We made it to the back of the room, where the largest

group of people were gathered around a small table. There was no game board on it, though. No playing pieces, or colorful dice.

Stacked dead center, in the middle of the table, was an oversized game of Jenga. The wooden tower was already very tall, with several blocks taken from the middle and re-stacked on top.

"Now *this* is something I can actually dominate," Shane grinned.

A young woman with hoop earrings and a half-shirt overheard his declaration. She whirled on him. "You really think so?"

"I *know* so," Shane boasted.

"Then go ahead," she challenged, adding a sly smile. "Take your turn."

The girl stepped back to the sound of whistles and whoops of encouragement, all around. All of a sudden, Shane looked only half-certain.

"Better get on with it," Darius encouraged him. "Can't back out now that they called your bluff."

Shane shrugged, approached the table, and carefully withdrew one of the lower pieces. As he went to put it back on the stack however, another player stopped him with an outstretched hand.

"You've got to do what it says, first."

My date's two blond brows knitted together. "What?"

"Read it."

He did. Those cute blond brows arched upward in surprise.

"Read it *out loud*," the girl with the half-shirt prodded.

Shane shrugged, turned, and looked back at us when he spoke.

"Take a body shot."

The crowd whooped again, and the girl immediately reached for the nearest bottle. Everyone watched as she leaned all the way back, earrings dangling, and braced one hand on the wall behind her. With her taut stomach stretched as tight as it could go, she deftly filled her navel with a small pool of crystal clear vodka.

Shane looked back at me questioningly. I smiled and nodded.

"Don't keep a girl waiting," I chuckled. "Go for it."

Shane did the shot with deliberate slowness, licking his way up from the smooth patch of skin just below the girl's alcohol-filled belly button. It was a hot thing to watch, especially with his eyes glued to mine the entire time. For a fleeting moment, I felt a sharp yet delicious pang of jealousy. Almost as if his lips should be kissing their way along my skin, and not hers.

By the time he closed those lips over her belly button and sucked it down, the crowd was already going wild.

"You got off easy," laughed Darius.

The moment was over, and collectively we began to shuffle away. But the man running the game stopped us the way he'd stopped Shane.

"You can't go yet," he pleaded, his eyes suspiciously locked on me. "At the very least *all* of you should play a round."

The four of us looked at each other. Before we could

say anything, Shane shoved Darius forward.

"Alright, then."

He extracted the next block and read it aloud: "Lightly run your fingertips across someone's butt."

"I've got this," Darius winked.

He moved in the direction of a cute little blonde, stopped, then looked my way. Teasingly, he cocked his head.

"Go on," I told him. "Fair's fair."

The blonde turned a little and stuck her ass out to accommodate him. But instead of reaching for her, Darius made his way back over to me.

"Do you mind?"

I smiled and turned sideways. His hand started at my hip, the fingers extending ever so slowly from one big hand. Then, tantalizingly, he dragged them downward. The electric feel of his fingertips hovering just barely above the fabric of my dress was absolutely exquisite. I broke out in instant goosebumps, as he went one step further to drag the flat of his palm over one whole side of my ass.

Darius was frowning now, perhaps feeling a sliver of the same jealousy I'd just felt. Which was interesting, all things considered.

Both my dates carefully set their blocks on top of the stack. Christian, who'd kept silent until now, stepped forward confidently. He chose another block, slid it out, and read it to everyone:

"Whisper something dirty in someone's ear."

He looked back at me, and my goosebumps intensified. But not for long, because to my dismay he moved to the other side of the table and bent to whisper in another girl's ear entirely.

What the hell?

The girl was grinning as Christian held his hand to her ear and began whispering. But then, slowly, her smile disappeared. Her eyes took on a far-away look, then went somewhat glassy. She didn't look nervous, or amused, or anything other than a single base emotion:

She was getting turned on.

Christian continued whispering and the girl's eyes finally regained a spark of life. Eventually they flitted to me. She was biting her lip.

"What the fuck is he *doing* to her?" swore Darius.

Eventually he stepped away, leaving her standing there stock still. It was a long time before the girl moved again. When she did, she couldn't stop staring at Christian… or me.

"You're turn, New York."

If I was envious before, I was damn near livid now. Only I wasn't really livid. The jealous part of my brain had tricked me into thinking I was. Especially since Christian's expression was all amusement.

"Fine."

I yanked a block free without even thinking, and read it just as haphazardly:

"Seven minutes in heaven with your current date, or the person you came here with."

The first time didn't register, so I read it twice. Then three times.

"Okay… so who's your date?" the guy who was

running the game asked.

For several seconds I just stood there. Like my brain was broken.

"I ummm… I guess I have *three* dates."

The entire pool house erupted at once, with the 'ooohs' and 'aaahs' drowning out all other conversation. Even the people in the hot tub looked over.

"Three dates, huh?" the host grinned.

"Uh, yeah."

By now it was obvious who my three dates were. Everyone was sizing us up, trying to figure out our deal.

"Well it's not like…"

"Right there," the host pointed over my shoulder. There was a door in the opposite wall. "That closet's the size of a laundry room. It should be big enough."

I turned, and the guys were already grinning. Even Christian's mouth had turned into a smirk.

"Here, let me help you fine people."

The host of the game walked over and cracked the door for us theatrically. He pulled his phone and began tapping the screen. "I'll even set the timer."

Shane shrugged, then stepped inside. Darius too. With the crowd cheering even more loudly, Christian reached back for my hand. I took it mechanically, as the host ushered us forward.

"You sure you don't wanna bail?" Christian murmured into my ear, on the way through the doorway. "We can you know. It's not like we owe these people anything."

For a second I hesitated, wondering exactly how much of a hand Kinsley had in this. Then I squeezed his hand and pulled him inside.

"Screw it," I told him. "It's only seven minutes of standing in a closet. What's the worst that could happen?"

THE AUCTION
is now available on Amazon!

About the Author

Krista Wolf is a lover of action, fantasy and all good horror movies… as well as a hopeless romantic with an insatiably steamy side.

She writes suspenseful, mystery-infused stories filled with blistering hot twists and turns. Tales in which headstrong, impetuous heroines are the irresistible force thrown against the immovable object of ripped, powerful heroes.

If you like intelligent and witty romance served up with a sizzling edge? You've just found your new favorite author.

Click here to see all titles on

Krista's Author Page

Sign up to Krista's VIP Email list to get instant notification of all new releases: http://eepurl.com/dkWHab